THE WEAVING SPELL

Also by Erin L. Snyder

Novels

The Citadel of the Last Gathering:
A Count of Five
A Tide of Ice
A Unique Sickness of Spirit
A Contest of Prophecies
A Sea of Sky
A Layer of Ash
Alaji the Witch
The Hut at the Towering Oak

For Love of Children
Facsimile

Short Fiction Collections

Tending the Fire
25 Christmas Eves

THE WEAVING SPELL

THE CITADEL OF THE LAST GATHERING

BOOK IX

BY ERIN L. SNYDER

The Weaving Spell, along with the entire series, is dedicated to my wife and editor, Lindsay Stares, who has poured countless hours over the past decade into making these books as good as they could be.

Thank you, for this and for everything.

1: THE HALL

The chamber had no visible openings or windows. The walls, floor, and ceiling were stone, but they were as smooth and sheer as metal. The enclosure was twenty feet across, but its occupant knew it could be bigger or smaller, as needed. The only source of light was a glowing ring of flickering energy suspended overhead.

The old crone smiled and turned slowly. All ways were alike here. She knew they would be coming soon, the people of this place, but beyond that, she did not really know what to expect—whether they would be scared or angry, or how much they'd know already. She did not know how long it would take them to reach her.

The air felt strange. It was warm and comfortable, but there was no magic in it. She did not need to whisper to her feather to know it could not have lifted her, nor did she need to invoke the spell of the hearth to know she could summon no fire. The magic sustaining this place was encapsulated in the walls itself, in the ring of light overhead, and in other places she could not see or touch.

While she waited, she reached into a pocket and withdrew a vial, which she dropped to the floor, where it broke open, spilling a viscous liquid. In any other era, it would have burst into flame hot enough to melt stone. Here, it did nothing.

From her belt, she removed a knife stolen from a murdered wizard during a barbaric age. It had been made for torture, and it had served her countless times in that respect. But she'd also used it in more merciful ways, to render enemies immobile rather than killing them. She'd lost count of the men she'd been able to spare because of it—thousands, at the very least. Or tens of thousands perhaps.

But in this place, it was just a knife she'd no further use of, so she dropped it to the floor. Others followed suit—enchanted blades she'd gathered or mundane ones she'd kept because she'd liked the feel of their handles or their weight. She dropped these, as well, and they clanked against the stone.

Because it was warm here, she removed her outer cloak and tossed it to one side. She was left with a patchwork of fabrics—leathers, wools, and woven cottons she'd stitched together with her magic or simply layered and tied down.

Lastly, she removed a satchel and tossed this to the floor, where its contents spilled out. Two intact talismans, along with most of the pieces of a third shattered one, rattled against the flat surface. And she grinned. And she waited.

"Greetings," a young woman's voice said from one side.

The old woman turned her head and smiled. One of the walls had vanished completely, revealing a short, dark hall containing a single individual. She was of medium build, with ornate robes and long hair.

"You are standing in the entryway of the Citadel of the Last Gathering Before the Falling Stars," the woman said. "I will tell you more of our purpose in a moment. My name is Reilla, and I serve as a specialist here. I do not normally have the pleasure of greeting guests, but some of your belongings are of interest to an investigation I am overseeing."

"I know where I am," the old woman said. "I know what this place is and what I carry."

"Some of these objects once belonged to friends of ours," Reilla said, glancing at the intact talismans.

"The old man and his student," the crone said. "I killed them long ago."

Reilla didn't even twitch. "Even so, I am hoping, with your help, to recover them. Perhaps others, too."

The crone shrugged. "I will tell you what I can—that is why I came here, after all—but it was long ago, and I took care to hide my path, even from myself. I'll warn you now, you will not find your people."

"I hope you are mistaken," Reilla said. "They have loved ones who would be grateful for their return."

"If Oadeth wanted to come back, he'd have found a way," the crone said. "He was more resourceful than Yemerik." She glanced at Reilla as she said the names and noted a growing expression of excitement on the young woman's face.

"I have yet to have your name," Reilla said.

"You have it," the crone said. "You've known it since I arrived. These give me away," she nudged the broken pieces of the shattered talisman with the butt of her staff. She caught the young woman suppressing a grin. "I am Alaji, the witch and sorceress. And I've come here, to the ends of time, to tell my tale."

2: THE MERCENARY'S PRICE

It was not an exaggeration to say Helgwin's face was misshapen. A mace had caught him on the left cheek fifteen years earlier, during the Battle of Exingles. He'd been left for dead on the field by his regiment and was the only of their number to survive as a result. If you believed the legends, he'd lived for three months on the island eating the flesh of his fallen comrades and evading the dragons left behind by their handlers. But those were exaggerations—he was found by a galley in under two weeks and sold as a gladiator, which afforded him the opportunity to truly make his name.

That was hardly the only scar he bore. And even without these marks, he'd have had a dark countenance from his protruding forehead, square jaw, and thick beard. So when he leaned forward and told the woman sitting across from him, "You've a darkness to your eyes," his words carried weight. She was unsure whether to take it as a compliment or an insult, but that hardly seemed important.

Alaji kept her eyes on the man who was at least twice her weight. She reached for the cup in front of her and lifted it slowly. Before drinking she said, "I am told you have been inside the ruins of Gretaila."

The mercenary snickered, grabbed a turkey leg off his plate, and ripped off a hunk of meat with his teeth. As he chewed, he asked, "Is that it? Are you writing a song or something?"

Alaji grinned. "I am planning an expedition."

Helgwin paused to chew the meal Alaji had paid for in exchange for this conversation. He inhaled through his nose, and it made a whistling sound, as it had since an ogre broke it in the arena during the fight that won Helgwin his freedom. If you believed the stories, of course.

"Last time, I took eight men. Best eight I ever had. Telvuk, alone, I once saw him break a gryphon's wing and kick it off a cliff. Not one in a thousand could manage that. Eight men, each chosen by me. And each of them is lying down there."

"Some perhaps," Alaji said. "There are slugs in the lower levels of Gretaila that will dissolve bone. There's likely nothing left of any who made it past the snare."

"How does a woman learn such a thing?" Helgwin asked, but she only smiled in response. He sneered and said, "I barely made it out alive."

"It is impressive you lived," Alaji said. "That's why I chose you."

He snorted through his nose, which made the same whistling sound as before. "I will go if you will," he said. "How is that?"

"Agreed," Alaji said instantly.

He snickered and tossed his turkey leg back on his plate. Then, noticing Alaji was still grinning, he squinted and said, "You know I was joking, don't you?"

"I wasn't," she replied. "Actually, I will go in there whether you accompany me or not."

"Then you'll die there," he said. "You will die in agony. Ripped apart from the inside by the sickened men. Or devoured whole by a serpent. Or just crushed in one of the traps. There's no number of men you could take down there and escape alive."

"You brought too many," Alaji said.

"What?"

"Eight men make too much noise, especially mercenaries. It's no wonder you attracted so much attention. I plan to take just you. And I plan to return."

"I don't expect to live forever," Helgwin said, "but when it's my time, I'm not dying there. I'll die in the open, not in some cursed dwarf tomb."

"It's not dwarven," Alaji replied. "Not most of it, anyway."

"Whatever it is, I won't go back."

"You will," Alaji said confidently. "It is only a question of price."

"There is nothing you could offer me worth my life," Helgwin said.

"You are right," Alaji said. "I don't know you nearly well enough to guess what to offer. So I will ask instead, what will it cost?"

"I told you, there is no amount of gold, no tract of land, you could promise me to change my mind."

"Then what would?" Alaji asked. "Come now. Think a moment and answer. What could I bring you to buy a few days' service?"

"I told you, there is nothing." He grabbed a biscuit off his plate, shoved it into his mouth, then washed it down with the remainder of his ale. "And I am out of food. Our talk is done." He rose to leave.

"You aren't thinking large enough," Alaji said. "You are thinking of what is possible. I am asking you to imagine beyond that. What is your price?"

Helgwin grinned and sat back down. "Fine then. You want to know what I want? I want revenge. Six years ago, I was sailing the Star Tide, off the coast of Viesalle. I was following the deposed king, Charyosh the Fifth, while he tried to outrun fate and justice. I was racing against the Berlians, the Feyinth, headhunters, and even his own former subjects. And my ship was fastest. I overtook him in a storm and boarded, and do you know what we found?"

"I believe I heard a bard say you cut a hole through his stomach and shoved his head through. It was unclear whether you cut it off first," Alaji said.

"Bards are fools," Helgwin said. "We found nothing. We found the blood and bodies of his sailors, and that's all. Charyosh was gone. To this day, I don't know what became of him. If he leapt into the sea and drowned, if someone else reached him first and killed him, then escaped unseen... I just don't know."

"Then what? You want the truth?" Alaji asked.

"I could shit on the truth," Helgwin said. "I want Charyosh. I want the revenge fate denied me." He grinned. "So there's your price. I'll take you into the ruins for that and nothing less."

Alaji shrugged. "Shall we say tomorrow then?"

Helgwin shook his head. "I do not like your humor."

"I will pay for your room," Alaji said, dropping a pouch of coins on the table. "See that you don't leave until tomorrow at noon. I'll meet you on the road and give you what you've asked for."

"And if I do leave?" Helgwin asked. "If I take your money for this insult and go, what will you do then, I wonder?"

Alaji grinned. "I'll bring you Charyosh earlier. I'll find you on the road tonight and throw him at your feet. It makes no difference to me. But I think it will make a better story if you wait."

He looked at her strangely, as if unsure whether she was mad or simply mocking him. But he sighed, lifted the coin pouch to test the weight, then said, "Tomorrow then. When you don't appear, I will leave."

3: THE INTERVIEW

The old crone paused her story to take a sip of water from a crystal glass. As she set it down on the table, she studied it carefully. In her other hand, she still clutched her staff, capped with a piece of broken stone.

"Would you like to know anything about our glasses?" Reilla asked politely. Yemerik had to concentrate not to show his irritation at Reilla's condescension. Everything she'd said since he'd returned to the Citadel had been encouraging and positive. It had grown downright cloying over time, even before Alaji appeared.

Alaji. Seated before him, as an old woman. Older than him, in fact. But he doubted what was underneath her wrinkled skin had changed so much. Instinctively, he brushed a hand over his cheek.

"She is thinking about breaking the glass," Yemerik said. "Of using it like a weapon."

He could feel Reilla staring at him in the moment of silence that followed his outburst. His presence here was, at least in principle, a courtesy. Until the crone arrived with the shards of his old talisman, he'd been little more than a prisoner. Now, he'd been assured he was something of a celebrity among the archivists. Not that he could verify that—he'd yet to be granted access to the archives or almost any department.

"Yemerik," Reilla said, in as close to a chiding voice as he'd heard from her. "There's no need to accuse anyone of anything. We are all safe here."

"It was more of a joke, really," he said, beneath his breath. "You will forgive me, Corrector, if my sense of humor has yet to recover from my time in the field."

"I was wondering if it would break at all," the crone said, flicking the glass with a fingernail.

"I would be happy to explain the properties of the room," Reilla said eagerly. "Or you are just as welcome to experiment."

The crone chuckled. "Are you certain that's wise? Inviting an old witch to look for holes in your magic?"

Reilla smiled and leaned closer. "It's my understanding we are safe from injury in this room. But, should you find a way to bypass those safeguards, any discomfort I'd experience would be a small price for the discovery. Please, do as you'd like."

Alaji pushed her glass further from her. "It was a passing curiosity. I have no desire to do further harm to your people."

"That, I do not believe." Yemerik regretted the statement as soon as he'd uttered it. But he couldn't take it back now, so he simply sat still and waited.

The crone threw back her head and laughed. "Oh, Yemerik. I have missed you!" she exclaimed. He glanced to his right and saw Reilla relieved.

He cleared his throat and said, "I only meant that my reckless-ness caused you a great deal of discomfort." He saw Alaji's face tense up at the word, so he immediately strengthened it. "Of sorrow. Pain. I would expect you to be angry. To want some form of revenge or another. It is natural."

"I bear you no ill," the crone said. "If anything, I feel I've done you a great wrong."

He shook his head. "I was sorry to hear about the agents. About Thomyus and Fimelsa. But they wouldn't have died if I'd been less careless about a number of things."

"Alaji has already provided us with a detailed account of their deaths," Reilla interjected. "We have a team of interventionalists and temporal theorists working to determine if it's possible to retrace a path to that era and recover our people. I do not believe it helps matters to assign blame."

"Blame?" Alaji asked. "I feel no guilt over their deaths. That is not the wrong I was referring to. What I did to Yemerik was far worse than that."

Reilla raised her eyebrows. If she felt anything about Alaji's callousness, she kept it hidden. "We would be grateful for anything you can tell us," she said.

"There's so much to tell," the crone said, leaning back. "It unfolded over all of time and rarely in order."

"You can start by telling us how you broke the talisman," Yemerik said.

Reilla cast him a quick glance, but quickly agreed. "We would be especially interested to understand how you accomplished that. It's something our best thaumaturgists have been unable to replicate or even explain. We would be extremely grateful for your help."

"I struck it," the crone said plainly.

"There should quite literally be no amount of physical force capable of cracking the exterior of a talisman," Reilla said.

"It takes very little force at all," the crone replied. "Provided you have the right tool."

Yemerik watched Reilla sit at attention, waiting for an explanation he doubted would come. Alaji was stringing her along, playing on her interest. To what end, he was not yet certain. She either believed there was something they might offer her or some trap she might trick them into. Or perhaps, in her old age she'd simply decided to do this for the sheer joy of frustrating them. That, at least, was a prize she might achieve.

Because here, in the Citadel, she could gain nothing else that would matter to her. The crone might be permitted to live out her natural life. The knowledge she gave them might offer some insights into bettering the Assembly's methods and tools. But she was in a place where her every action could be monitored and, if necessary, controlled. This interview was almost a formality, a chance for them to record information about an iteration of one of prehistory's most important and—until now—unknown figures.

But eventually, when they'd had enough, they would access her memories directly to learn what she'd omitted, unravel her lies, and hopefully piece together enough to recover their lost agents.

And then the corrections could be made. Yemerik's destructive act would be removed from history, and the timeline would self-correct. As he watched Alaji sitting there, he wondered if she realized this.

"I should tell you of the labyrinth under Medpak'id," the crone said, as her face brightened. "Of the thieves, Eroza and Rit'ka. They were interested in a jewel said to reside in the depths of the caverns."

"Wait," Yemerik said. "You were telling us about the broken talisman. And before that about some other caverns. And you never even explained what happened when you met your older self." He didn't really expect her to finish any of those stories, but he hoped to at least get some acknowledgment she was being evasive.

Instead, she smiled wider, revealing stained teeth. "You were the one who taught me to look beyond time for order. That events can cause those that came before. I am telling my story as best I can. We will come to those things."

"I would like to hear your account of... I'm sorry, it was Mepathid?" Reilla asked.

"Medpak'id," the crone corrected her. "The tunnels beneath the ruined city."

4: THE ARCHER AND THE SCOUT

Rit'ka sat not far from the mouth of the cavern, razor in hand, and shaved her head. All the while, Eroza knelt with an arrow nocked, staring into the black crevice. Aside from the scraping sound of Rit'ka's blade, they were completely silent, though the world around them was not. Birds called out from the woods behind them, and when the wind picked up, the caverns themselves sang.

After a few minutes, Rit'ka ran her hand over her scalp, cleaned her blade, and returned it to its sheath, which she replaced in her tightly bound pack. Then she removed a jar of dark gel, scooped out a handful, and smeared this over her head. She added stripes to her face, as well, not attempting to coat herself but to at least break up her features.

Once she was satisfied, she walked silently towards the last member of their small party, the witch calling herself Alaji. She offered her the jar, but the witch shook her head. "Most of what we find down there won't be fooled by that," Alaji warned the thief.

"How would you know?" Rit'ka whispered. But she turned away without waiting for an answer. She hurried to Eroza's side and asked, "Is it safe?"

"Listen," Eroza replied, as the wind grew in intensity. Once more, it whistled as it passed through the crags and through the twisted, rusted remnants of the once impassible gate. "You can hear it in the hollow. The whisper. Between the rocks and rustling sand. That's the song of bone."

Rit'ka whispered, "They didn't make it further than this?"

"It may not be from explorers. The bones might be from beasts or birds."

"Or there could be a damned hive of winged scorpions thirty yards in," Rit'ka said.

Alaji approached quietly and stood behind the women. "What is it?" she asked, louder than the other two appreciated.

"Nothing, maybe," Eroza replied.

"Or winged scorpions," Rit'ka said. "They aren't unheard of in these parts."

"How large are these creatures?" Alaji asked.

Rit'ka held her fingers apart a few inches. "It's not their size," she added. "They hide their eggs in their sting. When they hatch, they burrow their way to freedom. I saw a man dissolve once, not two days after upsetting one of their nests."

"What upsets them?" Alaji asked over Rit'ka's shoulder.

"Water. Fire. Light. Any of these will agitate them and send them into a cloud."

"There's nothing of the sort there," Alaji said.

Eroza's head tilted quickly to one side. "She moved," she said, surprised.

"What?" Rit'ka asked.

"Alaji just… I cannot explain it. I heard it, but… she moved."

Rit'ka glanced back at Alaji, who'd been standing completely still, as far as she'd been concerned. "What is she talking about?" she asked Alaji. But before she could receive an answer, she said, "Never mind. How can you be sure there isn't a nest of winged scorpions?"

"I am a witch," Alaji replied, shrugging. "That is the answer to both questions."

"It answers nothing," Rit'ka said, sighing. "Fine then. I will scout."

"There's a trap forty paces in. Past the stone cropping with a mark like this." Alaji used a stick to draw a circle on the ground and bisect it with a line. "If you step on it, a slab of stone will fall and crush you."

"These caverns have been here since the days of Ked'herd'datt,"

Rit'ka said. "Thousands of men have gone into that opening over the years. A few have even made it out. If there was anything so conspicuous, it would have fallen on some drunk ages ago."

"It did," Alaji said. "It has fallen on many."

"Then who do you think has been resetting it?" Rit'ka demanded. "The Order of Helgwin has been dead five hundred years, and they never passed the gate!" She kicked a mangled piece of metal at her feet. "Anything dangerous left in this place is here because it climbed in from above or crawled up from below—I don't care what scrolls you came across."

"We should listen to her," Eroza whispered to Rit'ka.

Rit'ka sighed and angrily ran a hand over her head, smudging the oily paint she'd applied just moments earlier. "Fine. I will look for your stupid trap." She hurried in ahead to scout, while Alaji and Eroza waited at the entrance, the latter with her arrow still nocked.

"It was a fair question," Eroza said calmly. "Who reset the trap?"

Alaji shrugged. "Perhaps Rit'ka is right. Perhaps I am speaking from old tomes and stories."

"Rit'ka is quick on her feet and thorough. She is the best thief I have ever worked with, and she is more perceptive than most. But she is not me. I hear your voice, and there is certainty in your words."

"Perhaps I'm simply too stupid to doubt myself," Alaji said.

"How do you know about the trap?" Eroza asked directly.

"Through experience," Alaji said.

"You told us you never came here."

"No," Alaji corrected her. "I said I'd never been to a place called Arusheld. I said nothing about Medpak'id."

"Medpak'id is part of Arusheld," Eroza said, tilting her head. It was an obvious statement, the type that should have gone without saying.

"But it wasn't always," Alaji replied. Before Eroza could respond, Alaji nodded into the opening and said, "Rit'ka is returning."

The thief emerged, dusting herself off as she stepped back into the light. "She was right," she said, staring at Alaji. "Forty paces in, right where she said it would be. I'd have seen it anyway, but… she was right."

"We should move," Alaji said. "The passages will grow more dangerous over time."

"Why?" Eroza asked.

"I think you owe us an explanation," Rit'ka said. "I don't know I'm going anywhere without one. Not even for the Heart of Ussell Varikhi, assuming it's really in there."

"You will find it inside," Alaji assured her.

"Even if Varikhi somehow hid it there before he was devoured by trolls, who's to say it hasn't been buried in a rockslide or taken by some beast?" Rit'ka asked.

"The warlock never came within a thousand miles of Medpak'id," Alaji said. "He wasn't the one who placed it inside."

Rit'ka leaned against the rock wall behind her and sighed. "You bring us here with claims of knowledge of the secret tunnels of Medpak'id. You tell us the Heart lies at its core, that you can help us reach it. But your stories are nonsense, and you give us nothing but vague answers and riddles. I'm growing tired of this. How do you know what's down there?"

Alaji glanced at Eroza, who'd returned her arrow to the quiver at her side and was studying Alaji carefully. "Because Galaize's expedition had a survivor."

Rit'ka snickered. "Galaize Oathpisser?" she asked. "Galaize Vomit-tongue?"

"Those were names survivors of the Order gave him," Eroza interrupted. "In Apelieg, he was well-loved. They still sing of him, of his tricks and games. He is a patron of thieves there."

"He was a murderer. A priest-killer," Rit'ka said.

Eroza shrugged. "It was a different age, with different values. I do not profess admiration, but there is little reason in applying the civilized values of an advanced age to the dark past."

Rit'ka scowled and looked to Alaji. "All right," she said. "Let's see proof."

"I am the proof," Alaji said. "I know what happened, what they saw, and how they died. I can prove it if we go in."

"So, no book. No scroll. That's convenient," Rit'ka muttered.

"I would at least hear this story," Eroza said. "You owe us that, I think, before we enter."

Alaji smiled.

5: THE PATRON OF THIEVES

The songs do not exaggerate—Galaize was beautiful. Men flocked to his band in such numbers, he dubbed them locusts. There are those who would later claim the name, "Galaize and his Band of Locusts," was meant to imply some sort of threat, or even that the term was an error of translation. But it began as a joke and stuck as the thief grew in renown.

It was more than looks he'd been blessed with. Galaize was shrewd, strong, and fast. He'd a love of challenge, danger, and excitement. But mostly he'd a love of hearing his name spoken aloud. It made little difference to him whether it was shouted in fury, whispered in reverence, or cried out in passion—only that it was known and spoken with conviction.

Some say that Ossariff, the governor of Yan'kulm, had once done him a great injustice, while he owed a great debt to the people of Apelieg for a kindness done for his mother in her youth. Perhaps this is so, or perhaps he chose at random one city to torment and one to champion, just to ensure he was loved and hated in equal measure.

He dressed like a man out of antiquity, adorned in a blue cape like the heroes of legend, and he rode a white horse. He humiliated his enemies in combat and in strategy, and by the age of thirty, he was legend.

But he was not content. He knew that his merits would wane with age: first his looks, then his strength, and finally, should he live so long, his mind. He'd decades left, but there was no escaping time. And, as notorious as his stories had become, he doubted they would last a century. His name was legend, but it was not immortal.

That was when he met the traveler.

Her name is lost to legend and song, because she desired no

such things. But she carried secrets and stories—she claimed there was a place where he might procure the immortality he desired, but it was guarded by beasts, traps, and horrors beyond telling. Even the entrance was guarded by the Holy Order of Helgwin, whose members were sworn on pain of death to keep those caverns sealed until the end of time.

Galaize was intrigued. He moved his company to Velincha, which in those days encompassed the caverns of Medpak'id, then split his Band of Locusts into two equal groups. He had them draw straws, explaining his reason to none.

When the knights of the Order found him, Galaize was alone, lying on the forest path. A trail of blood led into the woods, and when they followed it, they found his prized white horse, having bled to death from an arrow.

"You need to hear me," he said, when he came to. "I was once the duke of thieves, but now I am overthrown. My lieutenant, Buenharn, who once I trusted like no other, betrayed me. He seeks to steal the key to Medpak'id, so he might gain its treasures."

"There are no treasures in Medpak'id, save death," the knights told him.

"I care not," Galaize assured them. "Buenharn is shrewd, and he will come for you. I ask you this, take the key far from here, and accept my help in stopping him before you send word of my capture to Ossariff. I know my fate lies with the gallows, and I will not deny it is a just end. But, before that day, I would serve something greater than myself."

They agreed, but watched him carefully. The Order of Helgwin prized caution equal to honor. Yet they saw no sign of betrayal. Everything he told them was true, beginning with an attempt on their captain's life. With Galaize's help, they ambushed Buenharn's men and slaughtered them.

Galaize offered to draft a letter to Governor Ossariff himself, only to be told word of his capture had already been sent... but that the Order would not turn over the reformed thief. Instead, he was permitted to take the oath of the knights and serve beside them. Ossariff warned them they were being deceived, but as he'd no authority in Velincha, there was nothing more he could do.

For two years, Galaize served the Order of Helgwin honorably. He fought beside them, toiled with them, and shared in their sorrows. He was one of them, in all respects.

Until they trusted him with the location of the key to the gate.

Within a week, he'd assembled the remainder of his men, who'd been waiting for his command the entire time. With his knowledge of the Order, he massacred those who'd trusted him. Every knight who was present was killed, their monastery was burned to the ground, and the gate to their charge was thrown open.

6: THAT WHICH DRAWS BREATH

"Every child knows this story," Rit'ka snapped.

"Not all of it," Eroza said. "I have heard a dozen versions, and I've never heard of a woman being behind his fall, nor have I heard it said Galaize cared so deeply for his reputation."

"What does that matter?" Rit'ka asked. "What is the point of any of this?"

"You asked me to explain how I know what lies beneath us," Alaji said. "I know, because of that woman. She was there that night, when Galaize betrayed the Order. She went with them into the tunnels, and she alone survived."

"And we're to believe her account lasted five centuries in secret, and that it's still somehow relevant?"

"It is difficult to believe," Eroza agreed.

"Her account will last far longer than that," Alaji said. "One day, at the end of time, it will be told."

Rit'ka laughed out loud. "I should hope there are better stories to be shared on the last day than that!" But when she looked over to her companion, she saw Eroza staring intently at the witch. "Don't tell me you believe any of this."

"She believes it," Eroza said. "It is in her voice, as clear as the sound of wind scraping over the clouds. And while I hear a madness in her, it is a madness forged, not broken. I cannot yet say she speaks the truth, but I would hear more."

Rit'ka sighed but argued no more. A decade at Eroza's side had taught her to trust the archer's intuition. "Fine, then. Tell your story," she told the witch.

—

A third of Galaize's remaining men fell against the Order, and another third in the first mile of the caverns. Some fell to creatures wreathed in flame, others were swallowed by ice when their fingers drifted too close to hidden runes. As they descended deeper into the tunnels, they came across a lost city, buried beneath the ground. At first, it seemed safe enough, so Galaize gave his men permission to wander and look for valuables. Once they scattered, he was alone with the woman who'd convinced him this place held the secret to his name and legend enduring.

"The old tomes were right," Galaize said, examining a doorway. "In ancient times, dwarves were as tall as men." He paused, confused, to study a curved stone arch at the bottom of the door.

"This wasn't a dwarf city," the woman said. "Humans lived here."

"Beneath the earth?" Galaize asked. "I suppose it is possible."

"Humans have lived beneath the earth in the past," she replied. "But not here. These streets were once above ground. Far above."

"This is natural granite," Galaize said, tapping the floor.

"These streets," the woman said, correcting him. She pointed up, directly above them, twisted her hand, and summoned light. The ceiling of the passage was illuminated at once.

"Those… what are those?" Galaize asked, squinting at marks on the ceiling.

"Tracks," the woman said. "From the wheels of carts, most likely, carved into stone over millennia."

"If that is true… then this city… it was once upside down."

"No," the woman corrected him. "It was once right-side up. It flew through the air, like a cloud." She held her orb of light to show more of the ruins, how the ceiling was flat with signs of wear, how the doorways still intact were pointed down, how the scattered pebbles at their feet were the remnants of crushed roofs.

"What magic could have maintained such a wonder?" Galaize gasped. "I have never believed in the gods before, yet…"

"Do not start now," the woman said. "This city was held up by old magic and thrown to the ground by time. The only gods involved were ones we made, and most of them are long dead."

"One day, I would like to hear where your knowledge comes from," Galaize said with the same smirk that had drawn so many to his side.

"I do not know everything," the woman said. "In truth, I don't even know what lies ahead of us."

Their discussion was interrupted by a scream. "Illynson!" Galaize called out, recognizing the voice. He charged past the woman and followed the sound, meeting up with more of his men as he did so. They wound their way through the tunnels, using torchlight as a guide, until they found their companion, lying silently on the ground with his arm buried to the shoulder in an opening in the rock.

The woman Galaize had been speaking to moments before was kneeling beside the dead man. Galaize began asking, "How did you get here so quick—"

"Not now!" she snapped, keeping her eyes on the man lying still. Fragments of scattered bones lay beneath him, along with pieces of armor.

"He twitched!" Galaize said, grabbing Illynson's legs and pulling. His companions helped, though it took all their strength. As they dragged him, his arm emerged, bound in a metal casing. On the sides, small gears lined with barbs held tight while long needles penetrated his wrist and upper arm.

They fought against this strange mechanism, first trying to free Illynson's arm, then breaking the trap off from a series of cables extending into the wall.

"He's still moving," one of the other men said, as they lay Illynson on the stone floor.

"Can you hear me?" Galaize asked, lightly slapping his cheek.

Without warning, Illynson's eyes opened, but they were murky and dim. "Galaize," Illynson whispered.

"We'd thought we'd lost you," Galaize said, laughing, even as he shifted away from the man looking at him. "Rest a moment. You'll be fine."

"Galaize," Illynson said again. "Run."

Illynson's mouth opened, and black ichor bubbled out, pooling around him. He began quivering, while one of his friends dropped to his side, desperate to save him. But Illynson was already dead. His body deflated, like a wine skin being poured out, until it was just skin and bone. But by then the dark liquid had latched onto the man who'd tried to help.

The liquid stood, as if human, with legs, head, and arms. Its fingers were wrapped around its victim's neck, and it throttled the life from him with inhuman strength.

The others swung at it with weapons, but these sliced straight through without resistance, like they were cutting into a river. As soon as the first man was dead, the shade turned towards the next. But by then the woman had stepped between. She held a metal amulet, adorned with blue stones, and the silhouetted form froze. She plunged a second hand into a pocket on her coat and emerged with a glass vial, which she hurled at the being. The vial disappeared into its body like a rock thrown into a lake.

Then the woman uttered a quick incantation, and the form glowed a deep red. It began to boil immediately, and flames even flickered on its surface. Soon there was nothing left but a dark stain on the rock.

"What in the deepest hell was that thing?" one of Galaize's men asked, breathing heavily.

"I do not know," the woman said, returning her amulet to her coat. "But the Order of Helgwin were not the first to protect this place. Nor will they be the last."

Galaize was not as shaken as his men. "And that object you used to paralyze it? Or the potion that killed it? I would know more about those."

"The potion's recipe is older than these caverns. It is a spell of fire, bound in water, strong enough to melt stone. I have three more vials. I would offer to let you carry one, but I fear what would happen to you if you dropped it."

"I'm more interested in the object, to be honest," Galaize said. "Your trinket seemed to frighten that creature."

"It hasn't been made yet," the woman said. "It was a gift from a man I loved. He will steal it from someone who will spend eons perfecting this craft. By the time this will be made, its purpose will be forgotten, and its creator's mind will have all but shattered."

"Captain!" one of Galaize's men called out from the side. Galaize glanced back and forth between the woman and the man trying to get his attention.

It was clear he wanted more answers, but the note of concern in the young thief's voice was too strong to be ignored. "What is it?" he asked.

In response, the man held up a bent piece of metal he'd plucked off the ground. "Look at the symbol." He moved it close to his torch to illuminate the decorative piece of armor.

Galaize knelt closely but didn't touch the object. "I see the crowned head of a horse," he said. "And… the edge of a wing. The Order had a symbol like this at the base of the statue of Helgwin in the main hall. Each of the symbols represented…" He paused, concentrating to remember something. "Helgwin entered the caverns twice. The first time, he brought eight men with him. Mercenaries."

"Why would the holy knight of Rotokham keep company with mercenaries?" the thief asked.

"Because the holy knight was a mercenary for three decades before he found religion," Galaize said. "That's not important, though. What matters is this belonged to one of his men. Telvuk, I think."

"Then… these bones beneath Illynson… those belonged to one of Helgwin's companions."

"What does it matter?" Galaize asked. "Soon enough, the bones here will be a mix of Illynson's and Telvuk's. Or whichever of Helgwin's followers wore that thing." He motioned to the side, and the thief tossed the piece of armor to the ground, where it clattered among the rocks.

—

Alaji paused for a moment, noticing the expression of uncertainty on Rit'ka's face. "So then Galaize's drunken Band of Locusts dismantled a trap that killed one of Helgwin's men? Even if it's true, it offers little of value."

"They did not dismantle it," Alaji said. "They destroyed it. They wrenched the metal contraption from its hole and smashed it, then left it beside the bones of Telvuk and the bodies of the thieves."

"Her point still holds," Eroza said. "There is something missing."

Alaji smiled. "There was more than bones and pieces of armor against the wall of that cavern. Whether Galaize saw it or not, there was already a pile of twisted gears, rent wire, and rusted springs. Galaize's concern for his friend may have been a show for the others, but do you think Helgwin cared so little for the men who'd fought beside him for years? Do you think he tried less to save Telvuk, or that he left the contraption intact?"

"Then it was rebuilt," Eroza concluded.

"Or we should be less trusting of a witch's stories," Rit'ka suggested.

"There are things with an intellect in the depths of those caverns," Alaji said. "But not so near the surface and nothing that would wish to drive away invaders. The trap was not repaired; it healed. Those who created these caverns knew what the Order of Helgwin did not: that no being—living or dead—could be trusted to maintain this place forever. There are guardians down there, and monsters, too, but it is the rock itself that draws breath. The tunnels are veins, and the stone is muscle. It is a living thing."

7: A PAUSE

"Please. You need to calm down." Reilla, of course, was relaxed as she said this. Nothing in her tone reflected a hint of stress or even criticism. She spoke the words as if she was trying to help Yemerik, as if she legitimately had his interests at heart. Even worse, there was no reason for him to think that wasn't the case. For all he knew, she truly was as magnanimous as she appeared.

But the insinuation he was being unreasonable still set him further on edge. And, despite lacking a shred of evidence, he couldn't shake the suspicion that had been Alaji's objective all along. "I am fine," he said, with as much feigned sincerity as he could muster. "I am just... she was so different when I met her." He found his thoughts drifting for a moment and gazed out of the massive glass window at the world beyond the Citadel. In the far distance, he saw a mountain crack beneath a bolt of lightning as a geyser of lava shot into the air.

"She was younger," Reilla said from a bench behind him. He could feel her watching him, analyzing everything about him. But then his thoughts returned to Alaji, and the Corrector seemed to vanish.

"She was better," he replied, and regretted it at once. His mind raced, trying to think of a way to cover, but he was nowhere near fast enough.

"Better than what?" Reilla asked, as if it were merely a point of curiosity.

He could think of no lie, so he simply sighed and answered honestly, "She was a better person."

"The world is what the Gathering makes of it," Reilla said softly. "We cannot judge its people for limitations we've failed to prevent." He should have been offended by the statement—it was the sort of patronizing, self-evident drivel told to schoolchildren. But perhaps it was her tone that made him relax at last. Or maybe he was simply too tired to maintain so much anger.

"That's just it," he whispered. "I led her down this path. She was something… wonderful once. She saved my life so many times, and now… I don't even know."

"Whatever else she is, she is clearly fascinating," Reilla said. "And your discovery…" Her tone broke a bit, and he heard what was almost a laugh as she added, "While… unorthodox… has been an incredible gift to our comprehension of prehistory. There is little doubt that Alaji crafted the first temporal manipulation. I asked Thurles to test her hair to see if it's a match with Laur-Alem's. I'm expecting to have the results soon."

"Alaji wasn't royalty. She wasn't even from Rathara."

"No, she was from an area that would later house Hatharian colonies. Laur-Alem's father may have been Hatharian, but his mother was most likely from one of the conquered lands. It's completely possible one of Alaji's descendants married Timin-Laur and passed her knowledge onto their son. Given the information at hand, I would say it's more than possible."

"I suppose," Yemerik said, sighing.

"Yemerik, this discovery wouldn't have been possible without your actions. I can't condone every choice you made, but there is no denying the results. As I understand it, you're already something of a hero among the students."

"A few cycles ago, I was a pariah," he said.

"That's not true. You were as you are now—a man who made a difficult decision against the regulations of the Citadel. A valued member of the Gathering in need of correction and re-evaluation before returning to active duty. That's still the case."

"But now I can leave my room," he said.

"Did you feel like a prisoner? I would have made arrangements for you to be taken out, if I'd known."

"It doesn't matter. I deserved to be a…" He paused to take a deep breath and collect his thoughts. Reilla didn't give him a chance.

"It may be better if you skipped my next session with Alaji," she said. "I appreciate your unique connection with her, but I am concerned about your emotional state and possible effects on her willingness to cooperate."

"Ask her if she'd rather have me there," Yemerik said. "If she objects or doesn't care, I'll stay away. But she'll want me there. I'm sure of it. She's here because of me."

"I am skeptical that's true," Reilla said.

"She wants revenge. And, through the polished Jar, she deserves it."

Reilla was quiet for a moment, so Yemerik turned to watch her. She looked as though she was concentrating, though it was almost certainly an act. Finally, she said, "I cannot accept that. She's displayed a novel code of morality, but I've seen no evidence she's unusually vindictive."

Yemerik laughed out loud at this, covered his mouth with his forearm, then turned back to the window to try and regain control. He heard Reilla clear her throat behind him, and he managed a half-hearted apology. "I'm sorry… it's just… you didn't know her like I did."

"I think it's useful to remember she's had a lifetime since you last encountered her. She is not the same woman you knew."

"She once… she lit a man's head on fire. And I'm pretty sure she liked him better than me."

"Ulithaine," Reilla said. "I recall."

"Right," Yemerik said. Alaji had gone quickly through their adventures together when they'd first sat down to prove she was the iteration he'd known.

"Again, that was a long time ago."

Yemerik shook his head. "I know, but… why else would she come here?"

"She is old," Reilla said. "She may have realized that this is her last chance to obtain immortality in our archives. She alluded to something of the sort in one of her stories. You, yourself, said that was something of an obsession for her."

"Not immortality, exactly," Yemerik began, then paused, trying to formulate the thought. "It was more about existence for her. Remembering."

"She's had a long time to think things over," Reilla pointed out. "Perhaps she's finally realized that our recordings are the only form of memory that can last."

8: THE QUEEN'S CASTLE

"Have I told you of the Bleak War?" the crone asked as soon as Reilla and Yemerik were seated. An hour had passed since their last discussion, and a half-eaten plate of food sat to one side of the old witch.

Yemerik sighed and glanced away, but Reilla smiled politely, adjusted the magical recording device on the table in front of her, and said, "I would be grateful for anything you could tell us. I do hope you'll eventually finish some of the other stories you started, though."

"In time," Alaji said. "Very little of my life was spent from past to future; I don't see how my stories could be different. The war… this was long after the fall of the Bleak Queen, when she ceased to perceive a difference between her servants and herself… I met her once in those days. I hardly recognized her, even with the crown and throne. She still kept a palace—one floating in the skies, in fact. The inside was so similar to the other times we'd met, I could hardly believe it was a different building. But her castle in the cliffs was destroyed by the King with the Red Arm when they'd warred for… I think they were motivated by boredom, actually. At one point, I'm sure they wanted something from each other: land or magic or something, but eventually it turned into a game. Just something they did to pass the time."

—

Alaji landed on the walkway while wisps of clouds broke apart against the towers. Far above these, higher clouds cast a shadow over the flying castle and everything below. As soon as Alaji's feet touched the surface, a pair of serpents, each with six wings along their bodies, emerged from overhead and began spiraling towards her. They were quick, but she had more than enough time to walk to the stone guardian.

It was thirty feet tall, and it struck a pose, as though a statue. Alaji called out, "Greetings, Alabene!"

The sentry's head turned with the sound of boulders scraping together. Then, in a voice that echoed with sorrow and exhaustion, he said, "I bid thee well, Lady Alaji. Your coming here is unexpected."

Alaji glanced over her shoulder. The serpents were getting close. "I have no wish to hurt them," she said. "Call them off, please."

The stone giant looked up at the winged creatures. "Enough!" he called, and the creatures stopped in midair. "Return to your posts. This one is known to our queen! She is welcome!" He looked back to Alaji and smiled awkwardly. Pebbles and dust rained from his face as he moved. "I am sorry I didn't act sooner. It is harder for me to remember than it once was."

"You should send word to your queen," Alaji said.

"Oh, yes," the giant replied. He cupped his massive hands around his mouth and howled. A moment later, a shimmering form rose out of the ground. It looked like a middle-aged man with a full, brown beard and ornate robes. The giant said, "Go! At once! Tell the Queen she has a guest!"

The spirit opened its mouth and seemed to speak, but it made no sound Alaji could hear. The spectral figure then stood at attention, silently tapped its feet together, then turned, before heading towards the palace gate.

"Karshin will announce you," the giant said, nodding. "The Queen will be glad to set eyes upon you again," he added. But, even though his flesh was stone, his expression betrayed concern. "For now."

"I will follow him," Alaji said.

"Yes," Alabene said loudly. "Of course."

Alaji glanced at the stone creature. Once, long ago, she'd fought him to obtain an audience with the Bleak Queen, hurling him into a stone tower. She could still see the mark left along the back of his head and shoulder. She wondered how much longer he would endure.

She hurried to catch up with the spirit, who walked as if he still lived. It was an odd sight—his feet would pass through stones sticking out of the ground or land on air where a section of the road was missing, but he didn't seem to notice. He turned his head towards her and tried speaking a single word, but her translation charm did not extend to reading lips. Instead, she smiled back. But the spirit looked as sad and lost as the stone giant.

There was not much of a city left before the castle, but a few buildings had survived the eons of warfare, adventurers seeking wealth or vengeance, and natural disasters. There had once been far more: a sprawling metropolis in the clouds with a massive dock for airships. There'd been a time when wizards had flown here on conjured cyclones, warlords had come to barter on birds large enough to carry an elephant in each talon, and soothsayers would convince giants to stand atop mountains and hold them high enough to step on as the island passed.

Now, there was little left but a handful of goblins and orcs hunting rats and birds for sustenance in crumbling buildings. Even these wouldn't last much longer: this place was eroding, foot by foot, and eventually there'd be nothing. The Queen could stop this, of course. With a word, she could pull rocks up from the earth; with a glance, she could meld them to her city. She had the power to perform feats beyond the imagination of all but the most powerful of wizards. There'd been a time she'd have bothered to use it.

The once-proud gates creaked as they opened upon the hall. Light spilled in, illuminating clouds of dust thrown by the sudden influx of air. A pair of human guards, one old and one young, looked on in silent curiosity. Alaji wondered what strange turn of fate had brought them into the Queen's service, but she said nothing to them as she passed, nor did they speak or attempt to delay her.

She reached the great hall of the Queen, once a palace of pleasure overflowing with dancers, courtiers, food, and drink; now an empty, solemn expanse. The murals on the walls had faded, the pools and fountains were dry, and the tables were empty.

The throne, however, was occupied.

Alaji squinted in the dark. The Bleak Queen was there, resting her chin against her fist. The spirit stepped quickly into the room, bowed low, and gestured widely. He opened his mouth, and—again—Alaji heard no sound. But the Queen looked up.

"Alaji," she said, standing. There was little emotion to her voice, but she seemed strangely energized as she moved down the steps past her anointed. There were more than Alaji had seen before, which was to be expected. Each of the men, women, and children surrounding the Queen was connected to her. They held memories of her past lives; as they died and were reborn, they sought her anew. Their identity was subsumed by hers; their very souls were extensions of her being.

Alaji bowed her head quickly. "Greetings, Queen," she said.

The Queen reached her and placed a hand on Alaji's shoulder. "I am glad to see you here," she said. "There are matters I would discuss with you."

She was different than Alaji remembered. Her face appeared younger than Alaji had ever seen it. That wasn't entirely surprising—like most of her kind, the Bleak Queen renewed herself by dying and being reborn. But she would transform the flesh of each incarnation to match that she'd worn before. She still bore a resemblance to her past selves, but it was not as precise as Alaji was used to seeing. "There are things I need to talk about, as well," Alaji said.

The Queen nodded. "The time of my foresight is past," she said, softly. "I do not know if you knew that, because I cannot tell the order things have unfolded for you."

"I have not brought your anointed back yet," Alaji said. "I may do so after this meeting, though."

"Tens of thousands of years in my past," the Queen said,

pausing to look upon a mural so worn Alaji couldn't make it out. She inhaled deeply then added in an unwavering voice, "And perhaps a day in your future. Or not even that. I used to think I was the more fortunate between us. That, with all your power, your short life robbed you of great things. But I no longer believe that to be true."

"I am sorry," Alaji said. "I never thought that."

"I find myself wondering about my future now. I was once spared from such uncertainty, but now… it has come to trouble me."

"You want another of your anointed brought back?" Alaji asked.

"No," the Bleak Queen said quickly. "I do not desire that. You did me a great service once, but I believe now… it would be a curse. I only want to know if I return to what I was, if I know passion again. Or if this is to be my fate."

"There's no simple answer," Alaji said. "I've seen the future, but what I saw of you is not you as you know yourself. I think you had to choose between sacrificing those things you've acquired, including your very self, or continuing as you are. I will say no more—it seemed you made the better choice, and I would rather you come to it in your own way."

The Queen nodded. "Then I will trust in time," she said. "What is it you've come to discuss?"

"The Citadel," Alaji replied.

"Of course," the Queen said. "The only thing I have ever known to frighten you."

Alaji shook her head. "That was before. I no longer fear them. Things are more complicated now."

"They are no longer your enemy?" the Queen asked, raising an eyebrow in an unusual show of emotion.

"As I said, it is complicated. I don't fear them, but that changes nothing. I have spoken already with some of the others in depth. I cannot tell you everything, but I can explain a great deal, now that I understand it myself. But these words are for you alone, not for your anointed. They'll learn in time, but not through these memories."

9: THE PATH OF MUD

The old crone stopped talking somewhat abruptly. At first it seemed she was simply pausing to take a breath, then she looked to one side and saw the plate of half-finished food sitting there. She pulled it close and looked down.

"Is everything all right?" Reilla asked.

"I am just surprised," Alaji said. "There is not a single fly. Oadeth told me as much, but I don't think I believed him. It sounded like an idle boast. A joke at my ignorance. But I don't recall seeing a single insect of any kind since arriving. Not even…" She trailed off then grabbed a piece of something soft, like bread, but sweet and without crust.

"We don't allow them into the living areas," Reilla said. "There are select breeds in the gardens to ensure a proper environment, and a lab is maintained with countless different samples from multiple timelines for study. But there are magical fields in place to ensure they don't propagate elsewhere."

"Is that why you don't have any rats?" Alaji asked.

"How do you know there aren't rats here?" Yemerik asked. But before she had time to reply, he said, "Never mind that. What did you tell this 'Bleak Queen?' That's what you were actually talking about."

"It wouldn't make sense if I repeated it," she said. "Not yet. We are too close to the end of my story now. I will explain all of that when I'm closer to the middle."

Yemerik sat back, almost falling off his stool. He caught himself on the raised object, then shifted to try and cover up his mistake. He'd spent so long in the world outside the Citadel, he'd almost entirely forgotten how to interact with the environment he'd grown up in. He caught a glimpse of Reilla watching him out of the corner of his eye, but he felt a little more secure now, at least. As he'd suggested, she'd asked for Alaji's thoughts on the possibility of him sitting out these conversations. She hadn't told him what Alaji's response had been, but the fact he was invited back told him everything he needed to know.

"Rit'ka was like you in some ways," Alaji said, watching him as well.

"Clumsy and stupid?" Yemerik asked.

"No," Alaji said, chuckling. "Impatient. Or at least she acted the part. As the three of us descended into the caverns and tunnels, I began to think perhaps her demeanor was just a way of keeping me on edge."

"I take it we're returning to that story, then?" Yemerik asked, with as little sarcasm as he could muster.

"It is all the same story," Alaji told him. She wore a knowing grin that unnerved Yemerik to his core.

—

When they came upon the broken remnants of the trap, Eroza knelt quietly to examine the rusted gears and bones. "It is as you said," she told Alaji. "The city. The snare. Everything."

"And yet we still know nothing," Rit'ka interjected. "Even if those bones did belong to who she claims… she still hasn't told us how she learned all this. She hasn't shown us a book or document."

"There are no books," Alaji said.

"Here," Eroza said, lifting a rent piece of rusting armor. She studied it as best she could in the dim light of Alaji's magic and ran her fingers over it to explore its shape. "It is precisely as she described."

"A flying horse," Rit'ka said sarcastically. "And we're supposed to accept it was the symbol of… whichever of Helgwin's champions she mentioned in her story. I can't keep track of this nonsense."

"Telvuk," Eroza said. "This was his symbol, according to the Tome of Helgwin. I have read it."

"You've read everything," Rit'ka said, annoyed. "And we are wasting time."

Alaji released her ball of light into the air, whispering an invocation so it would remain in place. Then she began picking through scattered bones until she found a femur, mostly intact, and slid it into an opening in the wall. A moment later, a loud clank echoed out, and the bone was jerked from her hand. They heard the sound of turning gears, and the bone was dragged into the hole, until only the end stuck out.

"We should be safe," Alaji said. "The contagion needs living tissue to propagate."

"Your shadow monster, you mean," Rit'ka said.

"Shadow, blood, and spirit," Alaji replied. "It rends free the soul of the ensnared, then torments it before letting it loose in the body of its next victim."

"The Order of Helgwin would never create such a thing," Eroza said.

"No. Of course not," Alaji agreed. "And even if they'd wanted to, they lacked the techniques required. I told you, they were not the first to protect this place."

"I want some answers," Rit'ka said.

"This place is older than you know," Alaji said. "I know more of it than any living mortal, and I don't know a hundredth of its secrets. I know just enough to get us to the center. Beyond that, you would do better to pay attention. This place is riddles and answers both."

"At least tell me where you heard that bit about the trap. About it stealing souls."

"It takes much more than that," Alaji replied.

"Tell me!" Rit'ka demanded.

"From its architect," Alaji said. "From the King with the Red Arm."

Rit'ka scoffed. "There is no such person. The King is a myth from the old days. A story about a cruel fairy lord who conquered the world before losing it to his dark master."

"I am not so sure," Eroza said.

"He is real," Alaji replied. "And he still lives, though neither his mind nor ambition are what they once were. But if you ever come across a beggar with a scar on one arm, a long, deep red one that looks as though he carved it himself, you would do well to leave him a coin and hurry on your way."

"This is nonsense," Rit'ka said, scowling.

"She was right about the city buried upside down," Eroza said, pointing behind them. "I cannot explain any of it, but she has been right about everything."

"That's what bothers me," Rit'ka said, glaring at Alaji.

"We are wasting time," Alaji said. "And there's no telling what creatures may be drawn to the sound of us arguing."

"Fine then," Rit'ka said. "But if the Heart of Ussell Varikhi is not where you claim, we will have more than words."

"It will be in the labyrinth's center," Alaji assured her again. "You have my word on that."

Rit'ka glared at her, but she followed along as Alaji led them towards the next corridor. The passageway narrowed again, and they came to a stretch where a section of the ceiling had collapsed. Alaji paused, examining it thoughtfully.

"I take it this was not in your books," Rit'ka said.

"I told you," Alaji replied, "there were no books. But, no, this way was open in the days of Helgwin and Galaize." She considered this for a moment.

"We will not be able to dig through this," Eroza said, after shutting her eyes and leaning close to the rubble. "Are there other paths we could use?"

"There are," Alaji replied. "But I am unsure I like them."

"It's that or turn back, isn't it?" Rit'ka said.

"Not necessarily," Alaji said, thoughtfully. She glanced at the two women and found them watching her carefully. "But under the circumstances, we should probably just go around. I believe there is another path out of the underground city. Assuming we survive it, it should leave us not far from where this would have led."

Soon, they found themselves pushing through a damp corridor, wading through mud. On either side of them, dirt walls rose thirty feet before converging. "It's surprising this passage remains open at all," Eroza said, gripping her bow and quiver above her head.

"It means it's learning," Alaji said quietly. She held no light, instead opting to summon small orbs around them or even beneath the surface. With luck, it would either attract or repel anything hiding in the caverns or swimming underneath.

"I am not convinced the gem is worth all this," Rit'ka said, struggling against a slightly deeper section. It was a joke, of course—the gem they were seeking was priceless, though the two thieves had no intention of selling it. The object was a piece of history, a lost legacy of House Ewaltis. They were already as rich as any thieves alive, but if they returned this, it would buy them something money couldn't: a pardon.

Eroza whistled once sharply, and both she and Rit'ka froze in place. "Left," Eroza whispered and readied her bow. Rit'ka went for a blade at her side while Alaji clumsily shuffled backward.

A few seconds after Eroza's warning, Alaji heard it, too: a scratching sound, coming from the wall of dirt. Small clumps of soil began raining down at on them, and Rit'ka yelled, "Move!"

They dove forward as a section of the wall crumbled, and a curved, white beak appeared. It opened, emitting a loud squawk, as the three women lunged to one side. More of the wall broke apart, and the creature rolled out, landing in the muck, close to Alaji. It was fifteen feet tall, with a pale, awkward body. Two powerful legs ending in taloned toes lifted it upright, and it spread a pair of short, stocky arms with webbed hands.

Its beak covered its face entirely, then extended a few feet further in a crest. If it had eyes, they were buried beneath it. The creature sprung forward as the first of Eroza's arrows stuck into its side. It offered no response but faced Alaji and drove its head towards her.

As it struck the mud, a wave formed and splashed to all sides.

The light was extinguished immediately, though with a whispered incantation Rit'ka's daggers began glowing. The creature shifted forward, and Rit'ka hurled one of the blades, which whistled through the air as it spun. It moved in a great arc around the monster's body, then, with a flick of her wrist, Rit'ka commanded it to change direction and plunge into the back of the bird's naked neck.

It howled in pain as Eroza fired three more arrows into its stomach. The creature leapt up, kicking its powerful legs against the wall behind it. For a moment, it remained there, horizontal to the ground, then wriggled its head, burrowing into the dirt. As soon as its hands were close enough, it began clawing its way in, until it was swimming into the soil. It pulled itself deeper, kicking with its hind legs, until these vanished entirely. Eroza pointed her arrow at the place it had disappeared, in case it reemerged.

"How far?" Rit'ka asked.

"Twenty paces," Eroza said.

"Now?" Rit'ka asked, a few seconds later.

"Forty-five," Eroza said.

Rit'ka altered the position of her hand and concentrated. Then, she pulled her arm back, and as she did so the caverns shook. A moment later, her second dagger flew spinning out of the earth and landed directly to in her open palm. The blade's glow was muted by layers of mud and the blood of the monster.

"Alaji!" Rit'ka yelled, hurrying towards where she'd last seen the witch.

"She is unharmed," Eroza said, without needing to look. An orb of light appeared several yards away in Alaji's hand. She was no longer sinking into the wet dirt but now floated above it.

"I'm sorry," Alaji said. "I didn't expect that."

Rit'ka's expression shifted from concerned to angry in a heartbeat. "You can fly?" she said angrily. "Then why crawl through this mess?"

"It isn't her flight that should interest us," Eroza said. "She was standing right beneath that beast's beak."

"I thought it had you," Rit'ka said, cleaning her knife on a rag.

"It did have her," Eroza said. "Or it should have, by rights. What kind of a witch are you?"

"The only one of my kind," Alaji said. "Like you two. If I keep secrets, trust I have my reasons."

"I don't trust anything about you," Rit'ka said. Alaji glanced towards Eroza, but the archer shook her head.

"I share her sentiments," Eroza said. "You lure us with stories and promises, but withhold too much. That thing might have killed us."

"I wouldn't have allowed that," Alaji said.

"You could barely save yourself," Rit'ka replied.

"Neither of you will die here," Alaji said.

"Is that what you told Galaize?" Eroza asked. Rit'ka turned to stare at her with a confused expression, but she didn't say anything.

"No," Alaji said. "I told him he would leave a legacy that bards would sing of for three thousand years. I told him that if he came here with me, his tale would be known at the ends of time."

"There's that phrase again," Eroza said. "I am beginning to doubt it's figurative."

"You'd be surprised how often the truth is dismissed," Alaji said. "It's one of the reasons I'm so slow to offer it. If I'd told you as much when we met on the road, that I'd come here with Galaize and Helgwin after him—"

"Helgwin was fifteen hundred years ago," Rit'ka said. "He lived and died a thousand years before Galaize, not after."

"Are we to understand you're immortal?" Eroza asked. Alaji noticed she adjusted her grip on her bow as she spoke.

"No. Not immortal. I age, bleed, and die like you. I am human."

"A human who claims to have lived through myth and history," Rit'ka said. "But who doesn't know the order it occurred."

"Things are more complicated than that," Alaji said.

"Then explain them!" Rit'ka demanded.

"I am trying to," Alaji said. "But some things can't be explained with words alone. This place is story. You'll need to see it to understand."

"We should leave," Rit'ka said. "All of this feels like a trap, like she's playing us for fools."

"Not you," Alaji said. "Others, perhaps, but not you."

"Then tell us this," Rit'ka demanded. "Why should we believe the Heart is here?"

Alaji cracked a smile.

10: THE HEART OF USSELL VARIKHI

The warlock traveled light as he ran down the forest path. Behind him, he could hear his winged mount writhing on the ground. Perhaps he would be lucky, and his pursuer would be drawn to it. Perhaps she would perish in its jaws or by its fire. But he doubted such fortune would smile upon him. The witch had survived worse than his charmed dragon to follow him this far. She'd been the one to bring it down, after all.

But now he knew she was mortal. He'd seen her bleed, albeit from a mere scrape. Still, this meant she could be killed. It would not be easy, though. She'd dealt with everything he'd managed to place between them, and she seemed to know everything about him. His limitations, his magic… everything. And he did not even know her name.

He could feel his broken leg wobble, so he paused to adjust the straps binding a pair of wooden boards on each either side. Once he trusted they were secure, he stood again and started forward. He made it less than a hundred feet before he began to sweat—the pain was starting to return.

Ussell fished his mirror from his pocket and held it in front of his face. Then he chanted an invocation as he stared back at his own eyes, which began glowing. He concentrated on the pain, not his own, but that of his reflection. "I give to you all I feel. All my hardship is yours to bear," he said.

"No," his reflection begged, silently mouthing the words. "Please… no more."

"Be grateful," he said. His eyes dimmed as he returned the mirror to the pocket he'd pulled it from. His leg was almost entirely numb now, a welcome change from the torment he'd shifted to his other self. The spell wouldn't last long without being reinforced, especially with each step on his mangled leg weakening its hold. Ideally, this magic was intended for use in rest, though it served well enough in dire circumstances.

When he heard some rustling in the bushes near him, Ussell was briefly frightened. He breathed a sigh of relief when he turned to see a troll's arm emerge, followed by a head baring teeth and snarling.

As he met its gaze, his eyes began to glow. This made things difficult to see, of course—that was always an unfortunate side effect. But the troll's eyes remained in his view. The creature's eyelids were wide open, and it was staring back with a blank expression. Slowly, the warlock raised his mirror, passing it between them, so the troll was staring now at its own reflection. Ussell whispered his incantation, then lowered the artifact. Now it was the troll's eyes that glowed.

"There is a woman out there!" Ussell barked. "Find her! Kill her!" The beast turned in the direction Ussell had gestured, but the warlock had a sudden thought. "Wait! Are there more of you?" The beast turned back to look at him with a confused expression. "More trolls," he specified. Slowly, the enthralled monster nodded. "Take me to them first," he commanded.

Within a half hour, Ussell was sitting in the back of a shallow cave. The place smelled foul, and the remnants of a dozen animal carcasses littered the ground, along with numerous piles of dung. But at least his leg was resting, and he had protection.

He sat still for only a few moments before growing restless. The thought of eating in this place was horrific, but he wished he had some water or wine. Perhaps he should have commanded one of the trolls to bring him a servant before joining in the hunt for his tormentor.

There was nothing else to do, so he pulled out his mirror to check on the monsters' progress. He doubted they'd be able to kill the witch, but he trusted they'd delay her long enough for him to think of a better plan. At the very least, he was hidden here. He was safe.

He whispered a spell, and his eyes began glowing again. With another word, the image in the glass changed to show him the woods. He was seeing through the eyes of one of his trolls as it pushed over small trees and rooted through bushes. With another incantation, the scene changed to the view of another of the creatures. And another after that.

Then he saw her. Or, more accurately, the entranced monster saw her as Ussell looked on. It charged the strange woman who waited silently for it to approach. She simply watched as it rushed towards her. Then, just as it reached for her, she vanished.

The warlock watched the scene thoughtfully. If it was an illusion, it was a refined one. The troll turned from side to side, looking for her. Then there was a flash of light, followed by flame. The troll stumbled back, and its gaze found her overhead. She was floating in the air above it, moving her lips. Then she was staring into its eyes.

Ussell looked away at once to keep from being snared. He'd seen a flash in her eye; she was stealing the creature's will. By now, he knew he'd have lost it from his mirror, but he didn't need it to know what she'd do. She'd command the troll to lead her back here. He swung back onto his feet and took a step towards the opening. He'd have minutes before the creature managed to—

"Ussell Varikhi," the witch said. She was standing in the opening now. How she'd gotten there so fast defied reason.

He whispered an invocation to call his trolls back to him, though he doubted they'd be fast enough. Then he spoke the word to illuminate his eyes. He doubted the witch could beat him in a battle of wills.

But the witch was gone. The opening she'd been in was empty, and he was staring at nothing. He had just a moment to consider this when he felt a nick on his shoulder. He shifted forward reflexively, but he didn't have a chance to do more.

It caught him like fire. Pain, as intense as any he'd ever felt or inflicted, exploded in his veins beneath the surface of his skin. He fell, screaming, to the cavern floor, landing in the half-eaten remnants of a decomposing deer.

The witch stood over him and said something, but he couldn't hear her over the sound of his own screams. He felt his muscles tense, and he shook while she looked down pitilessly. In her hand, she held a simple knife. He did not doubt she could kill him now if she wished. Indeed, he almost hoped she would, just so the pain would end.

But she seemed content to wait. She wanted to torture him, he decided, and his rage billowed up from inside him. It could not overcome his pain, but it distracted him just enough to regain his wits. He grabbed for his mirror, which had landed beside him, and stared into it. With a screamed invocation, he called up his reflection, who looked on in horror.

"Take it from me!" he hollered, willing the pain out of his body and into his mirror image. He looked down as the silent figure's mouth stretched open in unrelenting horror. Then the warlock whispered again, glancing at the rock. He commanded it to move, and a stone spike extended towards the witch. But again, she was gone.

"Do you know what your magic does?" he heard her ask. He looked up and saw her back at the opening.

"It makes me… the most powerful… of us all," he hissed. It was an absurd boast, but despite the fact he'd forced his pain on his reflection, he was still exhausted and furious. He looked at her and began whispering.

"You entrap spirits," the witch replied. Then, without warning, she vanished again, appearing just beside him with her knife in hand. He looked down to see a deep cut in his side, but he no longer cared. His connection was open; it took nothing for him to push this onto his other self.

"I will make you feed yourself to the trolls piece by piece!" Ussell spat. He looked to the floor and tried to make it swallow up the witch's legs, but she simply vanished and appeared on his opposite side, where another cut appeared. Again, he channeled the oncoming waves of pain into his mirror.

"That is your own soul you've captured," the witch said, cutting him again. Ussell spun around and caught her wrist.

"Look at me!" he shouted, trying to glare into her eyes. But she vanished in front of him, leaving him grasping air.

When she rematerialized a few seconds later, right where she'd been, he tried to leap away, but she caught him with her blade again. He pushed this away, as he had before, though this time he felt something resisting him. His mirror seemed to be pushing back, fighting him. It was absurd—he simply pushed harder, forcing the pain into his reflection.

Then he heard a cracking sound. He looked down, terrified, to see a fracture forming on the glass. His reflection was bloated and pressed against it. "What did you do?" he demanded.

"You did it," the witch replied. "A long time ago. You should have just given me the stone."

"Stone?" Ussell asked, confused.

"I told you earlier," the witch said. "I am only here for the gem you pried from the statue of Brenseyd Ewaltis. The one you call your heart."

"You were sent by the Ewaltis?" Ussell asked angrily. As he spoke, he clutched at a pouch hanging around his neck with one hand. The other, still holding the cracking hand mirror, was shaking.

"No," the witch said. "It would take far longer to explain why I'm here. But I need the gem." She began approaching slowly as he stepped back.

The sound of straining glass grew louder. "Tell me how to stop this, and I'll give you the stone," he offered.

The witch shrugged. "If there's a way, I don't know it. I only bothered learning about the mirror's weakness before coming for you."

"Then at least tell me your name," he said. But as he spoke, he heard the glass shatter. His leg collapsed under him, and all curiosity was extinguished by a flood of pain as each knife wound exploded in agony. As he lay on the floor twitching, he saw the witch's form pass over him, kneel down, and take the pouch holding his stolen gem. Then she was simply gone.

Moments passed slowly as the warlock lay there without sense of time or being. Until, after what seemed like hours, he saw shadows appear in the cave opening. The trolls, free from his enchantment, had returned.

And all he felt was a vague sense of relief that his suffering was about to end.

11: REFRESHMENTS

"Well, that's horrifying," Yemerik said. Reilla cleared her throat, presumably to remind him that they weren't here to judge Alaji's actions.

"I always thought there was a poetry to it," the old crone said, smiling. "Ussell did horrible things in his life. I will not repeat the stories I've heard, but I do not think his death was unfitting."

"Phaesha hated that knife," Yemerik said. He felt a little satisfied when he saw Alaji's face sink a bit at the sorceress's name. The expression was short-lived, however.

"She was a fine teacher and perhaps the best friend I ever had," Alaji said. "But she still had much to learn. I wish I'd been able to stay with her and see her grow into her role. I think she must have made a magnificent queen."

"We'll never know," Yemerik said. "It's not a relevant point in time, so we'll—"

"Yemerik," Reilla cut him off abruptly, "I am sorry to interrupt, but Alaji should have an opportunity to rest." She said this as if she'd no ulterior motive. Then, turning to Alaji, she added, "I want to thank you again for sharing your story with us. What you're telling us is invaluable, both from an academic standpoint and as a subject of interest. I want to know if there's anything you'd like made available. It isn't an exaggeration to say we have access to an eternity of foods and drinks."

"Wine and water will be fine," Alaji said.

"Of course. Give some thought as to whether there's anything else we can do." She smiled and nodded to Yemerik, who sighed and stood up. Reilla stood as well, placed a hand on Yemerik's shoulder, and pushed him gently towards the door.

—

"I shouldn't have said it," he said, as soon as they were in the hall.

Reilla sighed, then shut her eyes tight enough to furrow her brow. Then she opened them, and her face relaxed at once. "Thank you for understanding. I think it's important we both take some time to ensure we're properly focused before we continue this interview."

Yemerik nodded. "She's smart enough to know why you pulled us out," he said.

"Of course," Reilla agreed. "But she'll realize we are trying to work through our cultural differences and meet her on her own terms. It's my hope she chooses to view that as a sign of respect."

"Respect," Yemerik echoed the word. "I really don't think she cares."

"She came to us," Reilla reminded him. "I remain optimistic she'll be more forthcoming once she feels comfortable."

"You caught that line about making fools of people?" Yemerik asked. "One of those parts about the two thieves in that cave."

"You mean Eroza and Rit'ka?" Reilla asked.

"I guess so. They were questioning her, and she had a line about—"

"Yes," Reilla interrupted him casually. "I did notice that aside. And I know what you're implying. It crossed my mind, as well."

"And?"

Reilla shrugged. "I'm not sure what difference it makes. Perhaps it really occurred that way, or maybe she intended it as a joke at our expense. Or it's just as possible the entire story is made up. I trust we'll learn the truth eventually and act accordingly."

"Don't you care? We're wasting time when we should be trying to locate Oadeth, Thomyus, and Fimelsa."

"Wasting time?" Reilla asked.

Yemerik sighed. "You don't have to say it. I was gone too long—I know. I started thinking like they do."

"You don't need to apologize," Reilla said, smiling. "I'm as interested in helping you reassimilate as I am in recovering our missing agents. Oadeth, Thomyus, Fimelsa, and all the others who have yet to check in since the timeline began to deviate."

"How many?" Yemerik whispered.

"I'm not at liberty to cite a number," Reilla said. "But they're all important to us, and we'll do everything we can to bring them home."

"You think Alaji knows what happened to them?"

"I sincerely doubt it," Reilla said. "My guess is the majority simply wanted an opportunity to explore the environment they wound up in. They'd have known if they returned here, we'd limit their access to the timeline, so they… wandered. I trust you of all people understand the impulse to explore, even when the rules dictate otherwise."

He chuckled. "That almost sounded like a joke at my expense, Corrector. Are you certain I've recovered enough to withstand such criticism?"

She smiled and said, "We should head to storage and find some wine. I don't want her thinking we forgot her request."

"She likes semi-sweet wines that are heavily alcoholic."

"I honestly have no idea how to judge the stuff," Reilla said.

"In this case, it should be easy," Yemerik said. "Just have me test it. When we find something I absolutely loathe, you can assume she'll love it."

12: CROSSING PATHS

The old crone sipped from her glass of wine, closed her eyes, and smiled warmly. "It is almost like Verow's Brew," she said. "This is sweeter, and not so rich, but if I am not concentrating so hard… it is similar."

Yemerik smiled, in part because his gambit had paid off, but also because he found himself warmed by her joy. This surprised him a great deal—a moment earlier he'd have sworn the woman before him was a corruption of the girl he'd cared for. But something in her face had endured.

"It's a flower wine," Yemerik explained. "I tasted a bit and noticed the similarity as well. I imagine it works better given how much time has passed."

The old woman tilted her head and looked at him curiously. "I drank a bottle of Verow's Brew just a month ago," she said. "Or did you forget?"

He sighed and rubbed his forehead. "I'm sorry. Of course. That moment on the mountain when your younger self recognized the drink. If you hadn't acquired it later in life, you'd never have been able to arrange the loop."

"Good," Alaji said, "You are thinking. I used to spend the day wishing you'd stop thinking, or at least stop doing so out loud," she laughed. "But as I've aged, I've found myself missing it."

"I still find it difficult to understand," Yemerik said. "Why would you have wanted the circle, at all?"

"Because it was something I'd done," Alaji said, grinning.

Yemerik tensed up. "That's not entirely dissimilar to something I read in Lundanta's journal." He watched Alaji closely, expecting a look of shock. But instead he received another smile.

"I am not surprised. She said something like that to me once."

"When you fought her in that library?" Reilla asked, speaking up for the first time in several minutes.

"No, no," Alaji said. "There was nothing cordial about that exchange. This was far, far later. Or, more accurately, earlier. It was… twenty thousand years before my people, about. Did you realize there were humans alive so far back?"

"Yes," Yemerik said quietly. "We don't interact with them, though."

"It's no matter," Reilla said. "We can correct for any minor issues that might arise."

"I wasn't quite so old as I am now, but this was years after most of my adventures were done. Long after that business with Galaize and Helgwin was concluded. I suppose I'd been putting it off. I am not sure I was still afraid of her, but I didn't welcome the confrontation."

—

The goblin stood stoically at the rocky crevice. Around him lay the corpses of his kin. He knew his own face from another six years of life in this body, each day of which he recalled clearly. It would be a bear that killed him after catching him in his sleep. He'd die watching the creature's jaws tear out chunks of muscle. He'd have more than ample time to kill it and perhaps even save himself, but this would serve no end.

Several of the dead goblins surrounding him shared enough of his features he could guess the nature of their relation. He was almost entirely certain the closest was his mother—she shared his eyes. And to one side, wearing an expression of shock and horror, lay a male he'd have bet was an uncle.

One day, he hoped to feel guilt for what he was about to do. But for the moment he had more important things to occupy his mind. Ahead of him, etched on a stone mountain in a human tongue that wouldn't exist for eons, lay the name, "Lundanta." That would be his name, in another life he'd lived in the future. It would be one of his most significant lives, one he'd never forget.

He waited quietly, surrounded by lifeless bodies, for another minute. Then he felt a familiar weakness overtake him. His head nodded forward, as his consciousness was pulled backwards. His eyes opened again, and he saw her standing there before him holding the metal amulet.

He leapt to one side, raising a hand and conjuring. He focused on the web of energies spilling off the amulet, deflecting his own spells as they formed. He prepared to charge ahead, hoping to knock her off-balance before she could react. It was a foolish hope, but then what choice did he have?

"Wait," he heard Alaji say loudly. "I am here to speak, not to fight."

"We are done talking!" the goblin said, running towards her. But as soon as he'd taken a few steps, she stepped to one side and kicked at one of the corpses near her. She knocked the dead body's arm to one side, and the goblin shifted slightly off-course as he felt a surge of pain cascade back in time. It wasn't bad, just a low ache in his head from the discordant shift, but Alaji had made her point. She already knew the structure of the future the goblin had come from. She didn't even have to touch him—she could change anything.

"There is no reason for us to fight," Alaji said. "Look at me. Not at my spirit—look at my flesh."

The goblin paused to focus on her actual features. She was as old as any version of Alaji he'd encountered over the millions of years he'd been searching. A memory he'd burned deep in his spirit surfaced, something he'd long ago made sure he'd never be able to forget completely no matter how many other things he experienced. He glared at her and whispered, "This is as you were."

"When we met in Tel-Ferach," Alaji said. "Your name was Mayulett. You were trying to save a village from a horde of the Bleak Queen's monsters, and I helped you."

"I remember none of that," the goblin said. "I only remember our discussion."

"Yes," Alaji said. "That was after."

"You asked me if I knew about the Citadel of the Last Gathering Before the Falling Stars. I knew only what I'd heard from the Bricklayer, how they existed to prevent things like…" The goblin paused. "I remember now. The Bleak Queen's forces. They weren't even there at her command. She'd left them after a war, and they'd just kept killing, moving from town to town."

"That's right," Alaji said.

"I told you… the Bricklayer had said that was the sort of thing the Citadel fixed. Then you told me the truth. That Graillinde had been right about them, that their benevolence carried a horrible price. The world I'd known, the people I'd loved, the things I'd accomplished… even saving that village… it could all just dissolve in an instant. Then you asked me if I knew how it had started."

Alaji nodded. "You didn't, so I told you. The Citadel came into being, because a woman uncovered the secrets of time travel. That power cascaded through time, like an avalanche, and the result was the Citadel."

"And you were that woman," the goblin said.

"It's true," Alaji said.

"So I set out to prevent it," the goblin said.

"The way I heard the story, you went to Red Arm and his council. Together, you decided to try and stop the first cause. He was the one to develop the magic needed, but he valued his well-being too much to use it on himself."

"There was more to it than that," the goblin said. "The council discussed the matter. The task… whoever was sent would have the same power over life, death, and time that the Citadel possessed. They chose me, because—"

"Because you were the best of them," Alaji said, interrupting. "They trusted you not to abuse your position. So they made you into the Anomaly. You knew what it was. You'd all have encountered it. I wonder how many times you came across yourself."

"I no longer remember," the goblin said.

"All to kill me before I could start the chain reaction that led to the Citadel's birth."

"I thought I'd succeeded," the goblin said. "I found you in Hathari and tore the spirit from your body. Yemerik made a mistake in… I do not remember the place."

"Iasyia," Alaji said. "It was when I first met you."

"Yes, Iasyia," the goblin said, glancing quickly at the name written in stone. "There was… a prison there."

"A sanitarium. We fought, and I killed you."

"Barely. And only after Yemerik told me of Hathari. I kept that word, held it with the most valued of my memories, until I began finding mention of it in books. I tracked it back, life by life, seeking information. Then, in the archives of the Syidian kings, I found a lost account of travelers who used gates to move through time. The details were absurd, but there was a kernel of truth. I traced it back to Hathari and found you."

"It was the wrong version of me," Alaji said. "You really weren't even close—that was a duplicate generated… it is a long tale, I'm afraid."

"One we won't have time to explore," the goblin said. He could already feel the weight of his condition setting in. His eyes grew heavy, and his head began to dip.

—

When he opened his eyes, Alaji was standing before him. Now she held her talisman, and she watched him carefully. He paused, unsure how to react. He fixed his mind on the beginning of their conversation, which for Alaji wouldn't have happened yet, and considered various strategies for arriving at that moment.

"We have as much time as we need," Alaji said.

The goblin shook his head. "I am sorry. I must not have been paying attention." He wasn't even sure if Alaji realized who he was yet.

"We were discussing the Alaji you killed in Hathari," Alaji said. "I told you it would be a long tale, and you said we would not have the time to finish it."

The goblin stepped back, dizzy. His mind railed against what he was hearing. "You aren't making sense!" he exclaimed. "The order... it's wrong."

"I am sorry," Alaji said. "I hadn't realized how much this would trouble you."

The goblin grabbed at his head, expecting waves of pain to strike him. But nothing of the sort occurred, because the moment was as it should be. Something else had changed. "What did you do?" he demanded.

"The talisman was able to match your time shifts," Alaji said. "I took care of that before you noticed me."

"Before?" the goblin asked.

"After, the way most of us view events," Alaji replied. "Before, the way you see them. The moment I appeared to you was the moment we began interacting relative to me. I thought it might make this easier."

"This isn't how things work!" the goblin exclaimed. "This isn't how I see things!"

"It's the only way I can think of to discuss what we need to discuss," Alaji said.

The goblin began sitting down before recalling he had been standing later. Everything was backwards now. He caught himself and focused, then took in a deep breath. "I am better now," he whispered, though he was uncertain if that was true.

"You killed a duplicate of me created when I crossed my own path. The people who made these..." She tapped the talisman and continued, "They knew they might fall into the hands of others who didn't understand them. They crafted them with rules to protect themselves while traveling in time. One rule generates separate timelines when one talisman intersects with another. The one already present exists in two realities at once, one where it was left alone and another where the new one exists. These realities can merge into a single timeline, providing the identical talismans are taken to different times. I used these rules to cross my own timeline, creating several versions of myself. One found herself in Hathari alone; the other… well, I am that other."

"Then you are the one I need to kill," the goblin said.

"That wouldn't affect the Citadel," Alaji said. "Even if you had found me in my original time—a few centuries before the time you murdered me—it would have done nothing. None of this is the timeline when the Citadel was created."

"If that's true, all of this was for nothing," the goblin said. Almost immediately, he corrected himself, "All of everything is for nothing."

Alaji sighed. "You have suffered at my hand more than any other. I am sorry for that, but it was necessary. It was as I'd done before, if that makes sense."

"The things we do… we do them, because of our circumstances. I have been in a position to see that, how the effects of my actions melded into their causes, but I have seen it in others, too. It is just that they are blind, while I've watched it unravel."

"I saw it in another form," Alaji said. "I saw time unfolding like a drawing on a wall, and I realized there was a path laid out before me."

"Fate," the goblin scoffed. "It is a lie."

"Not for me," Alaji said. "It has taken me a lifetime, but I forged it. Forward and backward through time, I built something. And you were a part of it. What you endured in your quest to kill me… it wasn't for nothing. You did something, just not what you imagined."

13: THE OLD MAN IN HATHARI

Yemerik and Reilla were leaning forward with mouths agape. It was Yemerik who spoke first. "You knew? About the version of you who died in Hathari?"

The old crone smiled. "Honestly, I didn't realize you'd found her. I suppose I should have assumed, though. Otherwise we never could have retained our version of the shards when we reached that age, could we? The talisman buried with the dead version of me would have been older, so to speak, and overwritten its duplicates. Unless, of course, it was already gone."

Yemerik leaned back, almost falling off the back of his stool again. Reilla spoke up with a quick, "I'm sorry. We should have told you about the body. We assumed you didn't know it existed at all. Honestly, we assumed there was a great deal you were unaware of."

"The invention of time travel, for example," Yemerik said. "How did you figure it out?"

"That was obvious," Alaji said. "Once I stopped hearing you tell me again and again that I couldn't possibly have figured it out on my own, I knew better."

"And your duplicate?" Reilla asked. "How did you learn about her?"

"We pieced the bulk of it together back in Hathari," Alaji said. "There were signs a version of me we couldn't explain had been present. Eventually, I wanted answers as to what it meant, so I went back."

—

Hund Korli stood gaping in disbelief at the woman before him. At first, he questioned his memory. This could not be the woman he'd known a decade before—the very notion was absurd. For one, she could not have been more than four or five years older, and she lacked the scar on her right cheek. But more than this, the woman before him was alive.

But she walked up to him, looked him over, and said, "You look like him. You are Ullin Hund's father?"

Her voice was unmistakable, but her accent was gone. She spoke Hatharian natively. Perhaps Alaji had a twin, he decided. Perhaps there was some other explanation. But, barring a better idea, he stuttered an apologetic, "Yes, I am Korli."

"Good. I am Alaji." She said this then glanced over her shoulder at a guard nearby. "I have reason to think we knew each other."

He stared, dumbfounded at the statement. He'd spent the better part of a year helping this woman learn enough of the language and customs of his people to survive. In return, she'd used her magic, unheard of in a woman, to save his brother's life after he'd been attacked by a group of thieves. "I know you," he said. "I cannot understand it, but I do."

"I do not know you," Alaji said. "I am sorry, but it is a simple truth. I cannot recall being here, and I would like to know what occurred."

"You died," he whispered.

Alaji nodded and asked, "Did you see it happen?"

"I buried you," he said. "I told the guard, but they thought I was mad. A doctor simply said you'd died of a sickness, but I knew better. I am sorry I could not avenge you. I should have tried to do more, but… I still can't easily explain what I saw."

"I am not here for revenge. Please, just tell me what happened."

Korli nodded stoically. "It was a woman, a beggar. Her name was Rora—she used to live around here. No one knows where she came from; she was not from this neighborhood, and I've never found anyone who knew her before she arrived. Until that night, I'd never had a reason to care."

"Tell me about her," Alaji said.

"There is not much to be told. She was tall and thin. She never seemed to care about anything. She would just sit on a corner or wander the streets asking for money. I saw Tenul-Hin strike her on a few occasions. Tenul—I don't know if you remember him—he despised beggars."

"I remember nothing of that time," Alaji reminded him.

Korli nodded. "There was something wrong with her. Rora was always odd—she would faint constantly, or perhaps only pretend to. It never lasted long—after a few seconds, she would stand again, as if nothing had happened. In the weeks before she... before what happened... she'd begun to lose her memory. She would forget names, places, everything."

"I understand," Alaji said. "Keep going."

Korli took a deep breath. "Rora came up to you on the street. We were walking together, and I thought she just wanted some money. I was digging out a coin to give her, but she ignored me. She just... she reached towards you, and there was a flash of light. Then she stood there until she collapsed. She looked down at your body, as if she was seeing it for the first time. She was ecstatic. I should... I should have done something. I was going to, but then she looked at me. It was like... she saw me and didn't. As though I was too small, and she was too happy to bother with me. I called for help, and she just... she wandered off. I tried to make the guard understand, but... they didn't care. You weren't Hatharian, so they just... I am so sorry."

"I told you," Alaji said, "I'm not angry. Not at them and certainly not at you."

"But I should have done something. If I'd known they wouldn't listen, I'd have... I don't know. I was so scared. That she'd do to me what she did to you."

"You were right to be scared. She might have, if you'd interfered. You're lucky she didn't kill you anyway."

"I can't believe you're here," he said. His voice lowered to a whisper and he asked, "How are you here? Did you return from the dead?"

"No. I believe I stayed dead. That me was different. I won't try to explain it."

"My son is receiving instruction," Korli said. "Ullin still mentions you from time to time. I could not bear to tell him what happened, to have him think his father a coward. He was just a boy."

Alaji shook her head. "That's best. Let him wonder."

"You mentioned him earlier," Ullin said. "I almost thought you'd spoken with him."

"No," Alaji said. "I have not seen him yet."

"Yet? Then you'll wait and speak with him when his tutor returns him?"

"No," Alaji said again. "I honestly do not know what damage that would do. Perhaps none. Or perhaps it would unravel everything I've worked for. Please, do not tell him you saw me. Don't tell anyone."

Korli nodded. "It is a shame. He was fond of you as a child."

"It was not me," Alaji said. "Not really. The woman he met died in front of you."

"I do not understand," Korli said. "Perhaps this is a matter for the gods. It is all a mystery to me."

"It would confuse your gods, too," Alaji said. "Thank you for speaking with me. You've helped a great deal."

14: JULTET

"But I don't understand," Yemerik said. He felt himself shaking—he was emotional, though he didn't know why. "Why did you think you had to follow this path you'd invented?"

"She told us," Reilla said before Alaji could speak. "When she was telling us about her encounter with the goblin: she wanted to do what her earlier iteration had done."

Yemerik knew Reilla was smarter than that—she'd be able to see the flaws in that logic as clearly as he could. What he knew and she didn't was that Alaji was smarter than that, too. He chose his words as carefully as he could force himself to. "But that shouldn't have mattered. The timeline she inhabited was stabilized by the talisman she was carrying. What difference would it have made if she'd deviated?"

"The talismans," Alaji said loudly. She paused then added, "You obviously recovered the one in Hathari, along with my corpse."

"One of our investigators found it there," Reilla said. "We were planning to use it to try and recover Yemerik when his reappearance rendered the matter moot."

"I've been wondering what happened to it. If it vanished when I arrived."

"Most of it did," Reilla said. "A few pieces remained. Which means a few pieces remain lost."

"It's because of the pendant she lost," Yemerik said. "She had some of the talisman pieces set in a piece of jewelry."

"One piece," Alaji corrected him. "The other I gifted to Phaesha."

Yemerik pinched the bridge of his nose. "You're kidding," he said.

"Of course not," Alaji replied. "I wanted her to have a way to leave her era if she wanted to."

"But that means every time you shifted in time after that, it could have generated another timeline. There's no telling how many variations of you were created."

"Eventually the Citadel would have begun collapsing them," Reilla said. "There are contingencies in place, after all." She cast Yemerik a glance to remind him to calm down.

"Of course," he muttered. He looked at Alaji and found her staring back. There was no concern on her face, nor was there regret, at least not that he could decipher. It was foolish; the sort of reckless behavior he'd tried to cure her of. Instead, it seemed to have consumed her. Was that the point? He'd failed her during the giants' attack, so she'd come here to show him she'd ignored everything he'd taught her. Was her final act of revenge a symbolic show of defiance?

He stared her in the eye, and she looked back. But she gave him nothing, not even hatred. Instead, she took another sip of her wine, smiled, and said, "I think about that other me sometimes. She must have wandered through the wilderness alone for years before finding a way to activate the talisman. Or perhaps she was drawn to Ilpinthi. You can sense those energies a continent away if you concentrate. It took me a lifetime to figure that out. But then I was never pressed to try. Either way, it's a stunning achievement, don't you think? She managed to travel through time on her own. Using the talisman, I mean."

"It is remarkable," Reilla said. "But then the things you accomplished have always been impressive."

Yemerik bit his tongue and fought against an urge to roll his eyes, but he couldn't stop himself from saying, "It didn't do her much good, though."

He was lucky. Alaji grinned before Reilla could chastise him. "It meant she got to experience Hathari, at least. It was likely an interesting life, even if it was a short one. I almost envy how exciting it must have been—leaping hundreds of years through time and finding strange cities without explanation! It must all have seemed miraculous."

"Miraculous," Yemerik repeated the word. "Most people would find that frightening."

She laughed out loud at this. "This talk of horror and miracles reminds me of Helgwin. The look on his face when he saw Charyosh alive, soaking wet, and scared. I think he'd spent years visualizing his revenge, only to have every shred of satisfaction torn away. I rather felt bad about it all."

"What?" Yemerik asked, unable to formulate any other thought.

"It's simple," Alaji replied. "When Helgwin asked for his nemesis, it was in jest. He'd every reason to assume Charyosh was already dead. When I brought the former king before the mercenary, Helgwin was too shocked to know what to do. When he finally killed him, it was almost an afterthought."

"No," Yemerik said angrily. "You need to tell us the rest about Lundanta. Or the goblin that she'd become."

"Yemerik," Reilla said louder than usual. "We would be happy to hear anything Alaji would like to share."

"I have every intention of telling you about the Anomaly. But it's not so simple as I'd like. The story is tangled. Lundanta, Helgwin, Oadeth, Yemerik… it wouldn't make sense in a straight line."

"But what happened?" Yemerik asked. "Did you fight her?"

"Him," Alaji said. "The goblin was male. It's confusing, because we tend to think of them as a woman, because that was the first form we encountered them in." As she said this, she grinned, and Yemerik was certain she was gloating at catching him in an error he'd corrected her on multiple times. The exchange made him feel a little better—at least he was briefly able to follow what she was thinking.

"My mistake," he said, nodding his head.

"But, to answer your question, we did not fight. We continued to talk. He had a difficult time doing so, in fact. After nearly an eternity having to interact backwards, a forwards conversation was harder for him than I'd expected. Every time he reverted and I was ready to continue where we'd left off, he was thrown off. But I managed."

"Managed to do what?" Yemerik asked.

"To tell him my story, of course. The same one I am telling you now. In the end, he understood, and we reached an arrangement. Then I helped him correct his temporal inversion."

"It was that easy?" Yemerik asked skeptically.

"No, it wasn't easy at all. He'd forgotten the primary details of the spell, and he required extensive assistance. I had to find the King with the Red Arm and get his help. And, even once I'd done so, the King was hardly an agreeable companion, to say nothing of his assistants. Then there was the matter of tracing the Anomaly to a point their spirit could be reflected. The only moment in a lifetime when their direction through time could be altered."

—

"Jultet!" Obertune said, exhausted from running. The goblin paused, panting, beside his worried brother. To their side, Asariba was lying in labor. She snarled in pain and clawed at the ground, but did not cry out.

"This is not the time," Jultet said, glancing up.

"There are monsters coming," Obertune replied angrily. "They pass by our best as if we were mist. Our spears to them are rain."

Jultet took a deep breath. "Asariba needs me here," he said.

"They are coming this way!" Obertune exclaimed.

"Then I will face them here!" he said, striking the leaning wall that provided shelter. He bared his yellow teeth, grinding them together in a show of determination. "If they are as strong as you say, what difference could it make? I would die watching over her! Perhaps the gods might take that in tribute for the lives of my family!"

"If the gods understood tribute, your clan's sacrifice would be enough," Obertune replied. He glanced around the wall back the way he came to make sure the ones following hadn't found him yet. "We need to move her."

"Move me, and you kill my child," Asariba growled. She lifted her head to stare him in the eye, then spat out, "I will gnaw your fingers off if you lay them on me!"

"This is where I stand," Jultet said. "Fight them where you like! Die where you like! Or kill these monsters at my side."

Obertune made a low, deep sound in the back of his throat, then he drew out a pair of stone knives. He handed the first to Jultet and said, "Tribute. For the honor of standing beside you."

"If I die now, I will die a grand death," Jultet said. "A better mate and better brother, no one has had." He looked up when he heard a sound he had never known. Then, stepping into view with Obertune, he caught sight of one of the creatures, and his blood went cold.

The creature was draped in what was neither hair nor the flesh of anything he could identify. It looked more like a deer skin than anything he knew, though it was jet black and moved like the leaf of a tree. At a glance, it didn't seem to be part of the creature's natural body, but he was far from sure.

The monster itself had pale, colorless skin, like that on a plucked bird. It was nearly twice as tall as a goblin, and its mouth was flat, showing no sign of tusks or protruding teeth. It called out to one side, and two more of the beasts stepped into the open. One was taller than the others and had something atop its head that looked like horns. These reflected the light seeping through the trees. One of his arms was bare, and he had a long, red scar running along it. At least now he knew the black layer was some sort of covering.

The third, Jultet assumed, was female. It was smaller than the other two, with curly hair and a darker complexion. Her clothing was different, too. There was more of it, and she carried something bulky on her back.

All three started towards Jultet, and his brother rushed forward to meet them. The one with the red scar simply stared at Obertune, and the goblin froze. Then, by some power Jultet couldn't begin to fathom, Obertune rose into the air.

The female called something out at the scarred male and grabbed his shoulder. The one with the scar said something back in an anxious tone, then rolled his eyes. A moment later, he gestured towards Obertune, who drifted back to the ground, gasping. The one with the scar then waved a hand to one side, and Obertune was thrown back and lay still on the ground. The female yelled again, but the scarred male just pointed. She squinted at Obertune's body, and Jultet did the same—his brother was breathing, at least.

"Wait!" the female called to Jultet, who was preparing for a similar charge to the one his brother had attempted. "We are looking for Asariba and Jultet."

"I am Jultet!" he shouted back.

"I am…" The female seemed to trip over her words. She shook her head and started again. "We are not here to hurt you."

"Then where are my kin?" Jultet demanded.

She tried to say something, but again there was something she couldn't form. "That was not… we came to find Asariba. Not to hurt her. They tried to stop us, and I am…" Her expression warped in frustration. The one with the scar said something in its incoherent monster-language, and the woman replied in kind.

"I will kill you if you do not leave!" Jultet shouted. The male with the red scar laughed at his boast and raised a hand. Jultet felt the very breath pulled from his body as he rose off the ground. He wanted to keep hold of his knife, but his fingers were no longer his to command. The knife fell and struck the dirt as he was pulled quickly towards the male with the scar.

The woman shouted something, but the other male pulled her back a step, and the two of them began bickering. Jultet cared nothing for them now, though—his focus was entirely on the scarred male with the gleaming horns.

Seconds later, Jultet found himself inches from the male's face, staring into his eyes. He wanted to show some sign of defiance, to kick or spit on it, but he could not even breathe by his own power.

"Show me Asariba," the scarred male commanded. Jultet's memory flooded his mind. It was as though he was again behind the wall with his mate. Then, as he snapped back to the present, he found himself suddenly able to breathe. He fell to the ground, struggling for breath, then worked his way to his feet. His clawed hand searched the ground for a stone or stick; anything he could use as a weapon. He felt a rock, but before he could lift it, he found himself staring into the eyes of the scarred male again. "Peace," the figure said.

And then Jultet felt nothing. The anger he felt towards the attacking monsters, the fear he felt for his family, and the love he felt towards his mate were sapped away. He no longer felt pain from where he'd fallen, nor did his chest ache. He simply was, desiring and rejecting nothing.

He heard the female arguing with the males as they made their way past him. He saw her look him over with a mournful expression as they went towards Asariba, and he heard her growling angrily at them until he heard that same voice speak that same, simple word: "Peace."

Jultet stood completely still. Time passed, but it did so only as images and sounds. A pair of birds fluttering by, singing. A group of hunters from his clan sneaking towards him, shaking him in a failed attempt to rouse him, then passing by. The sound of a goblin scream when one of the monsters caught sight of them. A mist of blood, followed by the female monster again berating the males. More of the monsters passing them by, followed by chanting. The cries of a newborn child.

Then, blinking, Jultet knew freedom. He stumbled forward and heard Asariba cry out. He ran to her, even as he heard his brother call to him, as well, and a chorus of goblin voices join in. "Prinhut," he heard one of them say, kneeling beside a smear of blood ending in a body torn open from the inside.

He would mourn his cousin later—for now, he collapsed near

Asariba, who was shaking in terror. "I could do nothing," she said. "I thought… I thought they would hurt him. But they just…"

"It is okay," Jultet said, though he'd no way of knowing if there was truth to that. He looked at the figure in her arms, and saw it looking back. Something about the expression in its face shook him, however. It looked on him with a quiet sadness, a stern love that implied an intellect it could not possibly have. Then the newborn child nodded his head, as if momentarily falling asleep.

15: THE STRANGER AT THE SALT MARSH

The grasslands shimmered like a wave. In the distance, Kaidul Medeak Faru could see the mound where a dragon lay buried. The beast's body had been left where it fell after she'd killed it to save her sister and father. At the time, Kaidul had been four. That was six years ago, and her father still looked at her like a thing possessed. She did not blame him, nor did she mind. It simply was as it must be.

"Kaidul Medeak!" she heard her older brother say, as he rode towards her on the back of a plated deer. He whistled to command the deer to stop then chanted a brief spell to keep it from running off while he dismounted. He leaned close and whispered another spell into the deer's ear, no doubt instructing it where and when to meet him again, then slapped the animal's armored hide, sending it running.

"What is it, Ruhklan Sharuza?" she asked, though she believed she knew the answer already.

"There is a strange woman in the salt marsh," Ruhklan said. "She is… a person who is no person. Shural Darlohn tried to kill her to claim her hair."

"Her hair," Kaidul said, shaking her head. "Did she kill him?"

"She had powerful magic. More like yours than that of…" Ruhklan trailed off without saying the word "mortals," but Kaidul was fairly certain that was what he meant. "She threw him from his deer with wind, then she calmed his deer with her eyes. The tree in Shural Darlohn's leg grows two ways now, but he lives."

Tree. They believed their bones were a kind of tree, and their blood was water. Kaidul had never seen a reason to correct them. "He was lucky. Did you tell father?"

Ruhklan scoffed. "If I told father, he would go after the woman himself. Or forbid you from going. If I told father, we would have no father by sunset. Just as we have no mother."

He looked at her expectedly. Their mother had died giving Kaidul life, a fact Ruhklan seemed to credit with her astonishing magic. Yet another notion she'd never seen fit to dispute. "I will go to her," Kaidul said.

"You will kill her?"

Kaidul smiled sadly. "I will. But not for more years than the trees will count. And she will live far longer after that."

"You speak like hares run," he said.

"Someday, people will have a word for that," Kaidul replied. "They will call it a 'riddle.'" Her brother gave her a confused look, and she added, "It is not how I speak, though. It is a way of saying that I am not going to this woman to fight her. And I will not return."

Ruhklan's mouth opened in shock. "No," he said, after a brief pause. "I will go. I will kill this woman who is no person. And if I cannot best her magic, I will lead her away."

"No. You will go home and watch after Accanmu Gulish. She will need you when I am gone. Father will need you, too."

He shook his head vigorously. "You have known ten springs. I thought this was a thing you could handle, because of the magic you possess. If I sent you to your death, father would throw me from his hut. And he would be right to do it."

"Father will be glad when I am gone," Kaidul said. "He will rest easier. It is not his fault. Most are like that. Now do as I say." She stared him down. If she'd needed to, she could have done more. She could have grabbed hold of his spirit and commanded him. She could have put him into a daze or tormented him. But despite the affection Ruhklan felt for her, he feared her as well. All of these people did. She trusted he would do as she commanded. Besides, what would it matter if he didn't, in the scheme of things?

When he left, she walked to the salt marsh. She felt no

compulsion to stop and look at the distant mountains or rolling hills, nor did she take a moment to appreciate the cool water washing over her bare feet when she crossed the river. She'd seen enough of these already, in this life and others.

She found Alaji sitting on a log near the edge of the marsh. The witch was in her late thirties, Kaidul estimated. And, unlike her, Alaji seemed to be enjoying her surroundings. As she approached, Kaidul couldn't help but note how vulnerable Alaji was, nor could she help that her pulse was increasing. Every instinct she possessed called for her to attack. But it was only an impulse, driven by eons of pursuit. She suppressed her reaction and spoke.

"You came, as you said."

"You weren't easy to find," Alaji said. "I spent months in the near future, circling the world, looking for pockets of humans or goblins, then asking them for stories of a child with strange abilities. So you know, you leave a mark on the people here. As did I, in fact. They blamed me for your disappearance and attacked."

"I hope you were lenient."

"Lenient," Alaji repeated the word. "I didn't hurt them badly. I think I did more damage to a boy who found me earlier today."

"Shural Darlohn Tuomith," Kaidul said, sighing. "He was my brother's friend in this life. You broke his leg—I imagine he'll recover."

"Good," Alaji said.

Kaidul couldn't help but chuckle. "I'm sorry. I'm not used to you like this."

"Like what?"

"Merciful."

Alaji nodded. "I suppose that makes sense. Whenever we met, there was pain and blood. I'm sorry for that business in Weithik, for what it's worth. I'm not sure you remember it."

"I remember Weithik," Kaidul replied coolly.

"I thought I had no choice," Alaji said. "I felt trapped, and you seemed so powerful."

"I was powerful," Kaidul said. "Less so as a result of that day. I do not know how many times you killed me in the library."

"As I said, I am sorry. I was still figuring this out. If I'd understood what was happening, I'd have been less cruel."

"And you'd likely have died in Iasyia as a result," Kaidul said. "You did not have the amulet then."

Alaji reached into a pocket and pulled out the metal object. "It is a strange thing. I've never found its match, not at this size. There were things far more powerful used in the Bleak War, but they were the size of buildings."

"I have no memory of such a time," Kaidul said.

"You wouldn't. It was long after Mayulett's era."

"It is strange hearing that name," Kaidul said. She found herself staring at the amulet in Alaji's hands.

"Would you like a closer look?" Alaji asked, handing over the artifact.

Kaidul accepted it hesitantly, then turned it around in her hands. She could feel its energy spilling out, swirling over the outside, then arcing back in towards the center. She laughed quietly at the absurdity of it all, of being handed the one thing in the world that could protect Alaji from her. Then she laughed again as she returned it.

"Have you considered what we discussed?"

Kaidul sighed. "I thought the choice would be harder. That once my spirit was realigned, I would find some joy in living. But it's all so disorienting. Things occur, and I can't see why. There's no sense of closure."

"We could set another time. Say, in a few hundred years or a few thousand. Once you've had a chance to adjust."

Kaidul shook her head. "I don't want to adjust. I've felt enough, I think. I'd experienced far more lives than most before I changed direction in time and came for... I guess it wasn't to kill you, after all." She shook her head. "Now, I am tired."

"Is there anyone you'd like to say goodbye to?" Alaji asked.

"Here? I've said enough, I think. And my other family… I've said everything I could to them."

"You mean the goblins?" Alaji asked.

"I am finding it difficult to reconcile. That they exist out there, as I remember them, right now. That another me exists, as well. I'm used to many strange concepts, but not that. This exact moment occurred twenty years ago." She sighed. "They loved me. Some of the people here love me, too, but I find goblins are better at loving things they fear. They never forgot the day of my birth. And I could never bring myself to apologize for the day they would die at my hand. You talk of regretting your actions," she scoffed.

"You didn't know," Alaji said.

"I knew enough, not that it matters," Kaidul said. "But they weren't the first family I killed then came to love. I hope it's worth it."

"It was," Alaji said. "I promise you, I was there. I saw it happen once, and I'll watch it happen again. You will, too, in the end."

Kaidul nodded. "Good. Then I am ready for that end."

"I can only take you so far," Alaji replied, returning the amulet to her pocket and pulling out a talisman.

"So long as I never have to live again," Kaidul said. "I have had enough of the enterprise."

"Preset five, me and Kaidul, two hundred and sixty million years, using minimal safety measures. Now."

The trees, the grass, and the salty smell of the marshes were gone, replaced with a blistering cold wind. Kaidul looked down to find she was standing in ash. She heard Alaji coughing first, then found her own lungs struggling against the harsh air.

"I'm sorry," Alaji said, between coughs. "I did not expect… it would be like this."

"It does not matter," Kaidul said. "Whatever death this place offers, I have endured worse."

"There shouldn't be anything after this," Alaji said. "Oadeth told me it all ended here."

"Oadeth," Kaidul said thoughtfully. "I think he killed me once." She shook her head. "This air will sicken you if you remain. Go."

"Do you want me to leave a knife?" Alaji asked.

"I don't need a blade to end my life," Kaidul said. Then, louder than before, she shouted, "Go!"

"Goodbye, Lundanta, Kaidul, Mayulett, Jelanure, and every other name you've held. I am truly sorry for the pain I put you through." Then, clearing her throat, Alaji held up the talisman, whispered to it softly, and was gone.

And a ten-year-old girl older than history stood alone, the last woman alive on a world claimed by spirits.

16: THE POISONED RIVER

"I have hundreds of questions," Yemerik said, when the crone paused to drink. Reilla was lost in thought—she didn't even turn to look at Yemerik.

"I would expect no less," Alaji said.

"What was she talking about? What was any of that… what did you say to her to get her to agree to that?"

"Him," Alaji said, correcting him. "When I convinced him of his purpose, he was a he. She became a girl in her next life, which she experienced at the same time, because the King with the Red Arm reflected the Anomaly's spirit forward through time at the moment of the two births. So he was truly born twice, rather than being born backwards in time into the body of a dying man or woman. It is not so complicated."

Yemerik bit his lip then said, "Him or her—I don't care. And I don't care about what this King did. What did you say to Lundanta to get her—him—to get him to stop fighting?"

"I've explained that already," Alaji reminded him.

"Right. Your story. This story. About an enchanted cavern and some thieves."

"You say that because you can't see it yet for what it is. The caverns are only a piece. I told him about us and the lakes. I told him about Oriv and the city of ice. About Iasyia, and Grestai before it. About the seas of sky, the wars of darkness and light, the rise of the elves… all of it. And he was far more patient than you," she added. "In fairness, he was immortal, so time was less of a concern."

"But all of this has a point," Yemerik said. "There must be something at its core. A promise or idea, something he believed."

"The Anomaly believed in my story," Alaji said. "So did the

King with the Red Arm. Not all who followed me did. Helgwin, for one, could grasp none of it. But then he never really trusted me. Even before we stepped foot in Gretaila, he looked like a man walking to his grave."

—

Helgwin knelt beside the body of Charyosh the Fifth lying at the side of an empty road. In all the world, there'd been no man he'd so wanted to see dead. But he felt nothing beyond a vague unease, a confused sense of empty wonder. He pressed at the bloody corpse with a finger, half-expecting it to turn to mist and dissipate. But it was as solid as he was.

"That smell," he whispered. "It is salt water."

"You will honor our arrangement?" Alaji asked.

"If I do not, will you deliver me to the man who most desires my death?" Helgwin asked.

"Of course not."

He sneered and stood slowly. "It doesn't matter. I have accepted payment for a job and now I must see it through." He stared at her for a moment and whispered. "How did you do it? How did you find this man? How did you even know that…" He trailed off as his gaze was drawn back to the body in the dirt.

"I knew, because you told me. I found him, because you told me where to look. There's no more mystery than that."

"What are you?"

"Beyond your employer? I am a woman. I am not a god or an immortal or anything else you are probably imagining. I am a witch, I suppose. And a sorceress, an assassin, a warlord, a thief… there is a long list, to be fair. I was once raised to fish."

"To fish?" Helgwin asked skeptically.

"I was decent enough at it," Alaji said. "Not as good as most of the girls from my village, but none of them could have accomplished the smallest fraction of what I've done."

Helgwin took in an uneasy breath, his nose whistling as he did so. "I will leave when you wish. But if it's permitted, I would return to the inn and stay another night. There are letters I would write to put my affairs in order."

"You are so certain the caverns will kill you?" Alaji asked.

"If not them, you," Helgwin replied.

Alaji burst out laughing. "You will not die on this adventure, Helgwin. It will change you, but you will survive."

"Even so, I would write my letters."

"Will this be a problem?" Alaji asked, nudging the body with her boot.

Helgwin sighed. "I will hide it first."

Alaji shook her head. "Don't trouble yourself. I can dispose of it."

"Are you going to turn into a snake and eat him?" Helgwin asked. There was no hint of humor in his voice.

Alaji laughed even louder than before. "Is that a story here? Snake-women who eat dead bodies?"

"Usually their meals are still alive," Helgwin replied.

"I've seen many strange beings," Alaji said. "But never one of those. I told you, I am only human." She removed a vial from her coat pocket, plucked the stopper out, then poured the contents over the corpse. Then she uttered a brief incantation, and the body erupted in flame.

Even from several feet away, the heat was almost unbearable for Helgwin. He looked at her, illuminated with light from the fire, and muttered, "Human. Right."

—

The next morning, Helgwin emerged from his room exhausted with a stack of papers, each folded and sealed with wax. He gave these to the innkeeper, along with a few coins and instructions to send them on to Rotokham. Then he sighed and stepped into the tavern, where he found Alaji finishing a plate of eggs.

"You look tired," she said.

"It will not matter," he assured her. "I am used to fighting while tired."

"I will say no more on the subject. You did whatever you needed to do?"

"I sent word to those I care for, to tell them it is likely they will not see me again."

"I am guessing this is not the first time you've sent such letters," Alaji said.

He shook his head. "I am a mercenary. It is my profession to die. The rest… it is only to delay fate."

"Mercenary," she chuckled. "If Galaize could hear such talk!"

"Galaize?"

"He was a man I knew, not long ago. You will not have heard of him." She grew quiet and shivered.

"He was a lover?" Helgwin asked.

"No," Alaji said. "I considered it. He was quite handsome, but I could not stand his arrogance."

"Then why do you look so sad?"

"Because I could not make him the same promise I made you," Alaji replied. She pushed her plate to one side and motioned for a waitress. "I have already paid them enough for both our meals. Get something to eat and meet me outside. I am going to claim our horses from the stables."

—

Helgwin ate a light breakfast and found Alaji mounted in front of the inn. Beside her, his horse stood at attention. He mounted without bothering to ask how she'd managed to tame an animal trained to obey him alone.

He said little as they started their ride. When they passed the corner of the road where he'd killed Charyosh the night before, he looked down to find only a dark smear of charcoal in a dent in the road. Not even bone fragments survived—it looked as if someone had started a bonfire on the side of the path.

"I give my word I'll go the rest of the way with you," he said. "I accept the payment," he added, sneering as he spoke the final word. "But I want to know if that was real, if it was actually him."

"That was Charyosh," Alaji said calmly. "I could not have faked it if I'd wanted to. I am no good with illusions."

He grunted and took a final look before his horse rounded the bend in the path. He believed her, he decided, though he took no satisfaction in her assurance. Perhaps he'd outgrown the pleasure of vengeance.

"You are still worried about the caverns," Alaji said.

"I am not scared," he replied, neither knowing nor caring if that was true. He cleared his throat and added, "It troubles me. The thought of seeing them down there. The bodies of my men. My friends."

"I'm sorry," Alaji said. "We will avoid those paths when we can."

"I was down there for days last time," Helgwin said. "It is a maze."

"I have seen worse," Alaji replied. "I could tell you of one such place, if it would put your mind at ease."

He shot her a skeptical look, but she started talking anyway, going into a tale about some ancient cathedral with incredible magic she'd infiltrated in her youth. None of it made sense, and he stopped listening halfway through. He'd other things preoccupying his mind, anyway: the tunnels of Gretaila, the sudden appearance and death of Charyosh, and this mad witch at the center of it all.

When she reached the end of her tale, with the destruction and shattering of her enemy's city (shattering? Had she said it was made of glass or ice when he'd lost interest?), she glanced back at him, and he felt he should say something.

"Have you figured out how we'll cross the Smelting River? It stands between us and Gretaila."

"I am unconcerned," she replied.

"The bridge was destroyed by goblins years ago, and the dwarf ports at the mountain forge are closed to outsiders."

"Then we won't cross, at all," Alaji said.

"In that case, we are on the wrong road," Helgwin said with an annoyed sigh. We should have gone south."

"I have the matter in hand," Alaji assured him. He simply shook his head in response.

—

He said nothing when they reached the shore at dusk, mainly because he didn't think he had to. Nothing grew along the river, which smelled of magma and boiling wood. They tied their horses to a stone to keep them from trying to drink from the poisoned river, then approached. Alaji found a stone that was warm, but not quite hot to the touch, and climbed onto it to look out over the water. Absently, Helgwin considered how easy it would be to shove her in and leave, mercenaries' code be damned. But it was just the idle thought of a tired man; he'd no intention of surrendering his sole principle to save something as trivial as his life.

"It is incredible," Alaji gasped, staring at the bizarre sight. Across the water stood the cliffs of Sern-Doltis. Streams of molten rock and metal spewed from tunnels burrowed into the rock. The glowing red substance flowed down, struck the water, and released billows of steam.

Helgwin was somewhat rattled by her reaction—for a moment, she seemed almost human. "It is dangerous here," he said. "There are things that can survive in that water," he added, gesturing to the simmering, discolored surface.

"Are they worse than what we'll encounter in Gretaila?"

"No," Helgwin admitted.

"Then if any come for us, they will make good practice. In the meantime, I would enjoy the sunset. I have seen many sights in my time, but never this."

"I've seen it too often," Helgwin said. "Damn dwarves know how to ruin a good river."

"What do they make in there?" Alaji asked.

"They say it's gold, but sometimes I think they're mining for mountains," Helgwin said, snickering. "Really. Half that mound poured out of their mines." He pointed to the cliffs. "They move rivers and land."

"Rivers and land move on their own," Alaji replied. "This is simply a faster path to the same end."

Helgwin shook his head. He'd no idea how to respond to her bizarre claims and notions. He still wasn't certain whether she was mortal, as she claimed, or some sort of god, but either way, he believed more than ever that she was mad. "We need a plan," he said at last. "We can't cross, and it won't be safe here after dark."

"I'd like a moment longer," Alaji said, "then we'll move back to the edge of the forest. It will be safe enough there to camp."

Helgwin laughed at this. "I do not like your notion of safe," he said. "Any number of beasts roam these lands, to say nothing of goblin packs or the occasional troll."

"You will be safe," Alaji said. "I will see to it."

"You'll see to it?" he asked, curling his lip.

"I will keep watch."

He chuckled. "I'll keep watch," he said. "I wouldn't sleep, anyway."

"I am in charge of this expedition," Alaji said, turning to stare the burly warrior in the eye. "I will decide who sleeps. And you need rest after last night."

He shook his head. "As you command, Captain."

"In the morning, we will push on," Alaji said.

"Back towards Eganhurd?" Helgwin asked.

"No. We will ride on towards Gretaila," she said.

"Do you think the river will be gone by morning?" Helgwin asked sarcastically. In response, Alaji simply smiled. The mercenary decided he was pushing his luck as it was and went to tend to his horse.

17: A GREEN GLOW

The slugs flickered a dim green, like fireflies, in the cavern. "I am going for the passage," Seigrisen whispered, as soon as Beralize's cries died down enough he could be heard.

"Go," Galaize whispered to the youngest surviving member of his dwindling Band of Locusts. But he gestured for the rest of his men to stand still while Seigrisen made a dash for the door.

To his credit, he made it further than Beralize had.

Seigrisen kept his eyes on the ceiling, watching for the flash of green the slugs gave off. He slid to avoid one dropping towards him, darted to one side, then hurried forward. But with a sickening swishing sound, green ooze splattered beneath his boot. He tried to keep going, but within seconds, the mucus had melted through his boot and reached flesh. He cried out in agony and fell, only for another splotch to appear beneath one hand. He screamed as three of his fingers dissolved before his eyes. Despite this, he tried to crawl on. But three flashing green lights dropped from above. Wisps of smoke appeared as he frantically tried to peel them off. He managed to pry one loose and fling it across the room, though the simple act cost him most of his remaining hand. The other slugs were already too far along.

Galaize stared at the gruesome sight as Seigrisen spasmed on the floor. The green light of the slugs was still visible, emanating through the dying man's body as their acid burned holes through his flesh.

The master thief glanced around at his surviving men. There were six now—just six—who'd made it past the massive beetle, the horrific traps, and the undead who'd come after them. He grabbed one by the collar and pulled him away from the wall, then gestured back at the slimy green creature which had crawled out of a hidden hole. The thief whispered his appreciation, then Galaize leaned close. "When I give you the word, make for the opening and come back with… with something. Anything we can use as cover." He'd already lost four men learning their packs, cloaks, and the like wouldn't work.

"Aye, sir," the thief said, swallowing nervously. He was about to step out when a light appeared at the other end of the room. Galaize wasn't sure whether to be relieved or more concerned.

"What is this place?" Alaji called, looking around anxiously.

"Slugs!" Galaize shouted. "They drop on you or come out of the rock! Don't let them touch you!"

Alaji glanced around the room quickly. Then, like the slugs, she flickered. Her light disappeared as she did so, but wind appeared in its place. It grew quickly, like a vortex in the caverns. Galaize and his men ducked behind a stone outcropping as several streaks of green light struck the wall opposite them.

"Go! Now!" Alaji yelled. Galaize didn't pause. He pushed his men forward and drove them on, deeper into the caverns. He glanced behind him, but Alaji wasn't following. When they rounded another corner and nearly ran into her, he was no longer even surprised.

His men froze in place, then began inspecting the ground for any sign of the slugs. They spread out as they did this to give Galaize room to step by. "We shouldn't stay put too long. There could be more of those things here."

"I haven't seen any," Alaji replied coolly. "You should not have gone off without me."

"You should have kept up," he answered, matching her demeanor. Perhaps she was right, and perhaps she was wrong—no one talked to him that way.

"I was handling the beetle," she said. "If you'd waited, the others would still be alive."

"They died, because you didn't warn us what was ahead."

"I didn't know," Alaji said. "I didn't see them the last time I was down here."

He grinned, glad for the information. He'd been piecing together the woman's powers since he'd met her back in Apelieg. "Then you don't know these caves as well as you claimed, do you?"

"Perhaps not. But if it weren't for me, none of you would have gotten by the slugs."

"I would have," Galaize said, staring her in the eye in case she could tell lies from the truth. He wanted her to know he believed that. He was the greatest thief who'd ever lived.

She glared at him, took a deep breath, then looked away. "We are wasting time," she said. "There are worse things ahead, most likely."

"Then lead on, great pathfinder," Galaize said in as condescending a voice as he could muster. As she stormed off ahead, he glanced up to see what remained of his Band of Locusts staring at him in disbelief. That, he was used to, but there was something else, too. He caught it in their eyes and read it in the curl of their mouths—they disapproved.

He kept his expression as unmoving as stone but felt a chill under his skin. He didn't begrudge their wavering trust, but it unnerved him. He'd watched men die for him without question. Not one of them hesitated to follow him down here, but this woman… she was siphoning off their loyalty.

She was earning Galaize's respect. And at the same time, she was becoming dangerous.

18: THE OGRE

It was not yet dawn when Helgwin awoke. He sat up quickly and breathed in the sulfuric air carried by the wind. Then, before he realized why, he leapt to his feet and looked around. Something was wrong, though he could not fix on the cause just yet.

"Good," he heard Alaji say. "You're awake."

Helgwin rubbed his eyes to clear his vision, and he began walking towards the river. After a few steps, he broke into a dash and didn't stop until he reached the shore. He gazed out at the dark water and the smoldering heaps upriver. "How?" he whispered.

"Does it matter?" Alaji asked from behind him.

He turned and walked back towards their camp, passing by her without a word. The horses, tied to different trees than he'd fixed them to, huffed as he went by. He went directly to the remnants of their fire pit, knelt beside it, and shut his eyes. He recalled the fire from the night before, the way he'd laid out the stones around it. He opened his eyes again and compared memory with reality. He didn't need to look to know Alaji was behind him—he'd a sense for such things, just as he'd a sense for the brush of the wind and the feel of the earth.

"This is our fire pit," he said.

"Of course," Alaji replied.

"I cannot understand how I came to pass from one side of the river to the other in my sleep, nor you or my horse. I can't understand it, but I can accept it. But the fire?" He shook his head. "This magic strains my mind. Tell me again you're not a god. I'm not sure I'll believe it, but I'd like to hear the words."

Alaji pulled a knife out from her belt, stuck the tip in the back of her hand, and drew blood, cringing as she did so. "I bleed. I'm human," she said. "And this is nothing to the things I expect to encounter in the depths of Gretaila."

"I've seen the inside of that place," Helgwin reminded her. "You are more frightening."

She laughed. "You've barely seen past the opening. We'll see if the rest doesn't change your mind."

Soon, they were riding again, heading into dry, mountainous terrain. Occasionally they'd come across a river or an oasis of trees, but for the most part they found little alive.

"There are dwarves beneath us," Helgwin said.

"You can hear them?" Alaji asked.

"What? No, of course not. But this is Sern-Doltis: there are dwarven outposts and mines scattered throughout these lands. If you care to look, I'm sure we can find a gatehouse. Sometimes they even welcome guests."

"We have no time for such things," Alaji replied. "I want to make Gretaila by tomorrow."

"Why the hurry?" Helgwin asked. "The denizens will be happy to devour us whole no matter when we arrive."

"The hurry is for your benefit," Alaji said. "I am trying to avoid startling you."

"Startling me," Helgwin repeated the phrase. "I'm not sure how to take that."

"The river was a test," Alaji said. "I wanted to see how you'd react."

"And?"

"You did not handle it as well as I'd hoped."

Helgwin chuckled. "Does that mean you've decided I'm no use to you, that you'll release me from our arrangement?"

"Of course not," Alaji said. "It just means we have to ride the rest of the way." She nudged her horse to make it go faster. Helgwin simply sighed in exasperation and did the same, wondering how he'd gotten himself in such a situation.

She glanced back, as if to say something else, but Helgwin

caught sight of something out of the corner of his eye. "Look out!" he cried, tugging on his reins to turn his horse so he was facing uphill.

There was a crashing sound as a boulder was struck from behind. Hairpin cracks appeared, and sections of stone cracked apart and slid forward. Another thud, and a cloud of sand billowed up, like dust on a drum being struck. For a moment, he feared the bolder might cascade down on them in pieces, but the thudding stopped. Instead, a figure, twenty feet tall and shaped like a man only bulkier and hairless, circled around the stone, dragging his palm against it. He looked at them with three eyes and opened a mouth to show his teeth, a third of which were missing.

"Ogre," Helgwin said, pulling his reins tight to keep his horse from panicking. He glanced towards Alaji to find her calm and relaxed, more interested in how he was reacting than in the beast. "Fine," he said, grabbing the broadsword strapped beside his leg. He pulled it free then tore away the blanket covering it. Then he called to his horse and kicked it to drive it towards the monster.

The ogre swept the ground with a massive hand, flinging small stones up at his horse and forcing the animal to lurch to the side. The ogre leapt at him, no doubt hoping to catch him off guard. But Helgwin was ready for this. As soon as his horse slid to the side, he kicked his leg free and used the horse's momentum to roll off and drop to the ground. Then, without turning to look, he struck the horse's hindquarters with the butt of his sword, sending it running, both so it wouldn't be easy prey for the monster and so his opponent would have two targets to focus on.

As he'd hoped, the ogre's attention was momentarily drawn towards the fleeing animal, giving Helgwin a chance to close in. He didn't quite reach it before it turned back towards him, swinging its hand.

Helgwin leapt back to avoid the strike but swung his sword as he did so. His blade struck the back of the ogre's fist and sliced into the grey flesh. The monster's hide was too thick for the blade to do any real damage, but it hollered in pain, pulled back its hand, and licked the wound.

Helgwin lunged, swinging his sword at the ogre's stomach as he did so. He cut, again barely drawing blood but still startling the creature, which wasn't ready for such opposition. It kicked towards him, and Helgwin spun to one side to avoid the massive leg and come closer in one move. He gripped his sword with both hands and hacked at the leg holding the ogre's weight.

The blade connected with the ogre's thigh, and it screamed with rage as it fell back. All three eyes opened wide, and it flung itself back up, springing towards the warrior. Helgwin simultaneously ducked, braced his sword in front of him, and slid forward to meet the creature.

The monster's cries of rage softened to confusion as its momentum slowed. Then, as it lurched to the side, Helgwin released his hilt and rolled away. He waited a moment for the ogre to stop moving then approached. His blade was completely buried in its body.

He turned behind him to find Alaji approaching slowly. She held the reins of his horse in one hand, leaving him wondering how she'd caught it so easily. If she was impressed by his victory, she offered few signs. Helgwin grabbed hold of his hilt, placed a boot on the dead ogre's stomach, and pried it loose. He held it up to display it, bent and warped beyond use. He tossed it to one side and said, "Now we have a reason to find a dwarf city. Unless you want me descending into Gretaila unarmed."

"I'll want to be quick," she said, "but we'll make up the time some other way."

"I hope I passed that test more to your liking," Helgwin muttered beneath his breath.

19: SIGNATURES

Alaji cut off abruptly as the light in the small room flashed green before settling back to a neutral color. Reilla started to stand but paused almost immediately. "It's okay," she said to Alaji. "It only means someone is outside. I'm going to check and see what they want."

"Of course," Alaji said, settling back down. "I was not expecting it," she whispered.

"The light is pure magical energy," Yemerik said. "We actually use it for a lot of things, but it more or less always glows, so there's no reason not to have it provide light."

Alaji was still gazing overhead. It looked almost like lightning flashing through water. "Oadeth told me," she said quietly.

"It turned orange everywhere when you arrived," Yemerik said. "It does that occasionally. Anytime there's an unexpected arrival or something we need to attend to."

"Orange means there's something requiring attention," Alaji said. "Red means there's actual danger."

"Yes," Yemerik said. "But how do you… oh. Yes, of course. Oadeth again."

"He told me many stories," Alaji said.

"If he told you he'd seen the lights go red, he was lying," Yemerik said. "We never had that kind of emergency in his lifetime. The last was when I was a boy. Someone had brought a small creature back for study and forgot to hand it over for procedural analysis. It turned out it had mass adjustment properties. I'm sorry, that means—"

"I'm guessing it could change size," Alaji said.

"Yes. That's exactly right."

"I've come across a few creatures like that in my travels. There was one, in a city beneath the ocean…" She smiled, thinking back, then waved her hand, as if shooing an insect. "Never mind that. Finish your story."

"There's not much more to tell. I didn't see anything, of course, other than the lights change. I heard later something that had been small enough to fit into a pocket had grown to a hundred feet long and done some damage to the archive. I think a few lives were lost, as well. It's still used as a lesson on the importance of following proper protocol when bringing unknown lifeforms into the Citadel."

Alaji couldn't help but grin. She started to open her mouth to say something, but Reilla reentered the room first, accompanied by a man Alaji hadn't seen before.

"This is Scotheck," Reilla said. "He's a spectro-alchemist who's been studying the fragments of the talisman you brought with you. There's a great deal of interest in how one of our talismans was broken. He was hoping to ask you a few questions."

Alaji looked him over. He was a young man, thin and short, with an oddly long face. "I do not think he is going to be satisfied with my answers."

"I'm sorry for interrupting," Scotheck said, speaking quickly. He was anxious, Alaji decided, and more than a little excited. "But our temporal signature readings are… somewhat intriguing, and we want to make sure we're not missing anything."

"Oh," Yemerik spoke up. "I think I can help. The pieces were separated and sent into different eras before reuniting. Their patterns won't align perfectly."

"I know," Scotheck said, shaking his head. "That was in the report. It's not that, so much as… the patterns don't match our records. The Dalanire pattern makes sense, given our understanding of its history, but the Kasanyo magnitude is completely wrong. It's so far off, it's not even resonating with the Citadel."

"That's absurd," Yemerik said. "Those things opened the gates. How is that possible if they're not from the Citadel?"

"No. You're not listening," Scotheck said. "The Dalanire pattern is exactly right. That means the fragments are definitely from the talisman you took. But the resonance is different. It's been altered."

"What does that mean?" Yemerik asked.

Scotheck shifted back and stuttered in an annoyed voice, "That's what I'm trying to figure out." Reilla placed a hand on his shoulder, and he took a quick breath. "We're operating under the assumption she transformed them somehow. And that whatever she did to them allowed them to be broken. More than that, they're interacting in ways we've never seen." He paused. "It might be helpful if we had the other piece."

"You'll want to speak with Tearna about that," Reilla said. "She's managing plans to recover the missing pieces, along with our people."

"No," Scotheck said. "I mean, the piece she still has with her."

Alaji clutched her staff closely. "This stays with me. Otherwise, I won't say another word."

"Scotheck," Reilla said. "I need to speak with you outside for a moment." She stepped back, still holding his shoulder and pulling him gently away. The door closed like a membrane behind them, and once again, Alaji and Yemerik were left alone.

"They'll need to examine it eventually," Yemerik said, motioning towards her staff. Alaji remained silent, and he added, "I wasn't actually supposed to mention it to you. Perhaps that was duplicitous, but no more so than you not volunteering the information. Unless you knew that we knew it was there." He paused again, then added, "They knew what it was before they ever confronted you. They knew a great deal about every object you brought here."

"Of course," Alaji said at last. "Oadeth described your protocols for uninvited incursions."

"Incursions," Yemerik laughed as he repeated the word. "Was that what you were trying to do?"

"I was trying to do nothing more than I accomplished," Alaji said. "To come to the entryway of the Citadel and introduce myself."

"You had to come to the entryway," Yemerik said. "The Central Operational Archive maps the spectral signatures of our agents and recognized guests. If those don't match an arrival, you're pushed to the entryway, even if you try and specify another location. Or did Oadeth neglect to tell you that?"

"It doesn't matter," Alaji said. "I specified the entryway."

Yemerik shook his head. "Why? Why… any of it?"

"I've been trying to explain since we started. You'll understand in the end."

"Will I?" he asked sarcastically.

"I am sure of it," Alaji replied.

"You can't be," Yemerik said. "I know what you're trying to do. You're throwing my own vague insinuations back in my face so I know how it feels. You're doing this to spite me."

"Am I?"

"Yes. And I'll tell you how I know. Because time here functions consistently. We're not in the normal flow anymore. There's no going forward and seeing how this conversation ends or what you give us. There's only us, sitting here, playing these games."

"This is a game to you?"

"No!" Yemerik shouted. He took a deep breath then continued, "No. But it is for you. I don't understand why you're playing it or what you want to get. But I know you well enough to see you're enjoying yourself. I know the look of satisfaction you used to get when one of your tricks worked, or you outsmarted some monster or warrior. And I've seen it plastered across your face since you got here."

"You think so little of me?" she asked, but she did so with a smile.

"I think you're brilliant. I think you've realized that yourself. But there are a lot of brilliant people here—Scotheck, for one, is smarter than either of us. Whatever you're hiding, he'll find it eventually, even if Reilla never lets him come within a hundred feet of your staff."

"I keep telling you, the explanation is within my story. In a way, the explanation and story are one."

"More riddles," Yemerik said. "More games." But he grew quiet when an opening appeared in the wall and expanded, allowing Reilla to step in. Scotheck was gone; once again, it was just the three of them.

"Am I interrupting something?" Reilla asked.

Alaji took some satisfaction in pausing to watch Yemerik's face turn white. "No," Alaji said, before he could try and explain himself. "Nothing of consequence, anyway."

"I'm glad to hear that," Reilla said. "Scotheck had to leave to attend to other matters, but he did ask that I inquire about the shard in your staff."

"If he can't work out the truth from the other pieces, this won't tell him more," Alaji said, clutching her staff.

"I thought as much," Reilla said, shrugging as if she didn't care either way. "But I assured him I'd speak with you." She paused thoughtfully, then added, "He also mentioned his team was surprised they didn't detect similar patterns from the complete talismans."

"I wouldn't expect them to," Alaji replied.

"Then the alterations were the result of the talisman being broken," Reilla said, watching Alaji as she spoke.

"No, no," Alaji replied, as if she were unaware Reilla was attempting to manipulate her into providing the information she wanted. "I was only able to break Yemerik's talisman because of what your friend saw." She glanced at Yemerik, who was watching her with an exhausted expression. She grinned slightly, as if to challenge him, or at the very least point out the irony of him accusing her of playing games.

"I see," Reilla said in a friendly, enthusiastic tone. "You found a way to transmute the talisman."

Alaji shook her head. "It's not so simple," she said. "I am trying to tell you about it. How it happened and why. The decision I made and the reason I'm here now."

"Yes, of course. I apologize for the interruptions," Reilla said.

Yemerik stifled a laugh then did his best to turn it into a cough. It wasn't at all convincing, but Alaji pretended she didn't notice. Instead, she smiled and asked, "Now then, where was I?"

20: THE FALL OF LEKSIASHA

The darkness moved like a coming storm towards the front lines, where nine men stood tall. To either side stood regiments of elves, men, and dwarves. The elves held bows nocked with arrows glowing white. Droplets of rain striking these arrows fell to the earth and blossomed with life, so patches of green sprouts lined the ground before them.

The dwarves had massive devices of war, enchanted with metal runes welded to the sides of ballistae and bolts. The rain that struck the runes never made it to the ground, but evaporated in wisps of steam.

The humans had the usual assortment of knights on dragonback, troops armed with magical swords ten feet long but as light as daggers, and wizards preparing to channel impossible power through their hands. But these, like the elves and dwarves, were mainly here to support the core of the army: the nine men standing ready.

Ahead of them, the darkness grew closer. They could see form in the coming tempest; images of men and beasts swirled in the encroaching black. Soon, it would break apart and choose its shapes. Soon, it would attack.

Behind them, Leksiasha, city of sunsets, glistened, shining against the night. Its walls were stone and metal, and at one time their glow alone could drive back the forces of its enemies. But a thousand years of war had strained its magic, and not even the Collective could replenish it fast enough.

So sacrifice was called for.

Marwye's voice cut through the rain. "In every generation, they have come, and in every generation, we have defeated them. The darkness is unyielding. It does not feel pain as we do. It does not suffer the same loss. If we are to win this war, it will be won with tears. How fitting it should rain this night!" The old man stepped into view in front of the nine. He stroked his beard thoughtfully and looked them over. "We look to our best to wear the Armor of Andotyn. You nine are the bravest, the strongest. If you would take up the mantle, now is your time!"

A cart was pulled before them, and a group of priests removed nine identical chests from the back. Each chest was placed before one of the nine warriors, then one by one, the latches were unclasped and the lids were lifted to reveal two objects embedded in violet silk lining. One was a small orb fixed to a metal spike. The other, a crystal vial.

"Before you lies the means to defend Leksiasha," Marwye said. "No obligation binds you. It is commanded by the Holy Collective that you may turn away from this call, and if you do so, you are to face no hardship. If any man or woman names you coward or challenges your honor, name them before the Collective, and they shall be called to pay restitution. For those of you who accept this burden, your names will be recorded twice, once upon the crypt walls and once in the Collective's Song, to be remembered for all time."

The nine men knelt in unison before the chests. In three hundred years, no man had declined this honor; indeed, these nine had competed for years to earn this right. They each took hold of a vial and raised them up. Then, when precisely three seconds had passed, they pulled off the stoppers and drank the contents.

"You are heroes, not only of Leksiasha and the Collective, but of all lands where life is sacred," Marwye continued. "You are…" He trailed off when he saw several of the archers shift position unexpectedly to aim at something behind him. He spun around and found himself face to face with a woman with tan skin. She smelled of moss and smoke, and she wore an assortment of peculiar clothes, none of which resembled those of any nation he knew of.

"I'm sorry. I hadn't meant to interrupt." She glanced behind her at the coming storm of shadow. "This looks like the place, at least."

"Who are you?" Marwye demanded. "What do you serve?"

"I don't serve the Bleak Storm," the woman said. "But I don't serve the Collective, either. I am here because I would speak with them both, and this will present a unique opportunity to do so."

Marwye stared at her, utterly befuddled. "There is… there is no time for this," he said. "Shoot her if she…" But she was gone. Vanished without explanation. His lips quivered, and he shouted, "Finish the rites!"

The nine removed the spiked orbs and held them in their palms. "The strength of land is life. The strength of life is will. Its wellspring is sacrifice," they said in unison. Marwye turned towards them. Behind them, floating over a group of dwarves, he saw the strange woman. He glared at her, furious that she'd interrupted. But he did not want to disrupt the ritual further by ordering her shot or captured.

The nine continued, "My blood is as the rivers. My flesh is as the earth. My breath is as the wind. For my country, land, and love, I sacrifice myself. May Leksiasha flourish until the end of days, and may the Collective pity those who mean us harm!"

They plunged the spikes into their chests. Some of them cried out; others merely grimaced as the orbs began to glow. The nine shook, and their eyes rolled back. One foamed at the mouth, while another began convulsions.

"The darkness approaches!" Marwye shouted, gesturing behind him but keeping his eyes on the nine men. "It is strong enough to break stone, to turn metal to ash! But your armor is stronger!"

Sparks of blue electricity appeared around the orbs, and the men rose to their feet. Even the one convulsing stood, though his body continued to quiver. They rose higher then, drifting into the air as the electricity formed pillars of light beneath their feet. Bolts of energy arced between their fingertips, between their arms and sides, and between their legs. Their eyes began glowing brighter and brighter, until they matched the orbs.

"Go!" Marwye called to them. "Go and show the Storm their folly in coming here!"

The first of the men stepped forward, and as he did so, the energy constructs surging around his body grew. The sparks were lightning now, formed in the shape of a giant. And in the giant's heart, the man could still be seen, shaking in awe, pain, fear, and glory. He bellowed, and a bolt of energy shot from the head of the construct around him. It struck the center of the approaching storm and burned a hole in it.

The other warriors followed, and as they moved, shells of energy grew around them, until they became towering, glowing figures, each a hundred feet tall. A few extended their arms, and blades of lightning appeared in their hands. The armies behind them cheered them on.

Marwye's attention, however, returned to the woman who'd interrupted the sacred rites of the donning of the Armor of Andotyn. Again, he considered telling an archer to shoot her from the sky or sending a wizard after her, but he knew that would be an act of rage, something more befitting a follower of the Storm than a servant of the Collective.

He stared at her until she looked back. By that time, the flashes of light had intensified, and the earth shook. The nine brave warriors were no doubt experimenting with their weapons, celebrating their newfound power while they could. The Armor of Andotyn was unmatched in strength, but it drew its energy from the lifeforce of its wearer. Marwye never doubted they'd find victory, but none of them would last the hour.

The woman drifted down towards him slowly. If she realized a dozen elven bows were drawn and aimed at her, she did not acknowledge it. Marwye raised a hand to signal the archers to hold. Then he took a few steps forward to make it clear he was meeting with the woman willingly.

"I will have your name and purpose," he said, making no attempt to mask his irritation with her presence.

"I will speak my name to the Collective when the battle is over," the woman said. "It would only complicate matters now."

"When the battle is over, assuming you aren't killed by a stray arrow or a shard of night, you will be judged by tribunal. Were I you, I should not expect to set eyes on the Collective in this lifetime."

"I'm sorry," the woman said. "You will not win this fight."

Marwye scoffed. "The city of sunsets has stood against the tide of darkness for a thousand years. It will stand long after you and I are dust and our names are forgotten."

"You are Marwye," the woman said, shrugging. "You will outlive the city, and your name will be spoken on the last day."

"I have had enough of this. Captain! Arrest this…" He trailed off angrily as she vanished again. Then, turning to one of the elves, he said, "If she appears again, you can put an arrow through her arm."

"Is she a spy?" the archer asked.

"Doubtful. What use would the Storm have with spies? She is probably just mad."

"Mad or not, that's an impressive trick she's mastered. I've never seen a mage teleport so quickly."

Marwye shrugged. "Why do you think I want an arrow through her arm instead of her eye?" He sighed and turned his attention back to the front, where the nine colossal figures of light stood before the coming waves of shifting black forms. "Better ready your men, Captain. In case some shards get through."

The archer nodded and hurried to marshal his troops, while the dwarven general solemnly finished reciting the Oaths of Stone, Sand, Blood, and Moss, then began rhythmically tapping his gauntlet against the metal edge of a ballista. Down the line, other dwarves did the same, creating a steady drumbeat for their soldiers. The wizards, meanwhile, chanted, summoning swirling violet lights above the armies.

Ahead of them, on hills beaten bare by centuries of war, the giants formed a line. Some hurled a few more bolts of lightning before holding out their hands to conjure incredible swords of flickering energy and shields to match. The bulging black shape struck the ground before them and took shape. Dragons with three heads, giants wielding clubs, and monstrous spiders the size of small mountains came forth. It was a fearsome if unambitious display: the nine wouldn't be so easily scared. A wave of smaller figures formed as well, shaped like ogres, wild dogs with six legs, and countless other monstrosities. The large figures would engage the nine glowing guardians while the smaller would attempt to rush through and do as much damage to the army as they could manage—it was hardly a new strategy.

"Maneuver sixty-two," Marwye said. The elven captain nodded and motioned for his troops to shift left, and subsequent divisions adjusted their positions in a cascade. Three dwarven ballistae fired to the left of the giant, glowing guardians. The bolts struck the hill with a distant thump, and Marwye turned away and plugged his ears as they erupted in an explosion which obliterated a large section of the hill, making the terrain nearly impassible.

A shadowy form shaped like a three-headed dragon jumped at one of the nine warriors and attempted to pin an arm with two of its heads. Perhaps the spirit commanding the beast hoped the warrior hadn't mastered his armor yet, or maybe it was simply more interested in being the first to engage than in achieving any kind of strategic advantage. The warrior simply stepped back, allowing it to grapple one arm made of lightning, then he twisted the serpentine neck to one side. While the beast was made of shadow and spirit, it was bound to the rules of its form. It struggled to stay upright while the energy coursing through the warrior burned its jaw. Then the armored giant butted the creature with his shield. The impact struck with a thunderclap, and a shockwave of wind swept over the armies behind Marwye. The dragon teetered back, giving the warrior time to lift his lightning sword overhead and arc it down, slicing the beast neatly in two. The creature dissipated into mist.

Another of the warriors charged at a spider, which towered over him. The monster was more than a thousand feet tall and walked on thin legs. The warrior, a tenth its size even in his magical armor, began hacking at the stalks. Another of the chosen joined him, pausing only to drag his blade through a group of smaller shadows first, destroying dozens. Together, they quickly managed to cut the spider down to size, then skewered it from below.

A wave of the smaller shards that had gotten past the massive guardians dropped to the glowing elvish arrows, which cut through them as easily as air. Another form, shaped like a troll, took a dwarven ballista bolt to the chest, staggered back, and exploded in a shower of black rain and mist.

To Marwye's eye, the battle was starting about as well as could be hoped, but he knew the Storm was far from finished. A massive maw shaped like a crocodile's head took shape and snapped onto one of the glowing figures. The bodiless maw, still connected to the cloud, struggled, trying to pull the warrior into its midst, but the figure fought back. Two of his companions plunged their blades into the shadowy head's neck while the trapped man strained. Every movement the man made, his glowing armor copied, and he managed to pry the jaws apart and wedge his shield between them. Instead of falling back, he allowed his shield to vanish. As the jaws began closing once more, he stabbed forward, pushing his lightning blade down the form's throat. Seconds later, it was fog and night.

Even so, the warrior did not relent. He took his sword in both hands and hacked into the dark storm cloud, cutting from side to side faster than it could take new forms. The others followed close behind, taking the fight to the Storm.

Marwye noted a group of small dark figures which had gotten through in the confusion and prepared to point them out to the archers. But the figures didn't make for the army; they paused on the field and circled back towards the massive warriors. Briefly, Marwye wondered if they were trying to flee, though he found it difficult to imagine.

The figures paused behind the great knights. Then, in an

instant, the black shrouds around them vanished, revealing instead figures glowing white. Marwye stared in disbelief for a second, then pointed and yelled, "Go! Take them! Kill them!"

But it was already too late. One of figures pointed to a knight, and a beam of light shone from her hand. It struck the lightning warrior right in its heart and passed through. There was nothing to fall but the charred remains of the man who'd been controlling it.

The other warriors turned on the white figures. One of them brought his foot down directly on the head of a woman, who simply raised her open hands and conjured a shimmering globe around her. The crackling lightning drove her into the ground, but it could not crack the barrier. He tried again, stomping down, only to find his foot stuck against the magical field. The woman reached up through her field and took hold of a pair of energy arcs as if they were ropes. A chain reaction began to flow up the giant energy construct. It affected only a fraction of the electricity coursing through the air, turning it from blue to a dull red. Then the woman tugged the ends in her hands, and the red strands snapped throughout the construct. Like the first to fall, the energy vanished, and the body fell, segmented by the transmuted wires of magic.

There were seven armored warriors left, and they did what they could. Most tried their swords; one even managed to crack the magical barrier around one of the small figures, but before he could press his attack, a pair of white-hot energy blasts converged from either side, vaporizing the majority of his body.

The shadow was not still, either. It surged forward, spilling into a wave of monstrous forms that charged blindly across the field. The large ones latched onto the warriors, holding them still while the robed figures finished them quickly, not caring if a few of their own troops were in the way.

The smaller shadows ignored the lightning giants and ran for the armies, which unleashed a torrent of glowing arrows into their midst, destroyed them by the dozens with exploding ballista bolts, cut them down with swords larger than their wielders, or burned them in their tracks with spells.

For a moment, Marwye almost let himself believe the battle could be won by force of arms. But then the beasts made of darkness began breaking through their lines. One leapt up, grabbed a wizard out of the air and crushed him against the ground. A group of dwarves were on it at once, splitting the monster apart with axes, but the enemy's loss was insignificant.

The next to fall was a group of elves, followed by two more mages. With a growing realization of horror, Marwye watched the front of the battle shift from the field between the armies to the ground beneath his feet. He barked orders as quickly as he could manage. "Send word to the Collective!" he screamed, hoping someone would live to carry out his command. Then he turned to the elven archer. "Captain. An arrow, through my heart. Quickly!" He stood tall, hoping to die with what little of his honor he could salvage. But he'd already waited too long.

The archer pulled an arrow from his sheath, drew it back in a flash, and released it. But something dark leapt out at Marwye, tackling him from the side. The shadow took the arrow meant for him as it knocked him aside. The dark form turned to mist as it died, and Marwye struck the ground, coughing and choking on the blackened air. "Captain!" he gasped, reaching towards his old friend.

The elf drew again and began to aim, but a shade in the form of a six-armed beast grabbed the archer. The arrow flew far off its mark, and the elven captain perished screaming in the monster's arms.

Marwye went for a knife strapped to his side, his last resort. He drew it and went for his neck, but another of the creatures was on him. It wrestled the blade away, threw it to one side, and fell on him.

It consumed him, and the world around him was dark. He felt the shadow's form shifting, moving quickly. He couldn't move or breathe, a fact which at least offered solace in the knowledge that he'd die. But even that was a lie.

He felt heat before he saw light, and by then it was a white glow. The creature which had been around him dissolved as he fell through dark mist. His lungs struggled for the air they'd been denied. His body, despite his wishes, refused to let him die.

"Marwye," he heard a voice say. It was a woman's voice, old and crisp. "That is your name, is it not?"

"The Accord of Temtaysia!" he managed to spit out between coughs. "You are violating… the Accord of—"

"Obviously," the woman said. "We are the Bleak Storm…"

"…If we choose to break our word," another robed figure said, continuing the thoughts of the first.

"…Then it is ours to break," a third said. "You hold secrets our brethren have kept from us. You will share these with us."

"I will die first," Marwye said, grabbing a rock off the ground and swinging it at the head of the woman before him. She caught his wrist as if she'd been waiting for him. Her hand glowed, and he screamed out, trying to drop his makeshift weapon. But by then it was molten stone, fused to his hand. The skin around it burst into flame, but the hand of the white-robed woman remained unharmed.

"You will not," she said. Then she whispered something, and he felt his neck and body go numb. He could smell the flesh on his hand burning, but he could no longer feel it. He'd no will to fight her, so his head leaned back, and he stared into her eyes.

21: THE RUINS OF THE LIGHT

Only sections remained of the towering walls that had protected Leksiasha for eons, and even these were lined with cracks. The glowing violet light which had emanated from the city of sunsets had gone dark, and the skies above were dyed red and green by smoke.

Men, women, and children ran through the carnage in a mad attempt to escape the thousand nightmarish forms taken by the dark cloud that had descended upon the once peaceful city.

Marwye's foot, acting on its own accord, took another step. His eyes glowed white without blinking, and his face bore no expression. Around him, the robed figures moved through piles of rubble and bodies while their minions served as guardians.

They'd barely gotten a hundred feet in when a group of guards poured out of a building, charging with curved swords. Most fell to white light pouring from the robed figures' hands. The magic burned away flesh and bone in an instant, before continuing to melt the stone foundations behind them.

The robed figures ignored the four who'd avoided this, allowing their shadowy minions to step in. The guards fought admirably, cutting through their monstrous opponents, but the numbers were far too great. Within seconds, the battle was over, and three of the guards lay pinned to the ground. The fourth's body lay crushed beneath the hand of a shade fifteen feet tall with long, gangly arms and a head like some sort of fish dragged up from the deep ocean.

"Kill me!" one of the guards shouted, as he struggled against the claws of three creatures which had taken the form of orcs. "Kill me, you cowards!" He looked up at their faces and found empty expressions looking back. Whatever intellect inhabited these creatures was beyond emotion as he knew it.

"His courage is admirable," one of the robed figures said, stepping towards him. She was a woman, young with long blond hair.

"Get away from me!" he shouted. Her head tilted to one side, as if trying to see him from another angle.

She knelt just behind him and lifted his sword to inspect it. "We must take care to avoid their blades. These bear strong enchantment," she added, turning it over. "They would not easily cut through our magic…"

"…but given the right hand," an older woman said, picking up the thought mid-sentence, "they might prove compromising." The young woman kneeling over the guard looked down at him. From his perspective, she was upside down, with the discolored sky behind her. She still held the sword in her hand.

The guard breathed heavily beneath the unliving arms pinning him. He stretched, craning his neck, so she would have easy access. "Go ahead, demon! See if you can remove my head in less than four cuts!" He tried to sound defiant, grinding his teeth and straining his muscles. But when the woman in white tossed his sword to the side, he seemed to deflate. "No," he whispered. "Kill me," he begged.

"You have a strong spirit," the woman said, reaching towards his head with fingers glowing white. He closed his eyes and tried to turn away, but she touched his cheek, singeing the flesh and forcing his head up.

His eyelids remained shut, but this did not deter her. She whispered a quiet spell, and he began screaming as his own eyes glowed in response. His eyelids were ash and smoke in seconds, and still he screamed. She reached down and touched his white-hot eyes with two fingers. As she pulled them away, she drew out a form of light, shaped like the man below her but made of crackling energy. Aside from its size, it was not entirely dissimilar in appearance to the nine armored warriors who'd fallen in battle.

"He is beautiful," one of the older robed figures mused.

"As they all are," the woman holding the spirit said. She began to chant, and sparks of red began coursing through the spectral form. It shook and its mouth opened in a silent scream, until it finally turned black.

"Do not fret," a middle-aged man wearing the white robes said. "This is a new kind of being."

"We welcome you to the Bleak Storm," the young woman in white said, lifting the dark form into the air and releasing it. "Someday, you may become as we are." The spirit shook, still feebly struggling as a powerful new gravity took hold and pulled it towards the bulging, shifting black cloud just beyond the edge of the city.

By then, robed figures were already kneeling beside the other two guards. Beyond them, shadowy forms were attempting to restrain prisoners to keep them from killing themselves or their own children.

—

It was nearly dawn when the robed figures reached the center where the massive marble dome of the Collective stood. A giant made of the same shadowy material as all the Storm's forces struck it, again and again. Its hands were cracking apart, but the structure remained undamaged.

"At peace," one of the robed figures said, raising a hand. The giant bowed its head and stepped away.

"Open the way for us," the young woman instructed Marwye, who walked forward, placed his remaining hand on the marble, and uttered a single word. A circular section of marble vanished, revealing a round hallway lined with violet lanterns. One by one, the other men and women in white stepped through the opening. Finally, only the young woman remained with Marwye. She paused to consider him, staring into his empty, glowing eyes.

"You will think this a kindness, and you will be mistaken: we will not take you into our fold. The Storm does not want your spirit among us. Perhaps, in another life, you may prove your value. But too much of our pain has been born of your acts." She reached out and touched his forehead, and a white light flashed. Marwye fell back, landing hard against the ground. "None of us will trouble you, nor shall our troops, unless you attack them. You may live out whatever years you have left, knowing the Collective fell through your weakness."

She turned and followed the other robed figures without bothering to look back at the general shaking on the ground and clutching what remained of his burned hand. She joined the others lining up along the wall of the amphitheater within the dome, where three dozen men, women, and children in similar garb were waiting.

"It is disappointing that the Bleak Storm has acted so recklessly," one of the Collective said from the center. The speaker was a child, no older than six, though her mind was as ancient as any in the room.

"We would hear your business here," a man nearing fifty said.

"…and if it does not meet our expectations," a woman in her thirties said.

"…you will join those of your kind born in our land," the girl said.

"You are in no position to threaten us," an old man from the Storm answered angrily.

"It is you who must answer for your crimes," the young woman in white said.

"You have imprisoned those who were once extensions of your own soul," another of the Storm said.

"…you have used forbidden magic," the young woman added.

"…magic which caused irreparable damage to its users," the eldest of the Storm added.

"…and injured the very spirits of our servants," one of the boys said.

"We have protected ourselves from your darkness with the tools at our disposal!" one of the Collective replied angrily.

"You have brought suffering to those in our care, and you have destroyed a city serving as a beacon to the whole of the world," the young girl added.

"We have been patient with you so far," another of the Collective said.

"…but that patience wears thin. You have given us no choice but to pass judgment against you." The eyes of the Collective glowed white in unison, and those of the Storm began glowing an instant later.

"We warned you," the boy from the Storm said.

"…you are not in the position you believe," the young woman added. The Storm braced themselves as a wave of force shot through the room. Everyone there, Storm and Collective alike, grimaced in pain.

"What has…" one of the Collective stuttered, terrified.

"What have you done?" another screamed.

"I can't hear you!" a third shouted. "I can't hear anything!"

The Storm raised their hands and rays of white light shot up, striking the underside of the dome. A section crumbled, revealing a massive shape in the sky overhead. The black cloud was directly above the dome now, and giant hands made of shadow held massive metal objects, pointing them directly at the robed figures below.

"What have you made?" one of the Collective demanded.

"Enough!" the young woman said. "Your city is fallen, and those held here will be freed. Once they have rejoined us, we will decide if your spirits are to take their place in your prison. But one way or another, the Bleak War ends this day."

"No, it doesn't." The voice came from the same hall those from the Storm had used to enter. They turned to look at the speaker, as did the frightened members of the Collective. And all of them, together, gasped.

"Alaji," the young woman in white said.

The witch stood there, watching them quietly. She was older than they remembered her, and her clothes were not as they'd last seen her. She walked in, eyeing them carefully.

"I am sorry you had to bear witness to this," the young girl from the Collective said.

"We are not… I know it seems as if we're in the wrong," the woman who'd controlled Marwye said. "But it is not as it appears."

"I don't care," Alaji said.

"Alaji!" one of the men from the Collective exclaimed. "Do you remember me? From the city beneath the sea! We spoke about the Bleak Queen! About her transformation!"

"I remember," Alaji said.

"We are trying to do better this time. We crafted a place where we could share our teachings, where we could elevate the spirits of all to join us."

"They lie!" one of the Storm exclaimed. "Their magic erodes the souls of their own chosen warriors! Ours is the true evolution of the Queen's dream!"

"I told you," Alaji said, louder than before, "I do not care. I did not come here to end your war or choose a winner. It has barely begun; before it is finished, it will shatter continents and kill millions."

The crowd went silent, and someone asked, "Which of us is responsible for this?"

"Perhaps both," Alaji said. "Or maybe neither. Before the end, more of the Bleak Queen's anointed will become involved, and other factions will form. Members of the Council you thought were gone forever will emerge and pick sides. As I said, I did not come to this place to settle your differences or lecture you."

"It is… complicated," the young boy said. "Sometimes you appear seeking help. Other times, you come to change the flow of history. And still others… it is a matter of ethics."

"This time, I came for another purpose," Alaji said. "This time… I am here to tell you a story and to ask for your help."

22: STRUCTURES IN TIME

"You were trying to do what we do. You were trying to manipulate time," Yemerik said. When the old crone gave him an amused expression, he sighed and continued, "That's where this is going, isn't it? You were there to tell them about the future of their world. At least one possible future. But you needed their help to achieve it. You wanted to construct some sort of utopia where everyone's spirit was connected."

Reilla cleared her throat to remind Yemerik that they were supposed to be present to hear Alaji's story, whatever it might be. But he'd said everything he had to say, so he simply sat back and waited for Alaji's response.

"They did go on to construct something of the sort," Alaji said. "Long after the war had ended, they joined millions of spirits together. They bent life itself to their whim. It lasted a few hundred thousand years. The parts I visited were quite lovely."

Yemerik nodded and looked to Reilla, who seemed disinterested in the information he'd uncovered. He decided she didn't understand the significance yet, so he added quickly, "She thinks this is the world we were looking for." He was silent for a moment as he waited for a reply. When he didn't get it, he said, "She believes we failed to find it sooner, because we were averse to darkness. That we suppressed too much pain and as a result never arrived at this grand convergence." He hadn't meant to allow so much sarcasm to infect his tone, but he heard it as he spoke.

"What are the readings in the Jar?" Alaji asked.

The question shook Yemerik. "I am... I'm not sure we should discuss that," he said.

"They are around four percent above non-interference," Reilla said.

"That bad?" Alaji asked playfully. "That is how it works, correct? Your measurements are based on suffering, so higher is worse. It has been some time since Oadeth explained it to me, so I'll confess I may be misremembering."

"No, that's right," Yemerik said, surprised by her lack of disappointment.

"I have more faith in your people than that," Alaji said. "I assume you've allowed countless iterations of spectromancy to develop so you could test the results. Probably things worse than spectromancy, too."

"We did," Reilla said. "Not in our lifetimes, but... the Citadel has existed for a very long time."

"A day," Alaji corrected her. "It only exists in a completed state for a single day."

Reilla grinned. "I apologize. I should not have tried to simplify matters. You are right, of course. The Citadel's temporal existence is limited to just this day. Its iterative presence has permitted our civilization—and our work—to progress for a relative period beyond measurement."

"Oadeth told me you didn't know," Alaji said. "That those records were destroyed."

"He probably shouldn't have told you that," Yemerik said. Reilla glanced at him, and he exclaimed, "You just said you wouldn't dumb things down for her. We can start with that. It's not like she doesn't know we have rules."

"There are many things Oadeth did with me he wasn't supposed to," Alaji said, glancing between Yemerik and Reilla, who took a brief, awkward breath. "Does it bother you when I imply we were lovers?"

"A little," Reilla admitted after a pause. "Relationships of that nature are not permitted with people through history. Our knowledge and power give us too much leverage. History is not supposed to exist for our benefit—we are here for it. To make a better world, as Yemerik was speculating you were trying to do."

"He is not entirely wrong," Alaji said. "He is mostly wrong, but not entirely. He is trying to see the matter through a prism he understands."

"Prism," Yemerik said, scoffing.

"Don't be surprised," Alaji said. "I've seen a great number of things since we split ways. I've seen more wonders than I can remember. I've known lovers who made me howl with delight. I've tasted foods so rich I lost control of my senses and wines that seemed to open new worlds. I've heard songs that left me in tears. And, among my travels, I had a chance to look through several prisms and learn a few idioms about them."

"Alaji," Reilla said, smiling, "if it's not too much trouble, I'd like to hear more about these things. About the places, food, and art you came across, and how they made you feel."

But Alaji shook her head. "I am sorry. I've drifted off topic. Those things were part of my life, but they are not part of the story I came to tell. If I spent my hours chasing those to their conclusions, I'd never be able to tell you enough to understand."

She was looking at Yemerik now, as if talking just to him. He nodded, unsure what to make of that. Then Alaji smiled once more.

"The dwarven city," she said. "Yes. That is next. The city of Xaryi. Or what was left of it, at least."

23: THE DENIZENS OF XARYI

"We've wandered into something else," Eroza said, as they stepped through dark passages. The three women were still covered in mud, though it had begun to dry and crumble off in patches. Between that and the remaining smears of gel on her head, Rit'ka barely looked human.

"This was a city of dwarves once," Alaji said. "They called it Xaryi."

"I've never heard of it," Rit'ka said.

"I have," Eroza said. "The Beratai list it among the eleven lost cities of their tribe. I have read of expeditions in the Olriane Mountains searching for it. But I never heard it was so far north, nor that it is joined to Medpak'id."

"It wasn't always," Alaji said. "The dwarves who settled here came from tunnels to the west. There is a string of ruins like the overturned city we passed through leading here. It must have been an island chain that came down together."

"You are still convinced that's where these came from?" Rit'ka said.

"Not Xaryi," Alaji said. "Xaryi was carved by dwarves. But it's easier to move through hollow paths than it is to tunnel. The dwarves had no idea where they were building or what lay beneath them. They made their city here and began mining for gold, gemstones, and iron. It was only a matter of time until they opened the wrong passageway and came upon Medpak'id. The old paths to the west are closed now, but the city's corpse remains."

"You are certain of this?" Eroza asked.

"I made it my business to learn the history of these caverns," Alaji said.

Eroza tilted her head. "Xaryi disappeared eleven thousand years ago."

"More or less," Alaji agreed.

"Then you see the contradiction. Ked'herd'datt lived about ten thousand years ago, unless the records are wrong."

"They are near enough," Alaji said.

"Then how could Ked'herd'datt's caverns have devoured a city before Ked'herd'datt's birth?" Eroza asked. Behind her, Rit'ka laughed.

Alaji, however, shook her head. "I told you this place was older than you knew. These tunnels were not made by Ked'herd'datt. He took an interest in them and devoted the latter portion of his life to their study."

"That's absurd," Rit'ka said. "Everyone knows he went mad in his later years and constructed Medpak'id as a testament to his power. If it had been an academic study, he'd have written a treatise on the subject."

"I assume he tried," Alaji said. "But it made no difference. He was not permitted to finish it. His obsession was his undoing."

Rit'ka scoffed. "Ked'herd'datt was the scourge of three kings. He kept dragons as pets and commanded rock to come alive and build him palaces. Nothing down here could have given him pause, let alone killed him."

"I would not be so sure," Alaji said. "But it makes no difference—it wasn't a beast or a trap that killed him. It was one of Medpak'id's architects."

Rit'ka threw up her hands. "Who then? What ancient wizard do you think built this, if not Ked'herd'datt? Did the gods themselves piece it together then hunt down Ked'herd'datt for defiling it?"

"It is not so impossible," Eroza said.

"Were your gods real, it wouldn't be," Alaji said. "Ked'herd'datt wasn't killed out of vengeance, and he wasn't killed by any god, at least not as you know the term."

"Who then?" Rit'ka demanded.

Their discussion was interrupted by a long, grinding sound, like stone scraping together. "This will need to wait," Alaji said, motioning ahead of them.

Rit'ka rolled her eyes but drew one of her glowing daggers with one hand. In the other, she clutched the torch illuminating the passage.

"What are we facing?" Eroza asked as she nocked an arrow.

"The people of Xaryi," Alaji said. "They were claimed by this place along with their city. I hadn't expected them to reform, too."

"Vampires, then?" Rit'ka asked nervously. "Common ghouls?"

"No," Alaji replied. "It will be worse." She paused, looking carefully at the pair of thieves preparing to fight beside her. "I am not sure this will work."

"We have fought the dead before," Eroza replied. "Rit'ka's blades will wound ghosts, and in my experience even vampires are useless if you rob them of their joints."

"This isn't like that," Alaji said.

"I would prefer if we actually knew what we are about to fight," Rit'ka said.

"If I could put it into words, I would," Alaji said anxiously. "Stand back, at least."

"I don't take orders from her," Rit'ka said, nodding towards Eroza. "And she's got the coolest head I've ever known. Do you really think I'm going to listen to you?" Despite her taunt, Rit'ka shifted away from the dark passage the sound was emanating from.

Alaji conjured a brighter light, calling it into being at the intersection with the tunnel. The entire area was illuminated, revealing the grain of the rock, as well as old stains and bits of debris. Rit'ka glanced around her, then tossed her torch to one side, deciding Alaji's magic was sufficient. She drew her second blade, which began glowing like her first.

"Do you trust me?" Alaji asked.

"What?" Rit'ka said.

Alaji took a quick breath. "Do you trust that I have access to incredible magic, and that I'll use it to aid you?"

"Yes to the first part, and no to the second," Rit'ka replied without hesitation. Alaji turned to Eroza and opened her mouth, but the archer spoke first.

"I am in agreement with my partner," she said. "You should not expect otherwise."

"No," Alaji admitted, "I suppose I shouldn't." She reached into her pocket and pulled out a stone object shaped like a large egg, as a massive shape shuffled into range of the conjured light.

"What in hell's cesspool is that?" Rit'ka shouted.

It was one being and many. Its body consisted of the bones of hundreds, if not thousands, of dwarves bound together by magic. It had no head, save for the skulls, each with glowing eyes, resting where joints should have been. An eerie aura of green gas oozed from its body, which creaked as it moved. It would have been more than twenty feet tall if it stood upright, but the low ceiling forced it to hunch over, putting its hands close to the ground. Its fingers were made of leg bones, segmented around skulls, ending in long femurs sharpened like spears.

Rit'ka backed away as the creature came closer. "I'm listening now," she said. "How do we kill it?"

"It wasn't like this last time," Alaji said. "Last time… wait. That's it—it was already wounded."

"I am not sure we can outrun it," Eroza said.

"I have a way," Alaji replied. "But we can't avoid it. We need to wound it, so Helgwin can beat it and we can get by before it rebuilds itself."

"Eroza!" Rit'ka shouted. "I hope some of that made sense to you!"

"It knew how to fight me," Alaji said. "I should have figured it out sooner."

Eroza fired an arrow at the creature, shattering a skull on its finger. As the tip of its finger fell, it reached down, scooped it off the ground, and hurled it at the three women, who barely managed to duck below the projectile.

"Preset two," Alaji said, "The three of us, fifteen hundred and eighteen years, minimal safety measures. Now."

24: THE FELLING OF THE BONE MONSTER, PART 2

Helgwin held his sword in one hand and his shield in the other. He knew Alaji was behind him, studying his every move. Was she still testing him? Was this all some sick form of entertainment to her? In the end, it did not matter. He was a mercenary, a sword for hire, and he'd failed to uphold the only rule that mattered—he'd taken the wrong job.

It didn't matter that he'd never intended to agree to this, that she'd somehow warped his sick joke into a sicker reality. He'd agreed to return to the one place he'd vowed never to step foot in for a price, and she'd paid him.

That, and that alone, was the reason he was facing a monstrous beast made of reassembled dwarf skeletons.

Helgwin was standing in a square room lined with stone pillars holding up the ruins of a balcony twenty feet in the air. He suspected this had once been some sort of concert hall or auditorium, but now it felt more like an arena. If he was to die here, at least he'd take some solace in the intrinsic irony of the situation.

He doubted that would console him long. As much as he tried to push the thought out of his head, he couldn't help but imagine the creature peeling the skin from his lifeless body and adding his bones to its collection.

The creature lumbered under its own weight. Many of its bones were cracked and bore scorch marks. Helgwin swung his sword at the creature's finger as it reached for him. He managed to crush a section of bone, but the monster's momentum knocked him backwards. He fought to right himself, even as he wondered why he was bothering. He knew better than to think he'd leave this place alive a second time—did it really matter which horror ended him?

Regardless, he dove to one side, avoiding a strike that battered bone and rock alike. He stood as ready as he could manage and put what trust he had in his reflexes, since he certainly had no strategy to rely on.

Then something occurred that he hadn't anticipated—Alaji helped him. She chanted quickly, and conjured wind began filling the room. Pebbles battered him, but the brunt of the force was directed at his opponent, who shifted backwards. Alaji then hurled something at the skeletal monstrosity. Whatever it was shattered on impact, igniting the creature.

Bones seemed to glow red-hot where the fires appeared, and for an instant Helgwin allowed himself to hope that would be enough. The green lights glowing through the skulls on the creature's body intensified, and the fires were pulled into them. Briefly, the skulls glowed red instead of green, then they went dark before reigniting in their original color. A foul-smelling smoke poured out from every crevice in the monster's body.

"I am not above hearing suggestions," Helgwin called out.

"I am thinking," Alaji replied. From the corner of his eye, he saw her fidgeting with some sort of metal object that had no effect. He sighed, then moved closer to the creature, trying to distract it and perhaps find an opening.

But it was quick for its size, and it was relentless. Helgwin managed to wound it slightly, but none of his blows did more than dent it.

"Stand away!" he heard Alaji shout. He charged to one side as he heard glass shatter against the creature behind him. When he looked back, he saw what appeared to be flowers dotting a section of its body. Were he not fighting for his life, the scene might have been comical.

A moment later, the flowers turned to vines, wrapping and winding between the bones comprising the monster's hips and upper stomach. They grew and stretched, straining then snapping bone. The monster, robbed of much of its form, toppled forward, catching itself with its hands.

Helgwin didn't hesitate. He leapt at it before it could shift its weight, then turned his sword over, gripping the blade in his gauntlets. He swung this like a mace, striking the glowing skull that served as its elbow joint and smashing it apart. The monster toppled forward, and Helgwin dove for the other arm, breaking that apart, as well.

Meanwhile, Alaji's vines continued to break apart its midsection. Helgwin targeted any joint he could find. When the opportunity presented itself, he traded his sword for a section of bone, which he used as a club until it splintered into pieces. But by that time, the monster was still.

"Come on," Alaji said, while Helgwin recovered his blade. He glanced back at the bones as she led him away, and he saw a faint glow of green light remaining.

25: THE FELLING OF THE BONE MONSTER, PART 1

Rit'ka blinked as the monster vanished before her eyes. The torch she'd tossed aside was gone as well, leaving them with only Alaji's conjured light. She glanced towards Eroza, hoping the archer would be able to offer some explanation, but her partner was leaning against the cave wall.

"Eroza," Rit'ka said, running to her. She'd rarely seen the archer show any sign of weakness or loss of decorum—on the few occasions she'd seen her ill, Eroza even managed to look refined vomiting— but now she was struggling to stand.

"I'm not hurt," Eroza said in a tone Rit'ka found disconcerting.

"What did you do?" Rit'ka demanded, turning to Alaji. Her voice was raised far louder than Eroza's. With luck, that wouldn't draw attention.

But Alaji was staring at Eroza. "You felt it," Alaji said.

Eroza was panting as she forced herself upright. "Every moment of my life, I have felt the world around me. When I was a girl, I spent a year locked in a cell beneath the ground, and I could still count the days. The hours. The minutes. Every second flowed by with a perfect rhythm. That rhythm is changed now."

"I'm sorry," Alaji said quietly. "I should have suspected. Your senses are the stuff of legend. Why shouldn't you see the flow of time, as well?"

"At least I know what you are now," Eroza said, cringing in pain.

"The headache will pass," Alaji said. "I used to experience them too."

Eroza stared at her. "I want to know the rest," she said.

Alaji shook her head. "I can't tell you everything. Even if it weren't for the monster."

"It's still out there?" Rit'ka asked.

"No," Eroza said. "It was still out there before. Now it's coming for the first time. That's right, isn't it?"

"More or less," Alaji replied. "We don't need to defeat it, not completely. We just need to damage it. It is difficult to explain."

"Can't we just sneak by?" Rit'ka asked. "If it hasn't found us yet, why do we need to confront it at all?"

"For the same reason I brought us to this moment," Alaji said. "We're a single year from the time Helgwin defeats it."

"And the future is immutable?" Eroza asked.

"It is worse than that," Alaji replied. "The future is easily changed. If we fail to align the events, they will cease to occupy the same chain."

"What does that mean? What are the stakes here?" Eroza asked.

Alaji shook her head. "Larger than I want you worrying about," she said.

Rit'ka sighed. Her frustration was tangible. "Are we actually treating any of this as real?"

"It is real," Eroza said. "We've moved through time. I do not understand how or why, but she's telling the truth about that. About everything, most likely. She was there for all of it. For Galaize, Helgwin... probably for Ked'herd'datt, too."

"I won't believe that," Rit'ka said defiantly.

"Good," Alaji replied. "I'd rather you didn't. Treat it like a game or a trick or some sort of complex con. Just get me to the center, so I can finish what I came here to do."

Rit'ka shot Eroza a worried glance, but the archer simply nodded and said, "We'll keep to our agreement, but we'll expect what we were promised."

"You'll find the gem when we arrive," Alaji said, "It hasn't been mined yet, but it will be there."

"I am starting to miss the bone monster," Rit'ka said, irritated. "At least it didn't torment me with riddles."

"This way," Alaji said, leading them on. "I am guessing it will be further into the city, closer to where I first saw it."

"We saw it here," Rit'ka muttered, being sure she was talking too softly to be heard. She'd figured out enough of the details to know she didn't want a response.

—

"This is truly Xaryi," Eroza said, pausing to run her fingers over a worn plaque beneath a statue half destroyed in a cave-in. Rit'ka glanced at the stone tablet Eroza was examining but couldn't make out a single letter or symbol.

Carvings on the walls on either side retained the images of dwarven warriors and maidens, along with ornate decorative columns. Doors and windows created the impression of buildings pressed together, separated by a city street. The detail and scale were staggering, as was the sense of isolation.

Rit'ka tightened her grip on her knives. Her hands were cold, and she found it harder and harder to fight off the sense that the weight of the world towered above them. It was absurd—she'd been in deeper places than this. She'd raided dwarven tombs and explored ancient caverns in her youth. But this was different. Alaji's warnings about Medpak'id were wearing on her.

As always, Eroza caught it first. The archer leapt up silently, drawing an arrow. Rit'ka slipped to one side, hoping to use a rectangular channel carved into one of the buildings as cover. Alaji simply looked ahead and waited.

Then came the sound, as before. A shifting, grinding noise, like two massive bricks slowly being rubbed together. Only the sound wasn't bricks or even rock—it was made from bones, slowly being worn down. If this was truly as far back in time as Alaji and Eroza had claimed, that suggested the bone must heal. Rit'ka shivered as she considered the implications.

Rit'ka leaned out to look at the monster turning onto the street, using its hands to feel the stone buildings on either side. She squinted, watching it in Alaji's light. Then she held one of her daggers behind her, pushed its tip into the wall, and scratched the surface.

The monster shifted, turning towards her, and she grinned. "It listens!" she called out. "It listens through stone!" She hurled a glowing knife, concentrating to command its direction. The spinning blade flew past the monster, ricocheting off the wall. A bony hand flew to where the knife had hit a moment before and scraped the rock.

Eroza released an arrow, splitting one of many bones forming its back. Rit'ka tried summoning her blade, hoping it would tear through the undead monstrosity's body, but it became lodged between its bones. She paused, giving it a moment to shift, then tried again, hoping her knife would be able to find a way to break free now that the angle had changed. Still, it was stuck.

She glanced over her shoulder and saw Alaji had risen into the air. The witch summoned wind, tossing stones in all directions, then threw a vial at the thing. It exploded into fire, which ate into the monster's side, turning huge sections of bone to charcoal. Eroza unleashed two more arrows, targeting the damaged section, which split apart.

"That is enough," Alaji said, holding the egg-shaped talisman. She began whispering to it, and a moment later the monster vanished. All that remained were a few pieces of scorched bone that had broken off.

Rit'ka gasped in shock. Even having experienced the magic, she still found it dizzying. A glimpse to her side reminded her Eroza was even worse off. The archer had leaned against the wall again, still holding her bow and arrow. Rit'ka looked at her, but Eroza shook her head.

"My knife!" Rit'ka exclaimed suddenly. "It was in the beast!"

Alaji shrugged. "Then let's go collect it," she said, motioning towards a nearby passage. They followed it cautiously, until they reached a room with a large opening, a stage, and a raised balcony. There on the floor lay a pile of skulls and bones oozing green fog.

Rit'ka reached out and whispered the incantation for her blade. Several damaged pieces of bone broke apart as the glowing knife returned to the thief's hand.

Eroza ducked near the bones for a closer look. She even ran her hands through the mist, allowing it to seep through her fingers. "We did not move so far this time," she said.

"No," Alaji replied. "A couple years. It is still recovering from its battle with Helgwin."

"That happened between… it was just a moment ago," Rit'ka said. "Just a few seconds passed."

"A few years," Alaji reminded her. "I moved us ahead."

"I understand," Rit'ka said. "I only meant it was seconds for us. For me, at least," she added, glancing at Eroza. "In a way, we helped him fight it."

"I'm not sure he could have beaten it otherwise," Alaji said. "At least not without depleting more potions than I was ready to sacrifice."

"It is good to know where our lives stand. In terms of value, I mean," Rit'ka said.

"I would not have let you die," Alaji said. "Or him. It is simply a matter of whether I'd have used other methods to get around the obstacle."

"You mean we didn't have to fight that thing at all?" Rit'ka demanded.

"It is complicated. We had to fight it, because I did fight it, here in this time," Alaji said, kicking a skull that had rolled from its pile. "I didn't piece it together until I saw it uninjured. Then I realized what we had to do."

"Because you fought it with Helgwin," Eroza said. "You'd previously battled the creature after."

"When I defeated it with Helgwin, my fire potion was useless, yet the monster was already singed. When I saw it otherwise, I realized it must have developed a resistance. We had to wound it before Helgwin destroyed it."

Eroza exhaled. "We could meet Helgwin," she whispered.

"No. You can't," Alaji said. "He is no longer down here, and I won't leave you behind. Once we're finished here, I'll return you both to your own time."

"Once we're finished?" Eroza asked. Her tone had grown more pointed than before.

"I always knew I'd have to move us back in time eventually, though I didn't know when or why. But this wasn't my final expedition here."

"There is something I remain unclear about," Eroza said. "Why did you bring us? If you are so powerful, if you can move through time with ease, then why bother with us?"

Alaji nodded. "It is a fair question. You're right—nothing we've encountered so far could have stopped me. I tried to do this alone once, long ago, but there are things down here I could not beat, not without help. So I researched this era for thousands of years in both directions. I found a list of names who might help me. You were on that list."

"As was Helgwin," Eroza said.

"Yes," Alaji replied.

"Then tell me this. What did he see down here that made him forsake his vocation and devote the rest of his life to keeping anyone alive from entering these caverns?"

Alaji paused and took a deep breath. Rit'ka didn't give her time to collect her thoughts. "What are you hiding?" she demanded.

"He saw a piece of something," Alaji said.

"We deserve to know," Eroza said.

"You do," Alaji agreed, "but I can't afford to tell you."

"Then we should go no further," Rit'ka said angrily.

"We are fifteen hundred years from the world we know," Eroza pointed out.

"What does that matter?" Rit'ka asked. "That means we've found a place we are not criminals. We can leave these mines without worrying about bounty hunters. Let the Heart of Ussell Varikhi rot down there with her secrets!"

"I am sorry," Alaji said. "It was a good gambit, but I won't tell you what you want to know. Not yet, anyway. All I can tell you is this, that if you'd seen everything I'd seen, if you saw the ends of time and had the same choice ahead of you, you would make the same decision."

"Would Helgwin?" Rit'ka demanded.

"No," Alaji said. "At least, I don't think so. As I said, he saw only a sliver, and it shook him. But even before that, he was the sort of man who saw the world in simple terms. I believe he would have preferred a simple solution."

Rit'ka sighed angrily. "It's not enough. Her word that we'd understand if we shared her vision? She's like every cultist we've ever robbed."

Eroza had been staring Alaji in the eye while Rit'ka had been speaking. The archer's expression had once again been cleansed of emotion. "We should hold to our compact," she said at last. "Take her the rest of the way, claim our gem, and return to our home."

"You trust her, then?" Rit'ka asked, sneering.

"No. Not really," Eroza replied. "But she isn't lying, and I don't welcome our alternatives. Besides, I have a feeling it wouldn't matter. In the end, we would help her reach her destination."

"What's that mean?" Rit'ka asked.

Eroza's head tilted the slightest bit, and she stared deep into Alaji's eyes while she spoke. "Is this the first time?" she asked. Alaji paused, so Eroza asked again, "Is this the first time the three of us have stood here and had a conversation like this? Here or elsewhere, have we spoken of these issues and discussed your plan?"

Alaji cleared her throat and glanced away. "We should move on," she said. "There's no telling what else is lurking in the ruins of this city."

26: DISCOVERIES AND LEGACIES

Yemerik and Reilla stood quietly on a floating walkway overlooking Archive Nine while they waited on the Second Order Director of Investigative Study, who was conversing with an excited ethereal specialist. The specialist was using a portable data crystal to project a brightly colored image of swirling lights and shapes. Yemerik neither knew nor cared what they represented—he had other things on his mind.

With a sigh, he glanced to his right. Below them, thousands of men and women hurried between shelves of artifacts, magically preserved data, and even old-fashioned books and scrolls. This was the first time he'd been allowed anywhere near the archives since his return. He'd forgotten just how beautiful they were.

The man they were waiting on dismissed the specialist and hurried towards them. Yemerik swallowed nervously, unsure what to expect. This wasn't a moment he'd been looking forward to, but he had no choice but to force an apologetic smile.

"It's good to see you, Melfirth," Yemerik said. "It's been… well, for me it's been a long time."

Melfirth looked him over and clapped a hand on Yemerik's shoulder. Absently, Yemerik noted they were no longer all that different in age. "It's good to see you, as well," he said, nodding.

"I feel I should apologize," Yemerik said.

"No," Melfirth said, shaking his head. "There's nothing left to apologize for."

"I took advantage of your trust," Yemerik pointed out.

Melfirth chuckled. "I suppose you did. But then I shouldn't have been so trusting. And the most absurd part is I'm glad I was." He laughed briefly. "If anything, I'm envious of your discovery. I'm only a glorified archivist here—look what you've accomplished!"

"Accomplished?" Yemerik repeated the word, surprised and confused.

"It's getting re-written," Melfirth said. "As we speak, they're studying the objects taken from Subject Seven-Nine-Six."

"Seven-Nine-Six?" Yemerik asked.

"I'm sorry," Reilla interrupted. "It's the designation they're using for Alaji. I should have explained that to you," she added, though Yemerik caught her exchange a look with Melfirth that suggested it was the Second Order Director who'd misspoken.

Regardless, Melfirth continued immediately. "We're comparing artifacts she had when she arrived with others taken from this timeline. We're hoping to be able to piece together her journey, both for academic gain and to recover our missing agents. It's going to change everything we thought we knew about prehistory. It's astonishing to imagine."

"Aren't we getting ahead of ourselves?" Yemerik asked. "It could all be coincidence. Or even temporal manipulation."

Melfirth smiled. "You didn't tell him?" he asked Reilla.

"I wanted to let you do it," she replied.

"The tests came back. We can now say for certain she was a direct ancestor of Laur-Alem. Not that there was much doubt."

"Is it really that much of a big deal?" Yemerik asked.

"Well, I think it is." Melfirth's tone had changed. It took Yemerik a moment to place it. He was concerned. Yemerik wasn't sure why—he was quite certain he didn't deserve sympathy. "Think about it," Melfirth continued. "Every history lesson about the development of Hathari needs to change. Laur-Alem will retain some significance as a historical figure, but he'll never again be considered the most important man who ever lived. His contributions were derivative, not original."

"Then what were mine?" Yemerik asked. Melfirth looked at him quizzically, so Yemerik continued, "I didn't find her."

"Of course you did," Melfirth said.

"No," Yemerik replied. "Whoever created that disk found her, and we're no closer to learning where it came from. If anything, we've lost the timeline it originated in. I broke that line, in fact. It's lost knowledge."

Melfirth exchanged another look with Reilla then said, "Yemerik. Have you considered the possibility that the disk was incidental to this discovery?"

"How could it be incidental?" Yemerik asked. "It led me to her."

Melfirth took a deep breath. "I'm not discounting that interpretation; I'm just not convinced it's the most likely. Stripping away everything else, the disk has three pieces of information that seem relevant: your name, a reference to the Citadel, and—if I understand your amended account—the name of a warlord from Alaji's time."

"It was a little more complicated than that," Yemerik said.

"I don't doubt that," Melfirth said, "but the names may well have been imperfect transliterations. It could have been an entirely unrelated text. Something religious or even poetic."

"That coincidentally brought us to the founder of temporal magic?"

"But it didn't," Melfirth pointed out. "It brought you to a warlord. You found Subject Seven-Nine-Six; the disk never mentioned her. At the time, you were looking for another Citadel, not proof our history was wrong."

"I believe that artifact was placed there as a trap. Or some sort of lure or something."

"Set by whom?" Melfirth asked, laughing. "Come on, Yemerik. It would take something with the resources of the Citadel to arrange such a thing."

Yemerik shut his eyes for a moment. Melfirth's analysis was foolproof—there was no getting around that. Still, it grated on him, and he couldn't understand why.

"I'm afraid you will need to face the possibility that there is no one who can be credited for this discovery other than you," Melfirth said. "I hope you aren't too disappointed to learn that you'll be a key figure in the ongoing meta-history of the Gathering. Or that I'll be remembered in a footnote as the stodgy old man who tried to stop you." He chuckled quietly.

"Thank you," Yemerik said anxiously. "I know... I realize you're probably right. It's just that I spent so much time in the past, I... I'm sorry. I'm blathering, aren't I?"

"It's okay," Melfirth said. "I'm not sure any of us can imagine the hardships you've gone through." He looked Yemerik over quietly and added, "I really am happy to have you back."

27: A STEAK

Yemerik sat alone, prodding at his food. Every now and then, one of the younger agents in training would approach and sit by him until he made it uncomfortably clear that he did not want company. This worked for the first twenty minutes or so, then Reilla showed up with a tray of her own. He tried not to take too much pleasure in the sound of discomfort she made sitting on the static stone bench.

"Good evening," she said in a tone that was pleasant, positive, yet not so enthusiastic as to appear threatening. If Yemerik had a lifetime to devote to the task, he doubted he'd be able to master delivering such a tone on command. He wondered how long she practiced each day.

He sighed and actually forced himself to take a bite of the meat in front of him. "It's wrong," he muttered, as he chewed and swallowed the food. He paused, waiting for her to prompt him, but she remained silent. "The beef, I mean. It's cooked too evenly. They'll never find anything like that out there." He motioned around the room without looking.

She had a similar meal on her plate, which she didn't seem interested in. "It was my impression this was intended as a halfway point, a chance for training interventionalists and temporal empiricists to gain some experience with the sort of food they'll encounter in their work."

"And recovering criminals who developed a taste for the stuff," Yemerik said sarcastically. He'd spent years longing to return to the Citadel and eat the magically generated foods he'd been raised with. Now, he found himself wanting eggs, meat, bread, and beer. This was as close as the Citadel offered.

"You are not a criminal," Reilla said, so forcefully Yemerik almost believed it.

"Of course I'm a criminal," he said. "I withheld critical information from the archives, I disobeyed direct instructions, I misused controlled artifacts, and I traveled to a forbidden era. I'm not sure why you insist on denying the obvious."

"Okay," Reilla said, "I was mistaken. You are a criminal. But our mission is richer for your crimes."

"Tell that to Fimelsa's family. Or Thomyus's or even Oadeth's. Or any of the others you haven't admitted are gone."

"Yemerik, we will get many of them back."

"But not all of them."

"No," Reilla admitted. "There will almost certainly be casualties due to this temporal divergence. But each of them knew there was a risk when they accepted their charge. I doubt any of them would dispute it was worth it. Besides, if we're judging you harshly, it should be acknowledged they failed to adhere to proper procedure. In the event of an unexpected temporal shift, agents are supposed to return at once."

"They were only curious. No one working in empirical induction would miss a chance to explore."

"The same curiosity that motivated you?"

Yemerik sneered. "I was motivated by egotism."

Reilla paused for a moment then said, "I think you should sit out the next interview with Alaji."

"Didn't we go through this already? She wants me there."

"She does," Reilla said, "but I'm concerned how it's impacting your recovery."

"You're kidding," Yemerik said. "What does that matter?" He hadn't realized his voice was growing louder until he looked around and saw several faces staring at him. He cleared his throat and said, "Besides, I'm fine."

"Are you?"

"No. Probably not," he admitted, sighing. "But if you pull me out of there, I won't be able to sleep or eat, because I won't be able to stop wondering what she's saying. If you're worried about my state of mind, you should let me contribute the one thing I still have to offer. I'm the only one here who has a chance of figuring out what's going through that girl's head."

"Girl?"

"What?" Yemerik asked.

"You just called Alaji a 'girl.'"

"No, I didn't," Yemerik said. "She's… what? In her sixties? Seventies?"

"We haven't attempted to age her spectrally," Reilla said, watching Yemerik carefully. "But mid-sixties would be my guess."

"If not older," Yemerik said. He felt as if it were hot, though he knew that was absurd. The Citadel's temperature was controlled carefully, even here. "The point is, I know her."

"You knew her," Reilla corrected him, "a long time ago."

"Yes. And I realize she's different. But the way her mind works… that hasn't changed."

"All right," Reilla said calmly, "what can you tell me about her last story today?"

Yemerik took a deep breath and sighed. "Fourth dimensional strategy. I didn't teach her that, if that's what you're wondering. I mean, I taught her how to send simple messages. I couldn't have given her the tools to do something like that—I never learned them myself. I'm not sure what she learned from Oadeth after… no. No, she couldn't have gotten that from him, either. Not at that level."

"Because he was too young. He wouldn't have been exposed to the concepts in anything other than theory."

"Which means she developed them on her own," Yemerik said.

"Why not?" Reilla asked. "She developed time travel itself. She would have made a great interventionist."

"If she wasn't psychotic."

"I don't believe that's fair," Reilla said.

"Of course, it's fair. She's a killer. And she's exceedingly good at it. She killed two agents of the Gathering before either could stop her. And she's killed… well, you're hearing the same stories I am," Yemerik said. "I know she comes from a barbaric time, but that doesn't change the reality of the situation."

"You're judging her in the harshest light possible."

"Maybe," Yemerik said, "but I have to. I once promised her… there was a time she wanted to work with us. This was back when she rescued me in the regressive civilization cynically calling itself Hathari. She'd just helped someone she cared about, and she was entertaining the idea of trying to join us. I told her it doesn't usually work that way, but at the time I couldn't help but wonder. She seemed so good back then, so pure. I mean, there was a lot I didn't know. I guess I allowed myself to believe in her."

"Did you fall in love with her?" Reilla asked, deceptively calmly.

"No," Yemerik said abruptly. But, almost immediately, he raised his hand to stop her from interrupting. "Wait. That's not… it's not untrue, but it's not complete, either. I wasn't in love with her romantically or sexually. But, yes, I suppose I was starting to love her. How could I not?"

"I'm sorry if that felt personal."

"The Gathering is owed answers, personal or otherwise," Yemerik replied with a shrug.

"I'm going to be frank with you—I'm trying to understand the nature of your relationship, not to judge you, but because I need a better understanding of how this is impacting your judgment and your health. You said a moment ago you didn't see why you matter. But the truth is my decisions will be reviewed for ages."

Yemerik shook his head. "Why?" he asked. In response, Reilla motioned her hand around the room. He glanced in time to see a dozen young faces turn away. He swallowed and whispered, "I don't deserve to be remembered as a hero. I don't deserve to be remembered, at all. The others, maybe. Oadeth and Thomyus are far more deserving of a legacy than I am."

Reilla nodded thoughtfully. "Perhaps that's true. But whether it's deserved or not, you're a central character in Alaji's story. And, regardless of what you deserve, I promise you I don't deserve to be dismissed as someone who drove you deeper and deeper into depression. There are more legacies than just yours on the line."

28: THE MOUNTAIN, THE LAKE, THE ICE, AND THE FIRE

Alaji walked along the steep path winding up the cliffside. Occasionally she'd catch glimpses of the watchers peeking their heads out of dark caverns. She didn't pay them much mind, though she cycled her count in case one of them tried something rash.

She paused to drink from her canteen, wiped her mouth with the back of her wrist, and considered flying the rest of the way or even using her talisman. It was a hot day, and the mountain offered little shade. But she didn't want to press her luck by startling the things around her.

The air began to cool as she walked, at least until she crested a rocky knoll and came across a field of wildflowers on the otherwise barren mountain. At least she knew she was in the right place. She continued forward towards a lake set against another cliff. Slopes of ice and snow lay sheltered in the shade, and even from a few hundred feet away, she could see cavernous openings.

She hurried around the water and acted as if she didn't notice the ripples that washed ashore whenever her back was turned. She reached the ice caves and selected the one she wanted almost immediately. It wasn't hard: each contained a trickling stream of water flowing in the center, with a single exception. She stepped in and conjured a light. The walls around her were patterned almost like scales. "How appropriate," she thought.

"Entering this domain was unwise," a voice rang out. A warm breath rolled over her, smelling of fish. A shadow her magic couldn't penetrate concealed the speaker.

"Is it really worth all this for some grand reveal?" Alaji asked.

"The illusion of darkness and all that… is there actually a single person who comes in here who hasn't heard legends of this place?"

The shadows shifted, and her light reached out, illuminating deep red scales, pale horns and teeth, and a green eye larger than a man's head. "You would deprive me of my satisfaction?" the dragon asked, flicking its tongue.

"Omagulis, isn't it?" Alaji asked, identifying the beast by the shape of a chip missing from its right horn.

"To the men. Do you know what the elves call me?" Flames flashed to either side of its mouth.

"No, and I don't care," Alaji said. "I'm not here for games. I'm here to speak with the Acolyte."

"If the Acolyte wished company, she would have told me of your arrival," Omagulis said. "Or perhaps she wanted to surprise me. She knows I enjoy the flesh of men."

"I'm Alaji," she said in an annoyed tone. "I trust you know that name."

The dragon paused, squinted, and stared at her. Then it said, "I do not know if you are who you claim. But the witch, Alaji, is said to have killed Peltolseid."

"The great wyrm of the western sea," Alaji said, using Peltolseid's formal title. "I've heard that story, too."

"And?" The dragon stepped forward as it barked the question. Alaji remained still. She had her count if she needed it.

"I've killed several dragons. If I killed Peltolseid, it was without learning her name."

"Or perhaps you haven't killed her yet," Omagulis growled. "That is what they say of Alaji. That she travels time like it was air. That eons are seasons to her, and what's passed may lie before her."

"I like that," Alaji said. "It's less grim than most poems about me."

"Did you slay her or not?" Omagulis demanded, spewing an arc of fire that licked at the ice overhead.

"Enough!" a voice bellowed from further down the tunnel.

Omagulis cringed, and the cavern shook. Small ice crystals showered over the dragon and Alaji both. "You are wasting time."

"Leave me to my charge, Varsemu," Omagulis said. But he was hunched over now, and his voice was almost timid.

"Troubling the Acolyte's guests is not the job you were entrusted with," the louder voice said. Alaji heard a scraping sound as a large form appeared behind the first. This one barely fit in the tunnel, which was fifty feet wide.

Omagulis made a sound in the back of his throat then spit to one side. A burning wad of phlegm stuck to the side of the passage and slid down, leaving a melted trail behind. "I was going to grant her passage," he said.

"It was never yours to grant or deny," Varsemu said. Then, glancing at Alaji, he shifted his head, as if commanding her to follow. He was too large to turn around, so he began backing up, scraping off sections of ice as he went.

Alaji hurried by Omagulis, who took up more than half of the passage. She was fairly certain she'd be able to teleport away before he could shift to one side and crush her, but she felt far more secure once she'd passed.

"Witch," the dragon said from behind her. "I will wait for my answer. One day, we will finish this discussion. Peltolseid was precious to me. Do you understand?"

"Fine," Alaji said. "We will speak again one day, and I will try to find out if I was—or will be—involved."

From ahead, she heard Varsemu chuckle. His laugh was like the quaking earth. "You may not enjoy the conversation, Omagulis," he said as he backed into a larger chamber. This one lay inside the mountain itself. Ice still coated sections of the walls and ceiling, but there was stone beneath it.

Alaji hurried to catch up and found Varsemu seated. He stretched his neck, and she heard joints pop like falling lumber. "Are you the Acolyte?" Alaji asked, and the dragon laughed again.

"I'd begun to think you knew everything. That you carried with you the knowledge of all kingdoms. It is refreshing to learn otherwise." He leaned forward, and Alaji's conjured light caught his eye. "I see it now. I should have seen it before."

"Then we've met," Alaji said.

"When I was newly hatched, barely an eighth the size I would grow into. You threw me into a wall with conjured wind. It broke my wing. Took ages to heal."

"It seems Omagulis isn't the only one I've upset," Alaji said.

Varsemu laughed again. "It was a powerful lesson," he said. "I do not think I'd seek retribution even if it were my right to challenge you."

"If you're not the Acolyte, where will I find her? Or him."

"Her," the dragon said. He motioned towards the tunnel leading on. "You will find her down there."

"Thank you," Alaji said. She began to leave, but Varsemu spoke again.

"You have seen eras before this?" he asked.

"Long before."

"Then tell me this: is it true there was an age when dragons alone knew the secret of language? When men were nothing but cattle for us to rule over?"

"If you dislike the answer, will it make my life harder?"

He chuckled. "I am too old to value pleasant lies."

"Then I'll tell you the truth. There was a time dragons grew no larger than gryphons and were no smarter than bears. Humans had intellect before your kind. But, if it's any consolation, goblins existed before men, and there were talking birds before any of us."

The dragon stared at her silently for a moment. Then he began laughing again, and Alaji simply walked on.

29: THE QUEEN OF THE KINGDOM OF DRAGONS

The mountain was hollow, a rocky shell concealing an expanse of crystals, running water, and growing fields. Alaji stood at the opening, gazing at the hidden world inside. Pillars of stone stretched thousands of feet, offering both support and beauty. Waterfalls spilled off ledges, feeding streams that supported an ecosystem of swaying grasses, bright flowers, and livestock. In the center of it all, a glowing light, like some miniature moon, illuminated the scene. Lining the cavern walls, Alaji could see dozens of dragons.

It was incredible and terrifying, even to her. Even with the thousands of wonders she'd seen, the world still had ways of surprising her.

She took an uneasy breath and walked into this kingdom of dragons, unsure what she was even looking for. She passed massive gemstones acting as prisms, catching and casting light in every direction. She came across statues carved by dragon claw and passed by murals scorched into stone. She watched as a dragon swooped down only a few hundred feet from her and snatched a goat in its claws, then carried the squealing animal off to devour it on a ledge.

Then, near the center of it all, just beneath the glowing light, she saw a human form. A woman wearing a silk dress was examining a group of flowers as tall as she was. Alaji wasn't entirely sure this was the person she was looking for, but it seemed as good a place to start as any.

As she approached, the woman caught sight of her and stared in shock. "I am looking for the Acolyte," Alaji said.

"I… remember you," the woman said, in a voice that rang with surprise. There was something off about her features. She wasn't quite human, though she was close. "It is harder to remember faces, even when they barely change," the woman said. "But I remember your face, Alaji."

"Irantinne," Alaji said.

The woman shook her head. "No. I left that name behind and dozens more after it. I am the Acolyte."

"So the others can keep track of you through the ages," Alaji said. "I understand the concept."

"I am not the first to take the name," she said. "But its prior owner went mad. Now, he exists as a statue overlooking the Cove of Duranya. Have you been there? Have you seen him?"

"No," Alaji said. "I don't even know what you're talking about."

"He grew tired of it all, of life and death, so he turned his body to stone. He is still alive, in a sense. A living statue, now and forever."

"Like a golem?" Alaji asked.

The Acolyte shook her head. "He is unmoving. Perhaps he is unthinking. Or maybe he is neither. Maybe he has simply slowed himself so a single breath will take him all of time."

"Why take the name of a madman?"

"Mostly because it was available," the Acolyte replied. She smiled and looked around her. "Do you like this? It is my kingdom."

"I didn't know what to expect," Alaji said. "I was told you lived in a kingdom of dragons beneath the mountain, but I expected something simpler. It's certainly beautiful."

"This took me ages. Three mountains collapsed before I perfected my method."

"I thought you'd be a dragon yourself," Alaji added.

"I would like to be," the Acolyte said. "When I joined them… back then they called themselves the Council of Eldest Days… one of them was a dragon."

"I remember," Alaji said. "The Limper. I was there."

The Acolyte looked confused. "I have no memory of you back then. I recall knowing you, but the details have faded."

"Do you remember this?" Alaji asked, removing her amulet. The Acolyte stared at it quietly.

"You gave that to us," she whispered.

"That's a generous description. But I lent it to you, and you put it to good use. I'm here so you can return the favor. I need the key Red Arm gave you before he forsook his kingdom."

The Acolyte shook her head. "There is nowhere you could take it safer than my kingdom."

"Of course there is," Alaji said. "But that's not why I want it."

The Acolyte stood quiet. Then, in barely a whisper, she said, "If you were any other, you would not leave here alive." She took a deep breath. "The key was entrusted to me by the council."

"The council fell apart eons ago," Alaji said. "It won't reform for some time, and it will never be as unified as it was."

"The council's decline does not lessen my charge," the Acolyte replied. Her patience seemed to be wearing thin, and Alaji wasn't the only one to notice. Several dragons passed above them.

"The council fell, but its purpose still matters, doesn't it?" Alaji asked. "You still want to see all of this protected."

"It is because I want to see this protected that I'm considering killing you."

"I've fought worse than you and lived," Alaji reminded her. "I've fought him, remember?" She stared the Acolyte in the eye and watched as she stepped backward.

"Sometimes, I worry you have been lying to us since the beginning. That you are playing a longer game than even we can hope to keep track of."

"In a sense, I am," Alaji said. "And I haven't told you everything. But the core of it is true. Enough of it is, anyway."

She took a deep breath. "If this is a lie, if you…" She paused and shook her head. "I have threatened you like this before. I remember this."

"It wasn't you," Alaji said. "It was the others."

"I don't remember it that way," she said quietly. "But I suppose it was more recent for you."

"I need the key," Alaji said, after a few seconds of silence.

"If you are lying... what became of the last Acolyte will be nothing. One of them will find me and exact a heavy price. I am powerful, but they are gods now."

"They are tired, scared, and losing control of their minds," Alaji said. "The same as you. Some of you will find ways to delay or even reverse this, but it is the price of the magic you've learned."

"Even so... their enemies will suffer for all of time."

"Unlikely," Alaji said. "Time is longer than any of you expected. That's what you're learning."

"I still think it was worth it. But it is only a matter of time, isn't it? Before I no longer believe that." She sighed uneasily. "Fine then." She shut her eyes and whispered. Then she paused until a form circled overhead, momentarily blocking the magical light above them.

The dragon spiraled lower then landed, beating its wings as it did so and tossing dust into the air. The Acolyte approached slowly, and the creature bowed its head. It was old, even for its race. Its scales were a greyish blue, and there was little left of its horns.

"This is Harbanthi," the Acolyte said. "There is no other here I hold in higher regard."

"My queen," the dragon said reverently.

"I've never heard of her," Alaji said, surprised. She'd spent much of the past year researching the names and descriptions of the dragons of the region in preparation for this day.

"There is no reason you should have," the Acolyte said. "She has never left this mountain. Never soared through the blue sky."

"All I have ever wanted for was here," Harbanthi said.

"Perhaps," the Acolyte said. "And still, I am sorry for what you've been denied. But I felt it necessary." She cleared her throat. "There is an object you were entrusted with, and I did not want to risk it being lost."

"You are speaking of what's inside of me," Harbanthi said sadly. "You know?"

"I have always known," the dragon said. "Since I hatched, I knew I carried something."

"I need it back," the Acolyte said sadly.

"I understand," Harbanthi replied. She lowered her head further until it lay on the cavern floor. The Acolyte extended the fingers on her right hand then whispered a short incantation. She plunged her hand downward, and there was a brief flash of light. The dragon's skull split open with a crack, and the beast's eyes rolled back. Its body shook violently, then went still.

The Acolyte's silk dress was now splattered in blood as she withdrew her arm. She clutched an object in her hand, which glowed yellow. "Give it a moment to cool," she said, uncurling her fingers to reveal a key.

30: THE FIRST GUARDIAN

"I'm confused," Galaize said, staring at a man in a suit of armor sitting beneath ornately carved stonework marred by an indentation melted into the vague shape of a human body. "Am I supposed to be intimidated?"

A mask concealed the face of the figure before them. Every inch of the armored warrior was covered in steel plate, though something was wrong with the metal. Areas were badly discolored and for a moment it seemed as if the figure would be unable to stand, but gradually he climbed to his feet.

"The Order of Helgwin promised three guardians," Galaize said. "I assume this is the last."

"I... am... the... first," the figure hissed in a voice sounding more like wind than anything human.

"Then what were those slugs? Or that snake? Or any of the other horrors we came across?" Galaize asked, drawing a sword so he'd have it ready if he needed it.

"I care not," the figure said. His voice was changing as he spoke. There was still something deeply wrong, like the words formed without throat or tongue, but he was speaking more naturally now. "Is there a leader among you?"

"Me," Galaize said with a shrug. "Or her, I suppose," he added, tilting his head in Alaji's direction.

"Her, I know," the figure said angrily. "My offer extends not to her. But to the rest, I offer you this..."

—

"One of you may leave," the knight in burnt armor said plainly to Eroza and Rit'ka. "I will permit no more. If you try and flee together, I will follow. I will hunt. And I will claim you. But if you choose amongst yourselves, by trial or by sacrifice, the other may go."

Eroza aimed her bow carefully. "I do not know what that is, but there is no man behind that mask," she said.

"It spoke the same words the other times I was here. It offered to release one of us if the others surrendered."

"Not surrendered," the knight said. "I will kill any who stand before me. It matters not if you bow or take up arms. You may die how you wish. I have leave to extend only the mercy I have offered: one of you may go, so that others may be warned of the fate of those who venture into this domain."

"I'm assuming you know her," Rit'ka said, gesturing towards Alaji. "So either she came here and accepted your proposition or she already defeated you."

"She was lucky once," the knight said. "And I have fought that battle again and again in my mind. It will not be as before."

In response, the first of Rit'ka's glowing blades flew spinning through the air and punctured the knight's armor. He offered a surprised grunt in response and stepped back a foot. Then, plucking the dagger from his chest and tossing it to one side, he said, "You have opted to decline my terms, then." He raised his sword and began towards the three women.

—

The knight stood stoically beneath an archway made of smooth rock. He faced Alaji and Helgwin and proclaimed, "One of you may leave. I will permit no more. If you try and flee together, I will follow. I will hunt. And I will claim you. But if you choose amongst yourselves, by trial or by sacrifice, the other may go."

Helgwin laughed. "I wish it were that easy," he said, holding his sword threateningly. "But I'm under an oath to follow her command. So, unless she decides to abandon me here, I'm required to fight."

"Be careful," Alaji said. "He is a better swordsman than you are."

Helgwin paused, unsettled by her remark, but he continued to approach. The knight closed the distance, as well, until they were within striking range. Both fighters held their positions for a moment, waiting for the other to make the first move.

—

"Iraksim," Galaize said. "See if you can take him in a fair fight."

The largest of the remaining thieves nodded, drawing his long sword with his right hand and a thick, pronged dagger with his left. "Think that armor will save you?" Iraksim shouted mockingly. Behind him, the other thieves subtly armed themselves and began inching closer as well.

Iraksim charged, swinging at his crippled opponent. But the knight acted quickly, shifting his arm to one side. The thief's blade struck his gauntlet and turned away with a loud gong. The knight shifted forward awkwardly, hindered by unyielding sections of his warped armor. That alone gave Iraksim a chance to avoid the knight's blade. Even so, the thief was left in a precarious position, with the knight's sword arm inches from his body. The knight's arm held there for a moment—if Iraksim tried to step back, there'd be nothing at all to keep his enemy from stabbing him in the throat.

The thief punched down with his left hand, trying to drive the point of his dagger through the dark visor in the knight's mask. But, inches from the opening, the knight's other hand caught his wrist. His grip was like stone, and he twisted the thief's arm. As the thief cried out in pain, the dagger fell from his hand.

The knight shifted in awkward jerks as parts of his mangled armor caught and scraped together. But while there was nothing fluid about his motion, his hands were always where they needed to be. As he twisted Iraksim's arm, the knight allowed his own sword to drop to the floor. As Iraksim's knife fell, the knight caught it in midair. Iraksim fell forward, and the knight released him. His arm snapped forward, and the stolen knife flew through the air, lodging in the eye of one of Iraksim's charging companions. By the time that thief struck the ground, the knight had recovered his sword and was chopping down at Iraksim. It took every ounce of strength the thief had to parry, and it left him kneeling with his sword raised over his head. The knight swung twice more, striking once on his enemy's blade then once on his hilt.

Iraksim shrieked in pain as sections of his fingers fell to the floor, followed by his sword. The knight didn't give him time to recover or dodge—in an instant, the knight's sword was buried in Iraksim's chest. He paused for only a moment before yanking it free and swinging his blade towards the next man coming at him.

The thief wasn't nearly close enough for the knight's sword to connect, but that wasn't the intent. Iraksim's blood splattered in the thief's eyes, and he stumbled, momentarily blinded.

—

The knight moved swiftly, fluidly, shifting towards Rit'ka, who hurled her second knife at him. He swung his sword, batting it aside, then shifted to avoid it when she called on it to change direction. Eroza released an arrow, but the knight turned his head, allowing it to deflect harmlessly off his helmet. Rit'ka swung her hands in opposing arches, and her twin knives closed together towards the knight. But he turned to one side, twisting his sword behind him to block one blade while he caught the other in his hand. Rit'ka called out to it, moving her hands quickly, but the knight repeated her spell, word for word, and the enchanted blade went still. He began to turn towards Eroza, then froze as Alaji appeared in front of him. The tip of her cursed knife stuck through his visor.

He paused, shaking, then began to scream. Alaji yanked her knife free and kicked Rit'ka's blade towards her. The thief called to it, and it began glowing again, then leapt into her hand along with its duplicate.

"He was about to kill me," Eroza said calmly.

Alaji didn't respond but pulled out a vial. She removed the

stopper and began pouring it onto the writhing knight's armor. Everywhere it hit transformed. Buckles and joints fused with plate, locking together into a heavy mass of metal.

"Will that kill him?" Eroza asked.

Alaji shook her head. "He hasn't been alive for eons. This will weaken him, though."

"Then he's immortal?" Eroza asked.

"No," Alaji said. "Unfortunately, he is not."

—

Helgwin howled as he fought harder than he'd ever fought in his life. Every move he made was countered with astonishing precision: the knight seemed ready for every strike, every block, and he never hesitated to offer a counter that was nothing short of astonishing. The word "artist" leapt to Helgwin's mind as he felt his own style deconstructed by an opponent who seemed to find the experience effortless. "This must be how others feel while fighting me," he thought, "just before they die."

He heard the sound of shattering glass as something struck the stone floor beneath the knight's feet. A layer of ice materialized, and the knight slipped. He caught himself almost instantly, but that moment was enough. Helgwin stabbed forward, driving his sword through the knight's visor. The knight went limp and dropped his sword, though a moment later, he began to stir again. But at least he was unarmed. Helgwin, still on stable ground, shifted his weight, sending the disoriented knight tumbling backwards into a wall. Another vial followed, exploding around him in fire. His armor turned red-hot, and the stone behind him melted. He struggled, but the molten rock held him.

"Come on," Alaji said. She was holding yet another potion vial ready, in case the knight managed to free himself. "That won't hold him forever."

"Wait," the knight said. "You would be better served dying here."

But by then Alaji and Helgwin were hurrying through the doorway.

—

The knight stepped on Iraksim's body as he made his way towards the nearest of the surviving thieves, who was still trying to recover from the gore hurled in his face. Another thief stepped bravely close in an attempt to slow the undead warrior's approach, but the knight's blade arched in ways the thief hadn't anticipated. It made no difference that he was awkward—every strike was precise. This thief fell back, leaving him as open as his ally.

But before the warrior could reach them, fire flared up right before his face. This barely slowed the knight, but even a little was enough to buy the men a second to fall back. The warrior's attention turned towards Alaji, who was chanting once more.

With a diagonal cut, the knight's blade struck the wall to one side. He turned to catch a falling piece of stone, which he hurled directly at the witch's head. But the rock simply struck the rock wall behind her—she was no longer where she'd been.

"Here!" Alaji called out from behind the knight. He turned to find her standing just in front of the entryway he was tasked with protecting. He lunged, but he was nowhere near close enough to reach her before she passed through the door. He hurried to the edge then froze, unable to follow her over.

"There are other guardians than—" he began saying, but didn't finish. Galaize slammed into him from behind, sending him sprawling forward over the boundary. The knight screamed in surprise as he fell. His sword dropped from his hand as he landed hard against the rock. The thief kicked the knight's blade to one side, then kicked the warrior squarely in the head.

"Stop!" Alaji said. "You'll kill him!"

Galaize didn't dignify that with a response. Instead, he kicked again, knocking the mask away. Beneath it, the face of a mummified corpse gasped. The knight tried to roll away, but the other thieves blocked his escape.

"Galaize," Alaji said. "He is important. We don't want others following us."

"Honestly," Galaize said, panting, "I don't care all that much. It's enough to know no other man will be able to accomplish this. A proud victory for Galaize's Band of Locusts!" He kicked one final time, connecting squarely with the undead knight's exposed face. With a crunch, the leathery form collapsed under the weight of the thief's boot. His men laughed, while Alaji looked on in scorn.

31: A DIFFERENCE

"They hadn't realized it yet—how could they have, after everything we'd been through—but we'd just entered the place we were looking for. The rest of it was… it was like moss growing around a tree. The creatures we'd confronted were things lured there or transformed by their proximity to the labyrinth. The traps were no different—I assume some had been set by the dwarves or even by goblins who'd stumbled in. Eventually, the labyrinth swallowed them. It swallowed connecting caverns, nests of animals, and colonies of insects. It was growing, feeding itself to grow stronger. The ones who'd built it intended this; they knew anything less would leave it at the mercy of decay. That was their mistake the first time; they'd made it strong but hadn't counted on it weakening over the ages. This was their attempt to fix that oversight, to create something that couldn't be beaten by time."

The old crone paused to sip her water. Reilla listened attentively while clutching the glowing object recording every word Alaji spoke and every twitch on her face. For all Alaji knew, perhaps it captured the inside of her body or the state of her spirit, as well. It hardly mattered.

"The labyrinth itself wasn't so different to look at. There were more inscriptions on the walls, older symbols conveying different meanings. Eroza realized something had changed, of course. Nothing got past her. In all the times and places I've been to…" Alaji sighed and shook her head. "I've never met another with her perception. That saved my life more than once. It helped that I couldn't lie to her. You never realize how useful that is until the truth—even a half-truth—can save your life. It was Galaize who surprised me, though. He was deceptive in a way few can match. He'd show you one face, one personality, and convince you it was all there is. Even to the point you'd see him act differently towards others, and you'd believe that was the lie. You used to play similar games," she said to Yemerik, "but not nearly so well. I wasn't ready for how smart he really was, not until—I'm sorry. I'm getting ahead of myself."

—

Eroza stumbled the moment after she stepped through the curved passageway. She veered to one side and caught herself. "Are you hurt?" Rit'ka asked, hurrying to the archer. Behind them, the dark knight lay on the dungeon floor, writhing in an attempt to stand, but his newly warped armor kept him pinned.

"No," Eroza said, clutching a hand to her head. "It is not me." She looked up at Alaji and squinted.

"I'm sorry," Alaji said. "It didn't occur to me."

"Will the two of you speak actual words for a change?" Rit'ka said angrily.

"I am trying to find words," Eroza said. Notes of frustration had slipped into her voice, and she sighed. "It is this place, I think. It is different, like when she took us through time, but more so."

"What is this?" Rit'ka demanded. "What did you do?"

Alaji shook her head. "This isn't me. I'm sorry, I didn't realize you would find it difficult to be here. It should have occurred to me, but there's a great deal on my mind."

Eroza forced herself upright and moved further into the corridor, using the wall for support. Alaji looked back at the knight, still struggling on the floor. "I'm sorry to you, as well," she added. "Both for this and for what's still to come."

"What was that, anyway?" Rit'ka asked.

"He's one of three guardians," Alaji replied. "He was left here to ensure strength of arms wouldn't be enough to reach this place."

"And what is this place?" Rit'ka asked, raising her voice. She took one of Eroza's arms and draped it across her shoulders so the archer could lean on her while she regained her footing.

"It's a place where something was stored away long ago," Alaji said.

"What?" Rit'ka demanded. "What could possibly be so valuable? What are you after?"

"It's not like that," Alaji said. "I'm not here to take anything away from this place. I'm just here to leave something."

"Leave something?" Rit'ka said. "What in the world are you so worried about losing?"

"It's not like that, either," Alaji said.

"Then tell me what it is like!" Rit'ka shouted.

"Stop," Eroza said. "I think I'm okay to continue on my own." Rit'ka paused while Eroza began to stretch and move around, as if she were rediscovering the lengths of her legs.

"I still want an answer," Rit'ka said to Alaji.

"Soon," Alaji said.

"Now!" Rit'ka demanded.

"It's okay," Eroza interrupted. "It's not the right question, anyway." Rit'ka gave her a confused look, so she added, "We should be asking her about the other guardians."

"Other guardian," Alaji replied. "The last—the worst—won't trouble us."

"It's dead?" Rit'ka asked.

"No. He'll be very much alive. But he's not like the knight or the heart. He's capable of rational thought, and he has no reason to stop us, not this time."

"Alive," Eroza said. "You mean there's a person living down here?"

"Person," Alaji repeated the word, as if trying to decide if it applied. "He's human, in most senses of the word," she said, "but he doesn't age."

"Like an elf," Rit'ka said.

"No," Alaji said. "Not at all like that."

"Fine. Then tell me about this 'Heart.' That's what you called the middle guardian."

"That's what the Order of Helgwin will call it," Alaji said. "It is not easy to describe. It looks more like an animal's stomach to me. Or maybe all the organs, stitched together. At least, that's how I remember it. I am unsure how it works. It seems to grow mouths, tentacles, and eyes as it needs them. It can see into your mind, and it can show you things."

"And it's down here with us?" Rit'ka asked.

"We won't reach it for a while," Alaji said. "It stays in one place. It's too large to move."

"How large?" Rit'ka demanded.

"The part I've seen…" Alaji paused, looking from side to side in the tunnel, which was about twenty feet across. "It's at least ten times as wide as this."

"And we cannot avoid it?" Eroza asked. "Even with your magic?"

"We need to confront it," Alaji said. "There's no other way."

"Fine," Rit'ka said angrily. "Where is this thing?"

"No," Alaji said quietly. "We'll see its children before we see the heart itself."

"Children?" Eroza asked.

"I do not know if the term applies," Alaji said. "They're… they are difficult to explain."

32: HEART SPAWNED

"What the hell are those?" Helgwin gasped. The creatures were malformed—asymmetric monstrosities the size of men but bearing little resemblance. They had the right number of arms and legs, as well as a lump atop their shoulders that could perhaps be described as a head, but their bodies consisted of pulsating bladders, stretched tissue, and a translucent membrane covering it all.

"They are poison," Alaji said, digging something out of her pocket. "Here," she said, handing a small stone to the mercenary. "Take this for now. It will offer some protection. But avoid their blood and the things growing out of them."

"Growing out of them?" Helgwin asked anxiously.

"You'll see soon enough. Cut cleanly and avoid their corpses. They are as dangerous dead as they are alive."

"I miss fighting ogres," Helgwin said under his breath, moving towards the three inhuman creatures coming towards him. Visible organs shifted, expanded, then contracted, stretching the slick skin over them. If these things had eyes, Helgwin wasn't sure where they were hidden.

He had no idea where to stab, so he aimed for a bulbous, pulsating organ on the left side of the nearest creature. He kept his distance and thrust the point of his sword in. The membrane parted, stretching around the tear left by his blade, and the organ burst, covering the tip of his blade in a brownish-yellow paste. A foul mist erupted as well, smelling like a mix of alcohol and rotting meat. The creature dropped to the ground, but the individual organs kept shifting.

Helgwin leapt away, coughing. He held his sword ready, in the hopes of fending off the others, but he felt his blade pull away from him. The strange mucus left by the creature was tugging and shifting from side to side. It was alive.

He swung at one of the other creatures, batting its arm. The pasty substance fixed to the monster, however, locked his blade in place. Helgwin pulled backwards with every ounce of strength he had and just managed to yank his sword free, bringing a torn section of membrane with it. A long, thick section of something that looked like intestine pushed out into the air through the hole and pulsated, as if trying to get free.

Helgwin stumbled back as the creature came at him with arms outstretched. His sword hit the corridor wall and the yellow substance reached out and latched on.

He felt his head shoved forward by a blast of wind sweeping over him and down at the creatures, forcing them back. He took the opportunity to tear his sword free then watched in horror as the substance on it crawled down the blade towards his hand. When he was almost ready to abandon his sword, the ooze burst into flame. It shook and made a hissing sound before falling away and landing on the floor. Helgwin stepped back further.

"Try to keep them back without cutting them," Alaji said, pausing between spells. If he'd had more time, Helgwin would have demanded she say how he was supposed to accomplish this incredible task, but the next monster was almost upon him.

—

"Stay back!" Galaize hissed through bared teeth. He was running low on men, and—unless he missed his guess—he was about to lose yet another. If he could keep the other three alive a little longer, he suspected his own chances would be better.

Regimir, a thief Galaize had been somewhat astonished had lasted this long, had rushed bravely into battle with the bizarre inhuman creatures coming at them. Regimir handled himself fairly well, all things considered, thrusting his twin swords into two of the creature's organs—one in its gut and one in the neck. For the briefest of moments, it had seemed as if the thief had won.

Then came the explosion of mist. It spewed from the creature's gut and filled the air around the thief, who began coughing. Seconds later, he started gasping and stumbling back. He reached out, as if begging for aid, which was why Galaize was so adamant the others stay put.

There was something happening to Regimir. His skin was growing puffy, and he was shaking. He tried to move, but he didn't make it far. He froze and looked down to see something small and white extending through his side. From where Galaize was standing, it almost looked like a worm of some sort. But then Regimir fell, offering a better view of what had occurred. A thin tendril had sprung out of the gut of the creature Regimir had stabbed. The monster had fallen to its knees, and it still had the thief.

A moment later, two more creatures grabbed hold from either side. Regimir tried to scream as they wrapped their arms around him, but he could manage nothing more than a faint gasp as the monstrosities squeezed.

Alaji stepped alongside the surviving thieves and began chanting. Out of the corner of his eye, Galaize saw her straining to get a look at Regimir. She'd be trying to save him, which would mean re-engaging the creatures pulling him away.

Galaize, thinking fast, grabbed her shoulder and said, "Wait! There's nothing more we can do for him!" He then pulled a dagger from his belt and hurled it at one of the creatures still coming for them. The blade spun, end over end, and stuck in the center of its head. There was a burst of sporous gas, followed by some sort of sticky goo that splattered on a wall and began shifting around. Galaize wasn't sure what it meant, but he felt reasonably certain it was too far away to pose much of an immediate threat.

"So, these are the 'heart', and those things spilling out of them are their 'spawn'?" Galaize said.

"I do not know," Alaji replied, pulling a vial from her pocket and hurling it at the creatures. The vial shattered, and the area around them erupted in flame. The creatures showed no pain. They continued forward, and it seemed as if they were unaffected. But as they moved through the fire, the clear membranes over their bodies dissolved. Their organs swelled and popped, spraying more mists, more tendrils, and more ooze. But this time, the expulsions were still—fire, it seemed, cleansed them.

The remaining thieves threw knives, fired arrows, and hurled rocks at the creatures while Alaji conjured fire to consume the monsters.

33: UNCOMMON THIEVES

Three of the creatures appeared at the far end of the corridor, and three arrows struck them in quick succession. Bladder-like organs burst, spewing the discolored slime Alaji had described, but this was nowhere near the three women themselves. Rit'ka swung her arm sideways, releasing a curved dagger emitting a twirling streak of blue light like a discus. It sailed between the wounded creatures, and she called out to the blade. She gestured quickly to the right, and the dagger changed direction, cutting into the creature and getting lodged in its gut.

Rit'ka pulled her hand to the left, and the blade ripped free and buried itself in one of the other monsters. Eroza fired another arrow through the head of another creature, which stumbled backwards. The shaft completely vanished into its face, which oozed some sort of pale mucus, while the arrow tip extended through the back. The creature, however, recovered and began stumbling towards the women, though its left arm hung limp.

"I once waded through a pool of maggots in the sewers of Avranthos," Rit'ka said angrily. "And nothing I saw or smelled there was as bad as this." She shifted her hands to one side, splattering sludge from the inside of one of the creatures as her blade broke free, almost cutting it in half. Quivering organ sacks spilled out, dropping to the corridor floor, and Alaji summoned fire to still them.

Eroza loosed another arrow, sticking it in the shoulder of one of the creatures. The monster paused, jostling for a few seconds before every one of the organs visible through the filmy skin covering its body erupted simultaneously. The body slouched over like a sack of water and lay trembling on the ground as the oozes, tendrils, and gasses mixed.

"There is a knot of pink tissue just beside their right shoulder," Eroza said. "Apparently, they cannot survive without it." She drew another arrow slowly, strung it, took aim, and pierced the next of the creatures in the same spot. Like the last, its insides deteriorated in seconds.

They finished off the rest then cleansed the walls and floor with Alaji's conjured fire. Rit'ka pulled her knife towards her, but left it untouched on the ground until Alaji could sanitize it. Then she kicked off bits of burnt tissue, wiped it down with a cloth, and slid it into its sheath.

"There will be more of those things as we approach the heart," Alaji said.

Rit'ka laughed sardonically. "Of course there would be more."

"Thank you," Alaji said. "That was easier than the other times I've been here." Rit'ka turned to give her a horrified look, and for once Eroza did the same. "I wish I'd known about the shoulder."

"How did you get by the guardian?" Eroza asked.

"It changes," Alaji said.

"It learns, you mean," Eroza said.

"This whole place learns," Alaji corrected her. "The heart, though… it's more complicated. I told you, it can see into our minds."

"How do you fight something that knows what you're about to do?" Rit'ka asked.

"It's worse than that," Alaji said. "It can see what you've done. It can read your memories and show you images."

"Like illusions?" Eroza asked.

"No, I don't believe so. It shows you memories. Mostly your own."

"So it can force us to relive our pasts," Eroza concluded.

"Not relive. It's more like flashes of memory."

"Why is that worse than being able to anticipate our actions?" Rit'ka demanded.

"Because I'm here," Alaji said. "And I've faced this creature in the past and future. The heart showed me images of all three battles."

"And we win?" Rit'ka asked quietly.

"Sometimes," Alaji said. "I told you, it changes. It shifts. The guardian uses my memory to send messages to itself."

"I am really starting to hate you," Rit'ka said, irritated. "I could have happily spent the rest of my life as an outlaw."

"Our best strategy is to approach without strategy," Eroza said. "To confront the creature and hope for the best."

"Perhaps," Alaji said. "It won't be easy."

"Neither was the knight," Rit'ka mumbled. "Or that bone creature. Or the tunneling bird."

"Alaji," Eroza said, "is this truly a fight we need to have?"

"I'm sorry," Alaji said. "This isn't like before. This is the reason I was testing you and the others."

"Others. You mean Galaize and Helgwin," Eroza said.

"Helgwin was the greatest warrior the world has ever known," Rit'ka said. "You were testing him?"

"I would take either of you into a fight before him," Alaji said.

"That is practically sacrilege," Rit'ka said, shaking her head.

"She is flattered," Eroza said, nodding towards Rit'ka who sneered at her. Eroza shrugged and added, "You are."

"I'm not flattered. Besides, she is lying. Definitely about us being better than him and probably about knowing him."

"Lies have a certain tone to them," Eroza said. "Truths, another. She is not lying."

"I am beginning to question your skill at reading people," Rit'ka said.

Eroza cracked a smile. "See? That is what a lie sounds like."

"He was strong and quick," Alaji said, interrupting their banter. "But there was a staleness to how he fought. He was like the knight in that way."

"Like the immortal knight?" Rit'ka asked. "The one who almost killed us, because he predicted our every move?"

"He predicted nothing," Alaji said. "He was dangerous because he'd practiced for eons. He'd mastered countless strikes and positions. That was how Helgwin fought, too—he turned action into instinct. That mindset is enough for the sort of opponent he was used to, but nothing more."

"And you think I'm better?" Rit'ka asked. "I'd be a common thief without these." She tapped the hilts of her knives.

"You'd be a fantastic thief without them," Alaji said. "And no one else could wield them half as well."

Rit'ka rolled her eyes. "That's nonsense."

"I told you," Alaji said. "I studied this era in great depth. The time before this, your age, and the future beyond. I am not guessing. You're not the first or the last to fight with those. But you are by far the greatest."

Rit'ka shivered and glanced back at the bodies. "We are wasting time with this," she said. "We should go. Even if it means more of those creatures. Or their creator."

34: WINDING AND UNWINDING

"Have I told you about the weaving spell?" The old crone asked the question seemingly out of the blue, and Reilla was momentarily caught off guard. She corrected almost immediately—it was her job to be able to adapt, of course. Her job and her calling.

Reilla smiled politely, as though she felt a deep gratitude that Alaji was willing to speak with her. Which, in a way, was genuine— she really was grateful for Alaji's cooperation. But she'd spent her life training to filter her thoughts and reactions through a layer of abstraction. What she felt could very well be faulty, and she couldn't risk contaminating an investigation this important.

For example, Reilla had found herself wishing she could interact with Eroza. There'd be no better test for someone of her training. The knowledge there'd been people with that sort of perceptive ability enticed her. She'd have loved to see if the archer from Alaji's story could read her so easily, and—if so—if there were ways of insulating herself further. But while this was certainly an understandable emotional response to an imagined challenge, it was objectively narcissistic. She'd learned long ago not to suppress such feelings but rather to exist above them.

She blinked once as these thoughts flooded her consciousness. Then, taking a breath to cover for the delay and flash of surprise, Reilla said, "You've told me several stories involving that spell. I'd be happy to hear another." That, of course, was less than entirely true. What Reilla really wanted were clear answers to the key questions— how the talisman had been broken, whether Alaji could assist in the recovery of their lost agents, and a conclusion to Alaji's life story in her own words. The first two were what Reilla's superiors demanded, and the last was what future generations would judge her on.

But pushing outright for those answers would be counterproductive. Strategically, it was more important that Alaji kept talking. Hopefully, she would get to those subjects in time.

Alaji tilted her head back and looked up at the ceiling. Reilla wondered how Yemerik viewed these mannerisms. She suspected they grated on him, which was as likely to be a problem as an asset. Alaji, like Reilla, was constructing a simulated personality. She was nowhere near as adept, but the signs were there. Yemerik was likely right that she wanted him on edge. That was why he might be an asset—as long as she got what she wanted, Alaji seemed eager to talk. But it also incentivized dishonesty. "The weaving spell," Alaji said, obviously feigning contemplation. "It is tradition for the girls of my village to learn it early. We need to know it before we're ready for the healing spell, which in turn we need for the spells of giving birth. These were said to be the core of womanhood. Gifts given only to us by our gods."

When Alaji had appeared, there'd been a dispute over which department should be assigned to interview, interrogate, and monitor her memory. In Reilla's opinion, Temporal Thaumaturgy had actually presented a better case than her own, but—fortunately for her—the Archivist Council disagreed. They concurred with Enforcement and Corrections' assertion that the details surrounding Alaji were first and foremost an extension of the ongoing investigation into Yemerik's desertion. The irony that said desertion would be effectively pardoned wasn't lost on Reilla, nor was the fact that Yemerik had no idea he was the sole reason Reilla had gained this enviable level of access.

"My mother was more practical," Alaji continued. "She favored the spells of the hearth. Fire. I did not fully understand why until she took me aside one afternoon and taught me to use them to fight. It was her teachings that allowed me to steal Yemerik's talisman in the first place."

Reilla saw Yemerik casting her a cynical expression, but she pretended not to notice.

"The things she taught me helped me many times over. But, just as I didn't appreciate the spells of the hearth, I didn't understand the weaving spell. Not really. It's no surprise—my people certainly didn't, either. To them, it was simply a method of unraveling and reconnecting threads of reeds or woven fur."

"It's a rare form of magic," Reilla said, mostly to prove she was listening. "My understanding is most civilizations never develop the spells you're describing, or they lose them along the way."

"No, I don't think they lose them," Alaji said. "I think they give them up. It is a matter of economics." She paused again to smile at Yemerik. "Another concept I picked up in my journeys."

"Along with theft," he said quietly. Reilla again pretended not to hear.

"Why train wizards to weave fabric when labor is cheaper? It would be better to have laborers master the spell, as my people did, but that's not how civilizations work. Magic, I've found, is inevitably hoarded by a few. It's easy to see why—it becomes a form of power, and even the innocuous forms are hidden away."

"I think that's a powerful insight," Reilla said, pretending it was a novel idea. She hoped Yemerik could restrain himself from calling attention to the diversion.

"But it's a shame. The weaving spell is powerful. Not because it can be adapted for flesh—I learned to brew far more powerful potions to achieve similar effects—but because of the mindset it requires. The ability to stop and slow yourself. To view things not as they appear but in their component pieces. Then to unravel them and weave them back together."

"I'm sorry," Yemerik interrupted, "is this going somewhere?"

Alaji didn't give Reilla a chance to chastise him. "Of course," the witch said with an enthusiastic smile. "It is all coming together."

"Because a moment ago you were telling us about some sort of magically engineered organism lurking in a deep cave, and I don't see how that relates to a spell that mends clothing."

"Not a cave exactly," Alaji said. "It was more a cathedral built underground. A cathedral and catacomb, both."

"Did you use your weaving spell to defeat this monster?" Yemerik asked impatiently.

"No," Alaji said. "I just told you, it's not about the spell. It's about how you learn the spell. How you have to train yourself to think." She pulled a bit of fabric off the tattered edge of her coat and held it up. "I wish I could demonstrate. But magic won't work for me here, will it?"

"I'm sorry," Reilla said. "We may eventually be able to arrange a room where you can show us your spells, but it's just not possible at this time." In the back of her mind she cataloged the dozens of individuals she would need to correspond with to set that up. The safety measures alone would require hours of preparation.

"That is all right," Alaji said with a sigh. "I think I have explained it well enough, anyway."

Reilla made a point of looking thoughtful and fidgeting with the device recording their conversation to hide her relief.

35: EVALUATION

Reilla sat before the desk belonging to Jeanda, the Director of Floral Archival Studies, and waited for the meeting to begin. Once again, she'd been pulled out of her interview with Alaji. To either side, a garden of trees shrunken to six inches tall soaked up light from hovering orbs. It was a lovely enclosure, if a tad indulgent, though Reilla imagined someone with Jeanda's status could afford to indulge in a little luxury, particularly when it could be passed off as related to her work.

Reilla naturally expected the director to speak first, but Scotheck, the only other individual present, took the initiative. "I'd like access to Subject Seven-Nine-Six," he blurted out, removing a small metal ring as he spoke. He stuck this in the ray of light overhead for a moment, pulled it back over the desk, and released it. Small runic symbols appeared on the object, which immediately began projecting images of the broken talisman shards, along with fluctuating charts and long series of numbers.

"I have no idea what I'm looking at," Jeanda said.

"These wavelengths demonstrate readings of Kasanyo magnitude we've taken from the individual pieces," Scotheck said. "But when we've registered them in conjunction..." He touched one of the illusionary images and pushed it to one side. As he did so, the series rotated closer to the director. "Entirely different readings. Dramatically different."

"I take it that isn't normal," Jeanda said.

Scotheck paused before saying, "No. It's very... we've never seen readings like this."

"That's to be expected, isn't it?" Reilla interjected. "Given the nonstandard state of the talisman, I'd expect to see something unusual." She was careful to conceal even the slightest sign of satisfaction at seeing how obviously shaken her intentionally inane statement left the spectro-alchemist.

"It isn't… this isn't even about normality. We can calculate the theoretical behavior of a broken talisman, and it shouldn't be anything like this. We're generating potential temporal rifts with non-standard magnitudes." When the director looked back at him blankly, he explained, "Potential rifts which don't conform to their own coordinates."

"You're opening doors in time without knowing where they go?"

"We're not opening anything," Scotheck said. "We're just generating readings. But they don't… it's like they point to a time that doesn't align with itself. We have no idea what these are or what kind of opportunities they hold. For all we know this could be used to develop alternate tracking methods."

"Are you saying you can use these to recreate the subject's path through history, even with her attempts to hide it?" Jeanda asked.

"I don't know," Scotheck said. "I don't even understand what these readings are yet. But if there's a chance of recovering our agents this way, shouldn't we at least try?"

Reilla cleared her throat. "I'm unclear why you think the subject could help directly. We've seen no indication she has anywhere near the level of technical sophistication to offer insight."

"Of course not," Scotheck said. "But she may have heard or seen something that would help. If we only understood how she broke the talisman, it would give us a place to start."

"I am working towards getting those answers," Reilla said.

"The slow way," Scotheck responded. "It would only take a few hours to directly access her memories and determine definitively what happened."

"Doing that now would risk the relationship we've cultivated with this woman," Reilla said. "She is beginning to trust us and is providing a detailed account of her life."

"Is that really as important as recovering our agents?" Jeanda asked, leaning forward.

It was a trick question. The honest answer would have been yes. But that wasn't the morally correct answer, so Reilla said, "No. Of course not. But as long as the current timeline is stable, there's no reason to rush this, not if it means sacrificing a unique opportunity."

"What opportunity?" Scotheck asked, growing noticeably upset. "What is this about?"

Reilla glanced at the director, who was staring directly at her. "This may be the one chance we have of capturing this woman's point of view. This woman invented time travel, broke one of our talismans, and proactively sought us out. She came here to tell us her story."

"I'm not sure the families of our missing agents are as interested in why she came here as they are in whether we can save their loved ones," Jeanda said.

"No, but future generations will care a great deal how we approached this."

"That shouldn't be our priority," Scotheck argued. "I'm only asking the council be convened to evaluate the progress Reilla's making and reconsider whether it's time to alter our strategy."

Jeanda tapped a finger against her desk. "Even if the council agrees, it will take time to pull everyone together. But I'd far prefer a solution agreeable to everyone." She looked to Reilla as she said this.

"Five days," Reilla said quickly. "That should give me ample time to get the information I need."

"That's far too long," Scotheck said. "I was hoping to begin the process immediately."

"Immediately was never an option," Jeanda said. "The council gave Enforcement and Corrections initial access, and unless they are willing to waive that access, it would require a vote from the council to revoke. Since you are speaking with me, I'll assume Reilla's superiors have already denied your request. I'm guessing I wasn't your first choice for a council member, either, seeing as my division has no direct involvement in this area."

"I believe… I think that makes you impartial," Scotheck said, sounding entirely unconvincing.

"Well, then. As an impartial observer, perhaps I can suggest a compromise. Shall we say another two days? If Reilla doesn't have enough information to assist you with your studies, she'll allow the subject's memories to be probed?"

Scotheck looked displeased, and Reilla was no happier. She certainly hoped to have the answers she was looking for in that time, but she had no way of knowing for certain. But if she refused and Scotheck pressed, she was fairly certain Jeanda would call for the Archivist Council to convene, and the vote could easily go against her. She'd lose access to Alaji in two days, one of which would be wasted testifying. So, lacking a better option, she nodded and said, "I can agree to that."

36: THE HEART OF THE LABYRINTH

The room was round, with a stone rim circling the edge. There was a pit below and one above, and part of the Heart lived in both. How deep the pits went and whether there was more to the creature was unclear. Perhaps the whole of its body was contained in this room, or perhaps it extended past the ends of the room, filled hidden caverns, and stretched into the depths of the earth. Perhaps it was the whole of the world.

Several more monstrosities with clear skin and pulsating organs stood along the edges. Tendrils fixed to their membranes tethered them to the Heart, pumping fluids in and out of their bodies. Here, they were one and the same. They were connected to the Heart, part of its body. The tendrils released them as Alaji and the thieves entered, and the creatures began a march towards the intruders.

Eyes hung in the center of the room. Long strands of tissue extended to the masses above and below. The eyes were shaped like ovals and held irises that would always seem to stare directly forward. At all times, they stared in all directions.

There were other eyes as well, floating on the flesh of the creature at the top and bottom of the enclosed space. The eyes did not blink, but occasionally a mouth would form around them, swallow up the eye, and digest it. Sometimes, these mouths would shrink, close, and open to reveal new eyes.

The Heart was never still. Its body quivered, and a soft whistle emanated, like a finger run over the rim of a glass. As she stepped onto the stone ledge along with Eroza and Rit'ka, Alaji felt a strange sensation sweep through the inside of her head. She'd felt it before, the other times she'd been there.

And she remembered.

—

The locusts had hurried in first. Galaize encouraged them, despite Alaji's warnings. She'd watched as the first fired an arrow directly into the nearest eye. The shaft sank in, and a white, viscous liquid spilled out into the fleshy mass below. The creature quivered faster, and the sound grew louder. Alaji's scalp seemed to itch, or perhaps it was beneath her scalp. Flashes of memories appeared—her and Oadeth naked on a hill. The smell of a potion brewing on a damp morning while Danwin chastised her for not feeling out the ingredients better. A battle with giants in a flying city...

Alaji stumbled forward, trying to focus on the fight before her, the one in the present. She heard Galaize laugh out loud and saw him bend over to lift a rock off the floor, carry it to the ledge and hurl it over. He leapt out of the way as a tentacle flopped up after him. A nearby thief shoved his sword through it, impaling the writhing appendage. Alaji bent over to look at the suction cups sticking out of the dungeon wall and wondered what had become of her companion. Phaesha and Elkelos were still waiting up ahead, and there was no guarantee the troll wouldn't return.

Alaji struck her head violently and blinked. Phaesha wasn't here—that was long ago. This was the Heart, playing tricks on her. She squinted, focusing on the opening on the far side of the room.

Memories continued pouring in at random. She was on a boat with Theojin, riding across the plains with Yemerik, fleeing from Krishind's hound through a forest. And, of course, she was facing the Heart. She kept trying to focus on this, until that fight drowned out all others. She was here, in this place, beside a muscular man with a misshapen nose and a scar on one side of his face. Who was he?

The warrior swung madly at the tendrils sweeping up at him while Alaji conjured fire to keep them at bay. The warrior bellowed loudly, calling out the names of men and women Alaji couldn't recognize. He hacked the ends off tentacles spotted with eyes and gaping mouths, then kicked them into the dark abyss, where they were swallowed by mouths below.

The memories were being fed to her, but they were real. This happened. "Helgwin!" she called to him. "Make for the door!" She started to follow when something caught her leg and pulled her off her feet. An instant later, she was dropping towards the horrible things below. She called out to her feather, and she was floating. She fought against the pull of the thing wrapped around her ankle, a thin, sinewy tendril trying to reel her into a gaping mouth large enough to devour her whole.

And through it all, more memories. A pair of women, one armed with a bow and one with daggers that flew through the air, leaving trails of blue light in their wake. The archer ignored the eyes in the center of the room, instead focusing on pinning tendrils and tentacles against walls. The swaying blades swung back and forth across the surfaces of the monster, slicing rifts along the top and bottom.

Did any of that help? Alaji couldn't remember.

"Alaji!" Eroza shouted. She shook herself to attention and saw the archer aiming at one of the eyes.

"Wait!" Alaji said. "The tentacles… aim for… no! Aim for the eyes!" She remembered it now. The two women focused on the eyes in center of the room. The creature went mad, striking out in confusion. "Look out!" she screamed, jumping back as a tentacle swept across the edge of the platform. Eroza stepped over easily, while Rit'ka jumped upward.

"I just… it's showing me my father," Rit'ka said. "I hated my father!" She moved her hands, and her swirling blades sliced through a web of sinew holding up one of the large eyes in the center of the room. The fibers below it collapsed, and the eye fell into the mass below. The quivering quickened, and the whistle grew louder. Eroza cringed and dropped to one knee, using her shoulder to block one ear even as she pulled back her bowstring and took aim.

"Wait!" Alaji called out. "The roof! Aim for the roof!"

—

Alaji remembered the sound of the archer's bowstring snapping, one note against the cacophony of ringing from the creature above and below them. She remembered the other woman screaming, "Behind you!" just in time for her to spin and conjure a blast of wind to slide against the curved wall and knock a pair of the monstrous spawn off the walkway. They toppled over into a mouth forming below, which swallowed them. Then she remembered the massive, thick tentacle forming from the center, rising up over the stone walkway. A mouth formed, and it disgorged the two creatures right between Alaji and the archer.

"Alaji!" Helgwin cried out as she struggled against the thing pulling her down. She looked up just in time to realize another, larger tentacle was descending from the ceiling. The creature wanted to pull her apart, mostly likely.

She struggled against the ache in her forehead, the exhaustion in her joints, and the mix of terror and confusion. She'd survived this before—she only had to remember how. She went for her cursed knife, hoping it would affect the creature, and sliced into the tendril. It released at once, and the creature began shaking. The sound went from a high-pitched whistle into a resonating drum. The memories intensified. They grew more vivid, more real. For an instant, Alaji thought she was standing among Galaize's Band of Locusts watching one of them get impaled by a tentacle. The man turned to his captain, the patron of thieves, with a look of shock and terror etched across his face. A moment later, the thief was pulled down into the waiting maw of the creature below.

Alaji screamed and held still in the air. She forced herself to focus on the now, the present, and found she was staring into a massive eye, not a foot away from her. She tightened her grip on her knife and sliced across the exposed white surface, which split open.

A thousand images struck Alaji at once. Men and women she'd

never met crying out in terror as they were devoured alive and partially digested until there was nothing left but a monstrosity covered in a clear film.

When her senses returned a moment later, she found she'd struck a wall. She landed on the walkway and saw Helgwin, cringing in pain, using the flat of his sword to pry one of the monsters loose and send it tumbling into the pit.

"No!" Alaji cried, looking over. She expected the figure to land in an open mouth, but instead it hit the creature's body and split open. She shook her head—that wasn't this time; it was another.

"I saw them!" Helgwin screamed. "I can see... I can see the monster's victims! They aren't dead!" he added with horror.

"The door!" Alaji pointed as she screamed. "While it's distracted!"

—

The thief was still screaming as the creature pulled him down and devoured him whole. Alaji looked up to see Galaize and his two remaining followers struggling to reach the other side. Sweating, she stood upright. Out of the corner of her eye, she saw a tentacle stretching down for her. She remembered remembering this. When she'd fought beside the man she'd heard herself call Helgwin, a name she already knew from this era's history. And she understood.

In her memories, she'd fought through this. She'd cut the tentacles with her cursed knife and had crawled to join Galaize. But she could see tendrils descending from every wall. Those, she did not remember.

She turned to the open pit, charged, and leapt off, calling on her feather as she did so. She conjured a burst of wind at her back to push her forward, propelling her past the hanging eyes and through the doorway.

—

"Behind you!" Rit'ka screamed, pointing. Alaji spun around to see a pair of the oozing spawn of the guardian coming at her.

This has happened before, she thought. But that wasn't right— it was happening now. The creature was reading her mind in this moment. And it would remember this for a thousand years when she returned with Galaize during her first visit. It would flood her mind with her own memories both to disorient her and to try and learn her weaknesses.

She summoned the wind, as she remembered doing, then immediately leapt towards Rit'ka and Eroza. When a tentacle shot out of the pit, she was ready. She sliced into its leathery hide with her cursed blade, and the room shook. The tentacle clenched up, and a yellowish slime oozed out as it collapsed.

"Run!" Alaji said, pointing towards the doorway out. "Quickly!"

37: MIRROR IMAGES

Alaji slumped against the wall of the corridor in three times. Once, Helgwin knelt to gently slap her face, thinking she was losing her mind. And perhaps she was, but she was struggling with more than that. In another, she heard Galaize's surviving men mourning the loss of their comrade. And in the last, Eroza was kneeling beside her, splashing water into her face.

"What are we supposed to do if she dies?" Rit'ka asked. "Or if she doesn't wake up?"

"I'm okay," Alaji mumbled, shifting in place.

She could hear an echo of Galaize telling her he didn't care and another of Helgwin sighing in relief. Then, louder, she heard Rit'ka say, "Then get up before those things come after us!" Her voice trailed off as she spoke, and Alaji realized the thief was looking at her with a baffled expression.

"What is it?" Alaji asked.

"You were mouthing her words," Eroza said. "Even as she said them."

"We need… we need to keep moving," Alaji said, standing. Her own words echoed through her head as well. "It's too close. It can still hear our thoughts."

"She's right," Eroza said. "I can feel it. It's weaker here, but it's still listening."

Alaji felt herself being helped to her feet in three different times. Then she led them on until all but the two women vanished like ghosts. She paused to scratch away the remnants of dried blood from under her nose. She couldn't remember when it had started bleeding, though that was far from the only thing fading.

"I can't... I can't remember what it looked like," Rit'ka said. "Even the things it showed me... I can't hold onto them."

"It did something to us," Eroza said. "To her, worst of all," she added, nodding towards Alaji.

"I have faced it so many times," Alaji whispered. "I still don't know why it does that. To learn maybe."

"How many times?" Rit'ka asked.

Alaji shook her head. "I don't know. I can't..."

"Before, you said this would be the third," Eroza said.

"Was it just three?" Alaji asked, astonished. She shivered and increased her pace. Occasionally, she'd turn to respond to one of her companions. Sometimes, she even found herself addressing someone who was present.

—

They followed twisting passageways that rose and lost elevation. They found traps along the way—some Alaji pointed out, while others Eroza spotted and disarmed. In a large square room, they were attacked by a pair of snakes, each a hundred feet long with scales blades could barely pierce. They killed one by tricking it into swallowing one of Rit'ka's knives, which tore apart the beast from the inside. The other died in ice when Alaji hurled one of her remaining potions at it. The encounter was almost a welcome diversion after what they'd endured.

Finally, they reached a long, open hall. Along the edges stood dozens of ephemeral figures. Their bodies exuded no light, but they looked as if they were formed of mist. Rit'ka drew her blades at once and whispered. The knives began glowing, and they seemed to pull at her hands, as if trying to break free.

"I can't kill the dead, but I can wound them," she said quietly.

"Wait," Alaji said. She was still exhausted from her ordeal, but her head was finally clear. "There's no need."

"Everything in this place has attacked so far," Rit'ka hissed.

"So far, everything we've come across has wanted to keep us out," Alaji said. "They want us to go on. They won't trouble us."

"These spirits harbor a corruption," Eroza said. "I can't describe it—it's like an infection."

"I know," Alaji said, leading them on. The hall progressed for miles, sloping down only slightly. As they passed, the spirits turned to watch them, but the ghosts neither approached nor spoke. The last of the apparitions stood to either side of a double door set in an ornate wall.

"The stonework," Eroza said quietly, "I would expect it in a church." Rit'ka glanced at her as if Eroza had gone mad, but she said nothing.

Alaji stepped forward and pulled out her metal amulet inlaid with blue stones, tying this around her neck. She took a quick breath, placed a hand on each of the doors, and pushed them open. As soon as they began to part, a crack of light appeared.

38: THE FINAL GUARDIAN

A body, once relieved of its spirit, holds some limited interest.

The third guardian kept a few around, collected from the few explorers who'd managed to reach him. A simple enchantment preserved the tissue and fluids, which he could use as material for the garden he kept hidden behind a wall only he could pass through.

Really, the bones were the best part, though. Sometimes he would craft them into magical beings, simplistic versions of the skeletal monster residing far above, which he'd send into the tunnels to serve as additional hunters and guardians in his maze. Other times, he crafted objects for his comfort. He'd a chair made from the skeletons of six elven brothers who'd battled their way to him only to be killed in seconds. At one time, he'd added ornate flourishes, so it would resemble a throne, but after a hundred years he decided it was too self-indulgent. He removed the decorations and reshaped them into game pieces.

He had dozens of games at his disposal. He took great delight in creating rules to play by. Most of the time, he had only himself to play against. He discovered he could manage this fairly well if he simply waited a few decades between moves, by which time he'd usually forgotten his original strategy. He'd then have to reconstruct both strategies, which could take days to accomplish. It was a reasonable facsimile of a challenge.

Occasionally he would challenge adventurers when they reached him. "Defeat me in this game, and you may pass to claim the riches beyond," he'd proclaim. Then he'd find ways of drawing the game out as long as possible by making absurd moves or even pretending he didn't notice when they were cheating. No one had ever beaten him, so there was no need to consider whether he'd make good on his promise and allow them to see the inside of the last chamber before killing them. It would probably be more merciful to kill them outright, so they'd never realize they'd died for nothing.

On the rarest of occasions, he was visited by one of the others. They were really there to ensure he hadn't abandoned his post, but he was glad for the companionship, however brief. He always asked if they would agree to relieve him for a time, but their answer was always the same. They would apologize and say there was too much going on. They'd promise to speak on his behalf to their old allies and ensure his time there wouldn't go on too much longer. Then they'd compliment him on his ability to retain his form and his commitment. He didn't actually expect more from them, but he'd discovered early on they were more amenable to his games if he asked.

It had been ages since one of them had come to see him and more than a century since a group of dwarves had fought their way through the labyrinth above. He'd passed the time as he always had, with his games and his thoughts, or by battling the monsters that would occasionally make their way to him.

Then he began hearing noise. He became excited almost at once, though he knew he shouldn't get his hopes up. In his time in these depths, he'd heard the sounds of countless distant battles, felt the ground quake from powerful magic, and seen scores of insects scurry from the walls on several occasions. Almost every time, the noises ceased without him encountering a soul. Either they were slaughtered by one of the monsters, cut down by the immortal knight, devoured by the eldritch beast, or they simply lost their way in the dark and starved to death—in any case, he was denied their company, their entertainment, and the components of their bodies.

As the sounds continued and he felt the ripples of the eldritch beast's psychic manipulations, he became more and more hopeful. He spoke a word known only to him that could be pronounced by no other tongue, and the door opened to his secret enclosure. A rock burned brightly with the force and heat of the sun, allowing his collection of crops to flourish underground, fertilized with the remnants of adventurers, beasts, and insects. He plucked a ripe grape off a vine and bit into it, savoring the richness.

He then hurried to his stone wardrobe and selected a dark robe he kept for such situations. He slipped it over his shoulders and stepped to his mirror to make himself presentable. He ran his fingers through his hair, pausing to pluck out a few grey strands. Then he spread his lips and picked a piece of grape skin from between his teeth. While he was there, he took hold of a crooked tooth in his mouth and pried it free, then threw it into the dirt of his garden. He concentrated for a moment, formed the hand sigils, and channeled his spirit through his flesh, transforming it as he did so. Within seconds, the missing tooth regenerated, fresh and straight. He wiped the blood away with his tongue, then used his magic to adjust his cheekbones—they were beginning to collapse—and to fix his complexion.

When he was happy with his appearance, he cleared his throat, tilted his head down, and said, "You have come far and faced hardships beyond imagination. A pity then your quest must end here, but never have you confronted one such as I! Should you wish, you may attack me, but no weapon or spell you have can overcome me. I offer you instead one chance—defeat me in a game of wits, and I shall grant you passage."

He was happy with his expression, but he could hear something was off in his inflection. He practiced the speech a few more times before he was satisfied, ate another grape, then grabbed two goblets and a bottle carved of bone that was full of a wine he'd made. With these in hand, he hurried back to the corridor, commanded the passage to his sanctum to close, and set his bottle and goblets down to wait.

It wasn't until he heard the whisper of voices in the hall of spirits that he knew he was in luck. He immediately poured some wine into one of his goblets, held it in his hand six inches from his mouth, wiped the excited grin from his face, and struck the most enigmatic pose he could manage. Then he called out a quick incantation, and a dozen orbs on a candelabra made of bone lit up.

He stood there for another minute until the left door swung open.

"You have come far and faced hardships beyond imagination," he said, bellowing to make himself heard. "A pity then your quest must…" He trailed off, paused, and squinted. A man and woman stood before him. He paid the man no mind, but there was something familiar about the woman, though he couldn't immediately recall why. But his gaze shifted to her hand, and he saw the object she carried. That, he recognized immediately, and through it he placed her. She was a little older than he'd last seen her (and his eyes had been those of a dragon's), but it was the same woman. He gasped, set his goblet on the table, and clasped his hands together. "Alaji!" he proclaimed.

"Hello, Limper," she replied warily. She held the amulet before her as she approached.

"Limper," he said, as if tasting the name. "The others rarely call me that anymore. I stopped doing that thing with my legs ages ago— we can tell each other apart by our spirits' auras these days." He glanced towards her companion, who was on edge. This was a bulky man with a mangy beard, an ugly forehead, and a nose so mangled he felt an odd compulsion to fix it, and only refrained from offering because he knew mortals were usually uncomfortable around such magic. "I am surprised to see you here," he said to Alaji. "This place… it must have been difficult for you. Please, feel free to have a seat."

"No. Thank you. I need to get past," she said, fairly dramatically.

"Oh, is that what this is?" he asked. "I assure you, our precautions are sufficient, but…" he stepped back, whispered a single-word incantation, and blinked. He saw Alaji's hand hovering near her blade, which surprised him, but he said nothing. He looked them over quickly and said, "You may pass whenever you like. As for him," he motioned to the warrior, "that's up to you. As a rule, I don't allow mortals who come this far to return alive. The last thing I want is for these caverns' reputation to lapse. But I'll certainly defer to your wishes. Consider it a friendly courtesy."

"Thank you," Alaji said. "I only need a moment, and we'll be gone."

"That's really not necessary," the Limper said, more quickly than he'd intended. "I actually have a collection of games of my own design I would be honored to share. And you're welcome to a glass of wine."

"I can't stay. I'm sorry," Alaji said. "I have too much to do."

With that, they passed by him. Despite his oath, the Limper briefly considered following to have a few more minutes of company, but he'd no desire to see the inside of that room again. Instead, he sat silently with his wine. He heard them speaking with raised voices for a short while, then they emerged again. The man she was with had turned pale, and he was staying several feet from Alaji, who appeared a little shaken herself.

The Limper looked her over, surprised. "Where is your amulet?" he asked.

She nodded towards the room she'd come from. "I'm leaving it here for now."

"Then you're planning to return?" the Limper asked, excited by the promise of company.

"Yes," she replied. "I'm not entirely sure how soon, but I'll come back."

"Perhaps then we can speak at greater length. I would welcome any news or history you can offer. And even a short game would please me to no end."

She looked at him with an expression he couldn't read then said, "Goodbye for now." And with that, she led her companion back the way they'd come.

The Limper poured his wine back into its bottle, returned his formal cloak to his wardrobe, and listened for the distant sounds of combat as she made her way back through the tunnels. Then, with a sigh, he returned to his life of games and gardening, punctuated by killing the occasional beast that made its way through the outer levels.

Barely any time passed at all—a year or two at most—before the Limper heard sounds of activity once more. He donned his cloak and grabbed his goblets, though he wasn't sure if he'd need them. This time, the doors leading to his abode swung open together, and Alaji appeared with a pair of women.

"Alaji!" he proclaimed, "it's good to see you again!" He looked at her closer and paused, momentarily confused. Around her neck, she wore the amulet with blue stones. As far as he knew, only one such artifact existed, and it was still in the room behind him. He was about to ask her about it when she cut him off.

"I need to go in again," she said. As she spoke, she glanced from side to side at the two women with her.

He shrugged and looked her over. "As I said before, I will not stop you. Though I find myself growing curious, why the interest? Do you no longer trust us?"

Alaji sighed. "I will tell you one day, and you'll understand. But for now, there's something I need to do here."

As before, she entered with her companions. And, also as before, the Limper heard sounds of disagreement. Then, after a few minutes, they returned, absent the amulet. He said nothing but shook his head in fascination.

"Will you come back here?" the Limper asked when Alaji refused his offer to stay.

"Yes," she replied quietly. "In a thousand years."

"I am uncertain if I will still be here," the Limper warned her. He was optimistic one of the others would replace him by then.

"I'm sorry," Alaji said, "but you will be."

The Limper felt as if a great weight had been placed on his shoulders. He returned to his life as best he could, though he did not doubt her in this regard. The following centuries were hard ones. The diversions offered by explorers ended entirely, and he wasn't sure why. After three hundred lonely years, he received a visit from the immortal who'd once called herself "the Farmer." Now, she inhabited the body of a half-orc diplomat. It was a simple life, as far as their kind were usually concerned, but she seemed to enjoy it immensely. The Limper did his best to conceal his jealousy, though he suspected she could tell. Still, she remained for several weeks, telling him news of the world, of distant countries ruled by the spirits of ancient immortals and a dozen other things. She told him of the Order of Helgwin, founded by a mercenary who'd descended into the caverns and sworn his life and fortune to keep any other from doing the same.

"He did us a favor," the Farmer said, gnawing on some dried meat she'd brought. "He's keeping his kind away. Saving you the trouble."

"Yes, the trouble," the Limper said thoughtfully. "I don't suppose you've given any thought to accepting this role for a time."

"I have some affairs to attend to first," she replied. "Once everything is in order, I'd be happy to relieve you for a few millennia."

She was lying. But if he confronted her, it would only dissuade her from ever accepting the post or even visiting him again. So he smiled as best he could, thanked her, and kept her there as long as she'd stay. When she left, he simply returned to his ongoing existence, passing the time as he waited for his next visitor.

The years dragged on. To keep busy, he collected more bones from the nearby corridors and constructed a grander hall for himself. In one of the side passages, he even came across a nest of wingless cave dragons that had tunneled in from deep beneath the earth. He was tempted to leave the tunnels they'd made getting in, since a group of dwarves might find them, and that was hardly an unpleasant idea. But he remembered his oath and collapsed the opening, then dispatched the creatures to keep them from digging more holes out. He took the skull from the largest and fixed it to the ceiling above his home. The others, he turned into additional pieces of furniture, including a shelf for the small collection of books the other immortals had brought him over the millennia.

When he finally heard sounds of conflict again, he'd long since lost his sense of time. He hoped it wasn't Alaji, not because he didn't welcome her company, but because the alternative would mean an additional set of guests. He readied a new cloak he'd made of dragon scales after his last deteriorated. Then he stood ready.

It was Alaji again, this time with three men, one exceedingly attractive, despite being covered in mud and gore. The Limper smiled, as he'd practiced constantly in the mirror. "Welcome, Alaji," he said.

"Who are you?" she asked, and he tilted his head. Then he laughed pleasantly.

"I am sorry. I hadn't realized our encounters were out of order. I believe the name you knew me last by was the Limper. We met in another life." He pointed overhead at the dragon skull above him. "But we are friends now. You came here twice before with other companions. You never told me why," he added. "Please, have a seat and a cup of wine. I have some vegetables from my garden, as well. I would offer you meat, but I doubt the options down here would appeal to you."

"I can't stay," Alaji said, shaking her head. "I only need to get by." As she spoke, she removed an amulet from her pocket. The Limper's gaze was briefly drawn to it—it was the same artifact that she'd left twice before.

"I could do with a glass of wine," the man behind her said, though the Limper couldn't tell from his tone if it was an honest request or a joke. "I am Galaize, trusted member of the Order of Helgwin." As he said this last part, the other two men chuckled.

The Limper cleared his throat, unsure what to make of the mention of the Order that was responsible for starving him of human interaction for a thousand years. But ultimately it made little difference. He nodded to Alaji and said, "Of course. You can go in and have a look around, for whatever good it will accomplish." He began to step aside then remembered the last piece of his oath. He shook his head, blinked, and whispered the invocation to transform his vision.

Then he froze. His mouth dropped open and his attention fixated on a magical aura emanating from within Alaji's pocket. "You have the Acolyte's key," he whispered. It was more an accusation than a statement. "If any other mortal had come with that, I would force them to tear themselves apart, piece by piece. But that would leave it here, so I will grant you the choice. Take it from this place and leave it on the edge of time, and I will allow you to leave those you've brought to suffer your punishment instead."

Alaji held the amulet in front of her and said, "Stay behind me." Two of the men did as she commanded, but the third, the shortest, inched away to one side. The Limper thrust his hand forward, weaving ethereal strands to counter the distance. He grabbed the thief by his very soul and gripped it tight. Alaji stepped forward in an attempt to cut his power, but the Limper was faster. He tore the startled man's spirit loose and pulled it to his hand. With a flick of his wrist, it transformed into a winding whip splitting into three prongs. He swung it at Alaji, but she held up her amulet, and the whip bent away from her.

The Limper shifted his grip, and the glowing whip changed shape, transforming into a long pickaxe. He didn't need it to hold its shape—if he could get close enough to reach over her defenses, he might be able to skewer her skull before his makeshift weapon fell apart. Somewhere in the back of his mind, the Limper was gripped by terror. In her own way, Alaji was older than history, memory, or any of his kind. She was as old as time, for all intents and purposes. What would the Collective say when they learned he'd killed her? Or the King with the Red Arm, for that matter, if he regained his senses?

They would understand. Anywhere else, they wouldn't, but here he could kill her. Here, he had no choice. Even with all that meant. Even with the artifacts she carried left behind. Power over time itself, available for the taking—even that was better than her taking the key in.

He charged quickly as she held up her amulet. He could feel it warping and twisting the energies in the spectral weapon he'd formed from the thief's soul. He could sense the spirit's pain as the Limper extended his own will through the spirit, compelling it to hold its form for just a little longer.

He needed only seconds more to end this. Alaji's full attention was spent resisting him—whatever weapons she had at her disposal were useless. He prepared to leap and swing the pickaxe down at her. Either it would kill her, or she would block it. And if she did manage to block it, she'd leave herself open. He could kill her with his bare hands if he had to.

Then he felt his ankle falter. A sharp pain shot through his leg, and he looked down to see the handsome thief below him drawing his blade through the front of the Limper's shin. It was a trivial wound, the sort he could heal in seconds with his magic. But it was enough to cost him his balance. He fell, and his strike swung widely off the mark. Alaji's amulet deflected it to one side, and the pointed ax stuck through the stomach of the third thief.

The Limper caught himself with one hand, shattering several bones in his fingers. He ignored that pain, as he ignored the pain in his leg, and he began pushing himself up, hoping to recover some momentum. But then he felt another blade cut into his forearm. He looked up and saw Alaji staring him in the eye. She actually attempted some rudimentary control spell, which he was easily able to subvert. He was about to return the magic in kind when the pain from her attack caught up with him.

Of course, he thought, as his flesh and mind caught fire, her legendary cursed blade. Legendary was generous—he'd felt worse. Whatever ancient conjurer had prepared this wouldn't be the last or the best to develop magical tools of torture. But this was enough to break his concentration. And before he could regain it, she'd stabbed him again. Then again. Over and over, her cursed blade pierced his skin.

He struggled to hold on, to keep this body alive, just a moment longer. To mutter an incantation that might kill them all, then hope he'd be able to return before any other mortal found their way to this chamber. But he couldn't form any such spell, and eventually his hold over his flesh failed him. Then, with a final exhausted gasp, he was spirit. Even then, he tried one last time to reach for her. But she must have sensed him. She lowered her amulet, and he felt himself hurled into darkness.

Somewhere in that darkness, he heard a heartbeat. He felt the warmth of a body, the flow of blood, and the absence of pain.

He couldn't reach her from here. All he could do was wait as his next body formed and was born. Then he would need to wait until he was old enough, at least to walk. After that, he would need to go in search of one of the others and confess his failure.

For now, he was trapped in another dark and lonely chamber.

39: THE TOMB

"Your gem is over there," Alaji said, motioning to a pedestal on one side of the hallway. Carvings depicting ancient wars lined the walls, along with writing in dozens of dead languages. "I have something to attend to, but you can wait here."

"I would rather see what is down there," Eroza said in an unusually forceful tone. She didn't even turn to look at the object they'd come for, though Rit'ka slipped over and pocketed it quietly.

Alaji turned with a reluctant expression. "I will not stop you," she said after considering for a moment, "but you will not like what you see."

—

"Is that what you came to do?" Helgwin asked a year earlier when Alaji paused beside the door, pulled out a large gemstone, and set it on an empty pedestal in the hallway.

"No. This… it's complicated. I've read about two women who are searching for this gem."

"And you're trying to lure them to their deaths?"

"I'm not trying to kill anyone else here," Alaji said.

"Anyone else. Is that an acknowledgment that you're going to kill me after all?" There was a dark humor to his tone. He was already resigned to die here, and he'd never believed Alaji's promises to the contrary.

"You live another thirty years," Alaji told him. "You'll go on to call them the only years of your life that mattered."

"Just know that when you inevitably turn on me, no matter how I look while I'm dying, I expected it all along."

Alaji rolled her eyes and started forward.

Alaji pretended not to notice while Galaize plucked a stone emblem off a pedestal in the hallway. It was likely invaluable, of course, but what did that matter?

"That was horrific," he said as he followed her onward. "My last two locusts killed by a wizard. Or whatever he was. Is warlock more accurate?"

"He was one of the immortals who built this place. He stayed behind to protect it."

"Immortal is clearly an exaggeration," Galaize said. "Don't get me wrong—that was one of the worst things I've ever seen, and most of his competition came earlier in this place. But that thing he did with Histear's life force. I'm assuming I'm getting that right—that the whip was made from his essence?"

"His spirit," Alaji said. "He made it out of your friend's soul. I don't know what a 'life force' is."

"It means the same thing, I think. Or not—philosophers are rather vague, and the whole subject is somewhat theoretical, as I understand it. But I suppose what I just saw qualifies as proof of a sort, doesn't it?"

"Think what you like," Alaji said.

Galaize chuckled at this. "I'd like to think the truth, whatever that is. I've heard a hundred stories of a life beyond this, and I generally took them all to be cons designed to entice us to spend our time as priests would like and not by our own whims. I've lived my life under that assumption—if it's wrong, I'd rather know the truth, just in case some corrective measure might ensure a more favorable continuation of my existence."

"You're talking about heavens and hells," Alaji said.

"Or maybe something less cliché," Galaize said.

"There are no such places." Alaji paused a moment then amended her statement. "No place but one. There's a spot at the end of time where souls are collected in something similar to what you'd call heaven, but it doesn't matter what sort of life you lead."

"Sounds like another children's story," Galaize said. "But I like the part about not needing to amend my ways."

—

"This is a mausoleum," Helgwin said, as he gazed around the dome. Alaji's magic illuminated the circular room, which had no exit but the one they'd entered from. In the center lay a massive stone sarcophagus. The lid was decorated with a carving of a man with his mouth open, as if screaming. Beside the carving's head was a keyhole.

Alaji hurried to one side and set her metal amulet on the floor, pointed directly at the statue. "It's done," she said.

"That's all?" Helgwin asked, suspicious.

"For now," she replied. "Once we're back through the worst of it, I'll return you to the entrance. After that, you'll never see me again."

"I just… I assumed there'd be something more dramatic. You're actually going to let me go? Assuming we make it back, I mean."

"I told you, you don't die here. Let's go." She began to leave, and Helgwin shook his head and started to follow. As he looked around, his eyes fell on an image overhead. And he paused, mouth agape.

—

Eroza's bowstring went taut seconds after she stepped into the room, and she aimed directly at Alaji's head. The archer's breathing grew heavy, and she began to shake. "Move and I kill you," she whispered. Rit'ka drew her blades in response to her partner, but she was looking back and forth between Eroza and Alaji.

"What is it?" she asked.

"That tomb," Eroza whispered.

Alaji froze. She locked eyes with the archer and said, "Please. Lower the bow."

"I know what's in there," Eroza said.

"What?" Rit'ka asked, but she caught sight of the painted ceiling before anyone could respond. Her mouth fell open, and she said, "But that's only a myth. He was never real."

"If you could see as I see," Eroza said in a shaking voice. "I can feel it. Smell it even. It defies words."

"Graillinde was real," Alaji said. "The last time he was defeated, he was imprisoned in this room."

"Are you here to set him free?" Eroza asked.

"I'm here, now, to delay his escape," Alaji said. "It's complicated, but that much is true. This amulet... it weakens him. This place does, as well."

Eroza lowered her bow slowly. Rit'ka whispered, "You're sure she's telling the truth?"

"She is. Mostly," Eroza said.

"He is going to escape one day," Alaji said. "No one can stop that."

"The Inesra monks believe in him," Eroza said. "Until now, I never thought there was anything to their faith. They say he is bound beneath the earth, that his freedom will mean the death of all."

"It didn't the last time it happened," Alaji said. "Or the times before that. I've seen the world dead, and I don't think it was at his hand." She slipped off her amulet, took it a third of the way around the room from an identical amulet, and propped it up so it was pointing at the center.

—

"So," Galaize said as he stepped into the room. "That's the resting place of the Dark Lord?" Alaji turned to give him a surprised look. He shrugged and added, "Deepest secret of the Order of Helgwin," he said. "Shared only with the most trusted of their number. But then Helgwin's notes weren't especially hard to steal." He patted his pack.

"You're right," Alaji said. "This holds Graillinde's spirit."

Galaize shivered, stifling a grin. "That's ominous, isn't it? The spirit of evil itself. The unstoppable force of darkness. I'll be honest, I wasn't sure I believed it existed until that third guardian. Before that, I thought maybe the Order was deluding itself. Or maybe Helgwin was mad. But there's really no treasure here, is there?"

"I never said there was," Alaji replied.

"No. You promised me… how did you put it? My name in song for thousands of years and a story to survive all of time."

"I told you your story would be told at the end of time. And it will be—I'm sure of it."

"Well, I'm pleased to hear that," Galaize said, chuckling. "It's hugely comforting. But, seeing as you're probably planning to release Graillinde now and end history immediately, it's more poetic than enticing." He reached for a throwing knife while Alaji pulled out a glass vial. Both held their objects ready and waited.

"I'm not here for the reason you think," Alaji said.

"You'll forgive my skepticism," Galaize replied. "I think I'll err on the side of caution."

Alaji held her potion up and looked at him menacingly. "Do not test me," she snarled.

Galaize just laughed. "Here's the thing—you're probably the most frightening thing I've ever seen, even more than the warlock. Or you were when all this started. Back at the beginning, when you were letting my men die whenever things got bad, you'd just appear and save most of us. You thought you were testing us, and—in all fairness—you were. But I was testing you, too. And—I hope you take this for the compliment it is—you did not disappoint. But after that knight—the first guardian, you called him—after that things changed, didn't they? No more vanishing and reappearing. No more incredible torrents of wind or fire. Just simple spells and potions, like the one you're holding now. So here's what I think—and feel free to slaughter me mercilessly if I'm wrong—I think this place counters your magic. I think here, you're just a witch."

Alaji began to step forward, but Galaize was impossibly fast. His hand shot out, and his knife shattered the vial, raining its contents on her and the floor. She grunted painfully as a small glass shard stuck in the side of her hand. Wisps of fog began spilling off of her, swallowing her completely.

"I want to assure you that your promise will be fulfilled. I just saved the world from the unleashing of Graillinde," Galaize said to the growing plumes of fog. "When I'm done telling the tale, it probably will last until the end of time!" He began to laugh, but a sound from the center of the fog caught him off guard.

He heard chanting.

He went for another throwing knife and hurled it blindly at the mist, hoping to hit the hidden woman, but he heard his knife strike the far wall instead. Seconds later, the fog billowed out at him, pushed by magical wind. He'd reached for another dagger, but his vision began to blur. He stumbled, trying to find a way out, but his sense of direction was distorted.

His legs wobbled, and he fell to his knees. The knife dropped from his hand, and it took every ounce of strength to keep himself from fainting. Then, through the fog, he saw Alaji's silhouette appear.

"You… you're alive," he said.

"It wasn't that kind of potion," she replied.

"There are… other…"

"I'm sorry," Alaji said, grabbing him by the back of his collar and pulling him. He slid, half asleep, towards the stone structure in the center of the room. "This was always my plan, and I'm sorry for that. You were the worst of them, at least according to the books, but that doesn't make this right. Not for you or your men."

"What?" he tried to ask, but before he could form a sentence, she stabbed him in the gut with a knife and pushed him onto the raised stone surface.

"I am sorry. But this will take a sacrifice."

He saw her produce a key and push it into the hole beside him. As she turned it, she stepped back. Then he felt himself grabbed. He felt his blood turn hot, and his wound expanded, as though something was crawling inside him.

40: A Meeting of Old Friends

The crone grew quiet for a moment. Yemerik was fairly certain he detected a hint of shame, which wasn't at all surprising. He cleared his throat and started to ask the obvious question. "Why—"

"Because I had to speak with him once more, and there'd never be a better opportunity," Alaji said quickly. Too quickly, in fact—he wasn't going to ask why she'd acted as she had (though he still had lingering questions in that respect) but rather why she was telling them this. Why speak of something so pointless? Or was there some reason she believed the act was significant?

"It weighed on me. It still does, even now, which is odd. I've made harder choices and killed better people. But rarely those who'd fought beside me. Even if it was always leading to that moment."

"You knew he'd betray you?" Reilla asked.

"No," Alaji said, surprised. "That I'd betray him. I took him down there for that purpose. I suppose it could have been one of his men, if any of them had survived that long. I think that would have been worse—I don't think any of them were as heartless as he was. They at least cared about him. He attracted that kind of loyalty against reason. Like Ulithaine, in some ways, but without any sense of responsibility."

Yemerik laughed out loud, but stifled it almost immediately. "I'm sorry," he said, "but I never found Ulithaine particularly responsible."

Reilla cleared her throat. "We'll want to make a note of that when we're compiling your reflections on these events." Her tone didn't contain even a hint of disdain while reminding him they were here for Alaji's story, not his.

"Ulithaine cared about his people," Alaji said. "Galaize saw them as a means to an end. But his men loved him. I think I was beginning to love him by the end," she added, laughing. "Even knowing what he was capable of, I couldn't help but be won over. Perhaps that's why I felt so bad about killing him."

"But you felt you had to do it?" Reilla asked.

"I did have to," Alaji replied. "Graillinde was too important. He was too powerful to leave out of it all."

—

It took longer for Galaize to die than Alaji had expected, certainly far longer than she'd hoped. And his screams left no possibility that his end had been peaceful. When those sounds ceased, others took their place. Of skin and muscle being unwoven and reformed, of bones cracking and being mended, of joints twisting and changing shape. She turned away, not wanting to be more on edge than she'd started. And long before it had ended, she retreated to the entryway and dismissed her light.

"I am free," she heard the ancient lord of darkness growl. "I am whole. Blood and flesh, once more. Sinew and spit."

"Do you recognize me?" Alaji asked, summoning another glowing orb to replace the one she'd dismissed. They stood facing each other. He was far less human than even their last encounter. His face bore no resemblance to the one Alaji had known. His skin was pale and stretched thin. Veins and muscles underneath pulsed, and black sparks showed through. He was no longer dead but not quite alive; a spirit taking refuge in a body built of dying flesh.

"I would not have," Graillinde said. "Were it not for these eyes. Their previous owner knew you, and I have swallowed his sight. Everything he was, everything he did... they are mine now. To me, you are a faded remnant of a memory—an idea without a face—but to him... I know you again, Alaji."

"Good," she said. "Because we need to talk."

Graillinde chuckled. "Oh, but we do not. I thank you for setting me free, for breaking my shackles, but I owe no mortal. I will swallow your memories, as I swallowed his. I will take everything you have seen, everything you are. If your words are more than lies, I will face whatever challenges await. But I have no use for those who do not serve me, and the one thing I remember about you is…" He paused, confused, as he attempted to shift forward. "What… what is this?" He demanded.

"I'm surprised you don't remember my amulet," Alaji said. "I used it to defeat you once."

"No mortal has ever defeated me!" he hissed.

"Phaesha did," Alaji said, but he only looked at her with a confused expression.

"You robbed me of a body long ago," he said. "You had something… a trivial object."

"It repels spectromancy," Alaji said, pointing to the floor beside him.

"I remember it now," Graillinde said. "It is not strong enough. Even weakened, I should—"

"There," Alaji added, pointing to his other side, where the amulet rested again. "Behind you, as well. I think two would have been enough, but I wanted to be sure."

"I have laid nations to waste," Graillinde said. "Do you think these will stop me forever?"

"They'll hold you for a few thousand years, at least," Alaji said. "But by then the others will learn what's happened. I don't think any one of them could defeat you, but a few will come and drive you back into your prison."

"And how long will that hold me?" he demanded.

Alaji shrugged. "Less than fifty thousand years this time. But I knew you'd only be held for so long before breaking free and tearing civilization down again. It's hardly the first time that cycle has repeated, is it?"

"This is the fourth such age," Graillinde said.

"It's at least the sixth," Alaji corrected him. "You can't even keep track of how many times you've been captured and broken free."

"You cannot fathom what I know," Graillinde said, "or how I know it."

"You learned from Lundanta. From the Incarnation Anomaly," Alaji added when he looked confused again. "As she stumbled backwards through time looking for me, you caught up with her again and again and traded what you knew about me for shards of her magic. Both of you thought you were swindling the other; you, giving her dates and details from the past, and her with trivial advances she knew you'd make anyway. But neither of you understood. Her teachings were rewriting her own past, pushing you further and further ahead. It must have been excruciating for her."

"I remember," he said distantly. "She was confused, hurt. Easy to manipulate."

"Exactly," Alaji said. "She was tumbling backwards in time, bleeding knowledge. You weren't the only one to notice. An entire branch of magic developed early. I saw hints before your birth."

"Birth?" Graillinde sneered.

"You've forgotten," Alaji said. "You were human once. You and Jaylarie both. Do you remember him, at least?"

"Jaylarie... he was the father of the betrayer. Of Ayalar."

"He was Ayalar," Alaji said. "You're confused."

"I remember everything!" Graillinde shouted. His eyes turned black for a moment, but they quickly faded back to milky-white. "You are a fool. And you are trying to trick me."

"You're wrong," Alaji said. "I came here to talk. To tell you my story and to strike a bargain."

"I have no interest in bargaining with the likes of you," Graillinde said. "You are nothing to me. Save your stories and know I will find you one day once I am free of your tricks. I will tear your spirit in half and be done with you. You and your Citadel both!"

"I'm not from the Citadel," Alaji said. "You're thinking of Yemerik."

Graillinde turned away with a sneer. "I will hear no more lies."

"Do you know how easy it would be?" Alaji said. "I have the power now to go anywhere, at any time."

"Not here," Graillinde said. "Here, your magic is as constrained as mine."

"I walked in, I can walk out," Alaji said. "Then I could go back a million years as easily as taking a step. I could keep going back until I found you, back before you ever became this thing. I could find you when you were a vampire, or even a man. Ayalar asked me to do that once, that or something like it. To wipe you from the timeline. To save the world from the horrors you unleashed."

"No," Graillinde hissed, "I would stop you." But there was fear in his voice. Even transformed and twisted, that remained clear.

"You have no idea how weak you were," Alaji said. "When we met, I could have killed you without exerting myself. I could have put a blade through your head, cut you apart, and burned the pieces. It would be even easier for me now. I have potions that could dissolve your body completely."

"You do not scare me!" he shouted.

"I'm not trying to scare you," Alaji said. "And I'm not threatening you. I'm trying to make you understand. If I was going to do that, I already would have. There'd be no you to debate with. But that's not what I want. It was never what I wanted. Piece it together!"

"Riddles," Graillinde snorted. "I have no taste for them."

"Fine. I've never been fighting you. I've been helping you—all of you. I tricked the Anomaly into going back through time to spread spectromancy through this timeline. I cultivated the magic that built you. I did this."

"That is absurd! What possible reason could you have for wanting me in the world?"

Alaji smiled. "That is the story I've been trying to tell since I woke you…"

41: A CIRCLE

"And next came the mysterious story you won't share with us?" Yemerik asked sarcastically, tilting his head to one side.

"I've been telling you the story this whole time," the old crone replied.

"Of course," Yemerik muttered. "I keep forgetting."

"What happened next?" Reilla asked, clearing her throat.

"Next?" Alaji asked.

"After your encounter with Graillinde. Did you just leave him there?"

"I had to," Alaji said. "I couldn't force him back into his prison. He was far too powerful. Besides, I knew some of the immortals would deal with him. Probably the Storm or the Collective, if none of the others reached him first."

"You knew, because you'd been to the future?" Yemerik asked. Without giving her a chance to answer, he added, "How did you know it was the same future?"

"I suppose I didn't," Alaji admitted. "But I hoped. And I trusted them to sort out matters well enough."

"The psychotic, self-obsessed immortal sorcerer kings?" Yemerik asked pointedly.

Alaji smiled. "It's as good a description as any. But yes, I trusted them."

Yemerik nodded. "And you made them? That's what you told Aengr—Graillinde, right?"

"They made themselves," Alaji said. "But I gave them the tools they would need."

"By sending Lundanta after you. It's… clever, I suppose," Yemerik said, ignoring several soft coughs from Reilla.

"Thank you," Alaji said in a tone Yemerik couldn't read. Then she added, "They looked after their world. They had to—it was all they had. To them, it was a small thing. I believe living that long changed their perspective."

"That's exactly why we don't extend our lives indefinitely," Yemerik said.

"But you still see the world as they do," Alaji said. "Something to adjust and control. It's small to you, beneath concern."

"Do you really believe that's how we view time?" Reilla asked in a tone implying she'd been hurt by the accusation. Yemerik knew it was an act, and he suspected Alaji did, too, but there was no doubting it sounded sincere.

"Of course," Alaji said.

"I'd like to think we work to nurture the world," Reilla said, "that our actions are fundamentally helpful."

"There's little difference," Alaji replied coolly. "If anything, you are worse. You would sweep entire timelines into oblivion the way Graillinde does cities. You do it for your measurements; he, for power."

"Our 'measurements' have a purpose," Yemerik interjected.

"I agree," Reilla said, though her tone was far more conversational than Yemerik could have managed. "We are working to minimize suffering. I'd like to think that's a worthwhile end."

"Oadeth once told me there were those among you who wanted to stop life itself from existing. That without life, there'd be no suffering."

Reilla took a deep breath and smiled. "I apologize. You are right, of course. Our mission is far more elaborate than a reduction in pain. We believe there is beauty in life itself, and in culture, music, and art. We measure more than just suffering, and we try to study the elements of existence that defy measurement." She leaned forward over the table and said, "That's what Thomyus and Fimelsa were doing. They were trying to understand the world they were in. They were trying to uncover just the sorts of things we miss here."

"I will tell you what I told Oadeth. I've done far worse than kill them," Alaji said. "And those words are far truer now than when I first spoke them."

"It's not a question of morality," Reilla said. "You did what you felt you had to, and neither of us can judge you for it." Yemerik managed to keep his face completely still when Alaji glanced at him. Reilla continued, "This is not a test or challenge. We are simply asking for your help and understanding."

"I understand fine," Alaji said. "But you continue to miss the point. I am defending that aspect of your philosophy. I share it. There is enough beauty in the world to outweigh the pain. I can say that after the giants, after the hound, after Theojin... I can say it after Hilleleah. The world is pain and suffering. But it's also song and drink and a lover beside a lake in the summer. I was taught that by the wisest people I met in my journey."

"Then you see why it's important we try and retrieve our people," Reilla said.

But Alaji shook her head. "I'm sorry. I'm not explaining this right. It's still tangled. Perhaps it would be better if I told you about the caverns. After I'd finished speaking with Graillinde, I fought my way past the Heart again." She shook her head. "It is still hard for me to remember. It crawls into your head. Touches your mind and shifts events. I don't think it was as bad going back through. It was already wounded, after all, but it was still horrible. It was no better the other times, either, when I went back with Helgwin, or when I had Eroza and Rit'ka. Their silence tormented me. When I reached the boundary that had been protected by the knight, I just used the talisman. But until then, there was nothing I could do."

"The complex was protected against temporal invasion?" Yemerik asked.

"Just like the first time I met Red Arm, before he became obsessed with ruling kingdoms and terrorizing his enemies," Alaji said. "In the cathedral during one of Graillinde's earlier reigns, just outside his lands. Not even the talisman worked. Even my count... I could barely hear it, and I couldn't move to it at all."

"Temporal control," Reilla said softly.

"It's similar here," Alaji said.

"It's necessary to maintain some control over where and how people come or go," Reilla said. "I apologize if it bothers you."

Alaji shook her head. "I expected as much when I came here."

"How?" Yemerik asked, before immediately answering his own question. "Oadeth, again. Of course."

Alaji ignored him. "Eroza kept glaring at me, and I wasn't sure if she was going to put an arrow in my back. But Rit'ka was scared, confused. And Helgwin, he was in a daze. Each time, I despised that place by the end. Even now, I feel ill talking about it."

"But you had to go back," Yemerik said. "You had to recover the amulets."

Alaji smiled. "That part was not so bad, really. I waited until after it was over. Once Graillinde had broken free, the dungeon was in ruin, and the dark magic had run its course, I returned. I walked through partially collapsed tunnels, through the room that had once held the Heart but was now only stone and rubble. I walked back through the halls of spirits, now emptied, and by the Limper's post after his carvings were dust."

"The amulets were still there?" Yemerik asked.

"Of course," Alaji said. "There was nothing left to disturb them. The immortals left them as added protection. As for Graillinde, when he finally gained his freedom and lived again, he understood that he had to leave them. Otherwise, it would all come apart. It is as I said—he understood the importance of it all. If he'd removed them, I couldn't have arranged them to begin with."

Yemerik took a deep breath and pinched the bridge of his nose. "Because you only had the one amulet," he concluded.

"I had to recover it three times," Alaji said. "Twice between expeditions and once at the very end. Each time, I went through the caverns, left the amulet behind, collected it in the future, then traveled to a new age."

"And recruited new companions," Yemerik said. "Yes, I see it."

"It wouldn't have worked," Alaji said, "if it hadn't been for their defenses against time travel. The same magic blocking me from teleporting or distorting time to avoid the dangers kept the talisman from overwriting the amulet."

"So you were able to make one object work like three," Yemerik said.

Alaji smiled and nodded. "Once I had the amulet, I waited years each time before going back. I attended to other matters until I could stomach the thought of returning. It was then I met with the Anomaly in goblin form, started my work with the Bleak Queen, and met with the King with the Red Arm. And also managed that business with the disk."

"Disk?" Yemerik asked.

"Of course," Alaji replied. "The invitation to seek the Second Citadel you found in the lava tunnels. I made it and left it for you."

Yemerik bit his lip to suppress a grin, but he couldn't keep quiet. "No," he said, "you didn't."

"Yemerik," Reilla said in a vaguely threatening way. "Perhaps we should listen."

But Yemerik knew Alaji wouldn't let him be thrown out, and he finally had her. "There is literally no way you could have done that."

"I crafted it from metal smelted by the Collective in their prime," Alaji said. "They created something that could withstand the heat of a volcano. I wrote it in Sansirian."

"You crafted a disk," Yemerik said. "And you probably managed a fair recreation. And maybe you found a similar tunnel to leave it in. But that's all."

"You're so sure?" Alaji asked.

"I'm positive," Yemerik said. "Because the Citadel moves one way relative to meta-time. There's a law of causality here preventing what you're describing. I returned here after I found the disk. Nothing I did after that could have altered anything before. Do you understand?"

"I fought my way through demons," Alaji said.

"You're not listening," Yemerik said, intentionally ignoring the looks he was getting from Reilla. "I understand what you thought you were doing. You were trying to connect everything back to you. A single, simple cause for it all. A circle in time, like I used to tell you about. But you forgot how the Citadel fits into it. We're not part of that here. For all intents and purposes, we're outside of it. So everything you went through to make a disk and find a demon-infested tunnel like the kind Oadeth told you about… I'm sorry, but it wasn't necessary. However the disk got there, it had nothing to do with you."

Alaji grinned. "I haven't forgotten," she said.

"Yemerik," Reilla said, looking over at him. "If you're not interested in hearing the rest, I'd be happy to listen alone."

"No," he said quickly. "That's okay. I just wanted to make sure we understood each other."

"I'd be happy to explain," Alaji said.

42: THE DEMON KING

Xazuel, the demon king, hovered over the river of fire, and his subjects, perched upon stone pillars, gazed at him with wonder. The hot air rising off the magma offered lift. All he had to do was hold his wings open and float there. On either side of him, the towering cliffs of his domain rose up towards the world above, where plentiful food and entertainment were free for the taking.

He looked across the faces and wondered what treachery lurked behind their eyes, what envy. He took pleasure in the thought, that each of them desired what was his, yet none were strong enough to take it. No greater honor existed in all the world, save the last, should he prove strong enough to claim it.

"Thulique," he called out. "Where is my most honored servant?" A rumble of laughter echoed through the ravine, but Xazuel silenced it with a glare. His eyes scanned the cliffside until he spotted the malformed fiend, hunched in a shallow cave near the surface of the burning river. Xazuel stared at him until Thulique stood on shaking legs, leapt up, and opened his two working wings. The demon struggled to gain elevation and move towards the impatient king.

"It is unwise to keep me waiting," Xazuel howled, taking joy in the way the fat demon quivered at the sound of his voice. Thulique had hatched wrong. He was fatter and slower than his kin, with a face closer to that of a pig than a true demon.

"Forgive me," Thulique begged.

Xazuel grinned. "I will do more than pardon you," he said, pausing to enjoy the look of fear on the lesser demon's face. "I have chosen for you a high honor. I hunger and desire food. Go find me a human, then roast it over the slow stone. Do this, and you may stay in your nest another day."

"Yes, Lord Xazuel," Thulique said, bowing his head. Then, cringing, he added, "I thank you for this honor."

"I am glad to grant it," Xazuel said, smiling cruelly. "You have always been a favorite of mine." More laughter came from the other demons, who were all too happy to celebrate the humiliation of their most maligned member. This time, Xazuel let them enjoy his cruelty. Balancing his subjects' need for sadism with discipline was the most important part of ruling. If he was too strict, he would force more challenges than he wanted. If he gave them too much leeway, there might come a day when they frenzied and attacked in mass. Either would end in his body being broken, his wings being torn off, and him being thrown into the river below.

He eyed the boiling magma and breathed in the rich aroma. Someday, if he lived so long, he would be ready for the last swim. His ancestors were born in hell, and like all of his kind, he longed to return. But it was said only the strongest could hope to survive to reach it. If there was any weakness, he'd burn up and be swallowed by the molten stone.

"Lord Xazuel!" he heard Thulique call from above.

"If you've returned without meat, I shall need to claim your nest," Xazuel said. "I wonder if you can survive closer to the fire." It actually might be an intriguing proposition to test, he thought.

"But Lord, there is a human here!" He pointed overhead at a woman floating in midair.

Xazuel beat his wings twice and overtook the lesser demon. He struck Thulique with the back of his claw, sending the fiend spiraling towards the rock wall. The fat demon's lame third wing struck frantically at the air. "You would have me fetch my own meal and cook it like a hatchling?" he shouted. "You are banished from my kingdom! May the wild gryphons pick you apart slowly!" A chorus of cheers erupted around them, and he called out, "Will any among you capture a meal for your king?"

Several demons took off at once and headed for the flying woman. Part of Xazuel was curious to know more about her, but he knew better than to risk keeping humans alive when they knew magic. Before Xazuel killed him, his brother used to say there was nothing more dangerous than a witch or wizard, and there was certainly truth to that. They'd encountered survivors who'd escaped human masters. Demons were highly prized by humans capable of controlling them.

As the three demons nearest to the human converged on her, she vanished, like an illusion. The demons paused, holding steady in the air in case she reappeared, while Xazuel squinted. Something small fell between the three of them. One reached out to try and take it, but before his hand closed around the object, it exploded in a shower of mist, coating all three.

For a moment, the fiends just seemed irritated. They swooped away, screeching and yelling. But their shouts turned to painful cries as frost engulfed them. Their joints locked, and they began falling towards the fiery ravine below. None of the others moved to catch them, of course—who would risk being contaminated? One by one, they plunged into the magma. They screeched as they tried to fight their way out. The strongest of them managed to swim to the edge and begin clawing his way up the wall, but it was a futile act. His wings had burned off, and most of his body was burned beyond use. He made it a few dozen feet before the soft stone he was clutching melted and he fell backwards into the molten rock.

Xazuel looked up and saw the woman once more, floating above them silently and peering down. "Kill her!" Xazuel commanded, and the air was thick with his subjects. As for the king himself, he flew towards his own home: a deep, winding tunnel cut in the rock. He dove in, landed in a dash, and hurried on until he reached his private arsenal. He grabbed the hilt of a sword embedded in the stone floor and pulled it free. It was eight feet long and made of iron. Even he required two hands to wield it. He turned back, preparing to return to the ravine and kill the woman himself if his subjects hadn't already done so.

But he didn't need to go far. She was there, standing in the tunnel, watching him. "Sorceress," he hissed. "I'll roast you until your skin peels! I'll devour your bones and send your soul to hell to warn our enemies we are coming!"

She began to chant, so he charged. But he'd barely taken a step before she vanished again. He began stumbling to a stop when he felt a gust of air nudge him from behind. It was a pitiful spell, too weak to trouble even a hatchling. He began to turn, but as he did so, he felt the wind increasing in ferocity. By the time he was facing her, it was deafening. He grabbed hold of the wall with one hand, and his claws bit into the rock. The woman was flickering, vanishing and reappearing faster than his eyes could trail her. She was a blur he couldn't follow.

He felt his wings caught by the wind, until one was forced open. His hands were ripped away from the rock wall, and he was hurled back. His sword bounced against the floor as he slammed into a bend in the corridor. He heard a snap and cried out as his wing was twisted and wrenched from its socket. The force of the witch's spell carried him further, scraping him against ridges in the passageway.

It took all his strength to stand. One of his wings was broken, and he suspected his right leg was no better. He began limping away in an attempt to reach the ravine and call on his subjects for aid. As he approached, he saw a figure before him. "She is behind me!" he shouted. "Kill her quickly!"

As the figure lumbered towards him, he recognized it. Thulique had followed him in. "This is your chance," he told the fat demon. "Tear her head from her body and redeem yourself!"

Only when Thulique grabbed him by his horns and threw him to the ground did Xazuel realize it wasn't the witch the pig-demon was after. Xazuel cried out as his broken leg collapsed under him. Still, he had some fight in him. When Thulique charged, Xazuel raked his claws across his enemy's face, drawing red-hot blood. Thulique bellowed in rage and pain and slammed into the king, pushing him against the wall and crushing his broken wing. Xazuel cried out again, and Thulique hurled him to the ground. The pig-demon began kicking him repeatedly, concentrating his blows where the king was already wounded. After a minute, Xazuel blacked out.

When he came to, he was being dragged over stone. He looked up and saw fiends he knew staring down at him with a look of awe and reverence. "Kill the traitor," he said, but they didn't move. He strained to turn his head and saw Thulique pulling him towards the opening. "Wait," he said, but his pleas were wasted.

He felt a sudden sense of weightlessness and tried to open his wings, but only one moved at all and even that just slowed his descent. He saw the light of the magma approaching and tried to find his strength. There was a life beyond this for those strong enough to swim to it. A life in a world of fire that burned those given to the fiends and never the fiends themselves.

He plunged into the scorching magma and sunk deep. He tried to swim down, but he found he'd no strength with which to do it. He felt the fires dissolving him, bit by bit, melting his eyes and seeping into his ears, mouth, and nostrils.

And, in those last moments, he felt himself doubting. How could any demon be strong enough to go on? Just before the end, his faith returned to mock him. It was his doubt that made him weak, he realized. That alone would keep him from ever reaching the promised world.

43: THE COURT OF DOLLS

"I used a potion housing the essence of fire to melt the rock around the disk. Oadeth told me that was how they'd found it, that they'd had to cut it free with magic." The crone kept glancing at Yemerik, who was doing his best to hide his irritation.

"We have a tool that creates an intense ray of heat," Reilla said. "Most of our magic is contained in such devices. It lets us store magical energy and instantly channel it in ways that would otherwise require elaborate rituals."

"I will confess, I never fully understood your magic. Oadeth tried teaching me the different kinds once, but there were so many. To be fair, I wasn't able to teach him how to work magic the old way, either."

"I'd be happy to go through them with you," Reilla said. "Once we're finished collecting your story."

Alaji looked at her with what almost seemed like pity and said, "I do not think that's possible, nor would it matter. I do not need to understand the intricacies of your magic to use my own."

"But you can't use your magic here," Yemerik reminded her. He said it in a passive, academic voice, but he still said it. "Perhaps you'd find some of our tools helpful," he added quickly, before Reilla could respond. "I'm sure there'd be limitations to what we'd be able to share, but we have devices that can conjure food and drink." He glanced at Reilla, who was eyeing him skeptically. "Once you've finished your story, of course." He concluded with a smile, as if nothing he'd said had been condescending.

Alaji shook her head. "Finished," she said quietly, as if there was something humorous about the word. "I have only a bit left to tell," she said, pausing when the light overhead shifted to a shade of orange.

"Don't mind that," Reilla said quickly. "It's just something that happens from time to time."

"I remember," Alaji said. Then she cleared her throat and said, "I will tell you of the Court of Dolls and the reign of the King with the Red Arm. It is not a pleasant piece of the tale, but it is necessary, I think. He is a part of all this."

—

There was no ceiling in the King's court, at least none that could be seen. A wall of stone twenty meters tall formed the footprint of a castle, while towers rose from each corner. The parapets were lined with men standing perfectly still. They held weapons but made no move to act or even blink.

Alaji moved cautiously, not daring to risk using her count or talisman to cover the distance. She'd heard stories of this place and time, and she knew better than to risk startling the King or his servants. She could feel herself being watched, and she clutched her amulet, still dusty from eons beneath the earth.

There was music around her. Beautiful music that filled the court. An orchestra stood atop a stage holding instruments, but they were as still as the guards. The music came from elsewhere.

Not all was still. Hundreds of men and women dressed in fine fabrics danced in perfect harmony with each other and the music. Every step was precise, every bow in tandem. But unlike the music, there was little beauty here. It was too perfect, too wooden. They were like moving statues.

In fact, that was just what they were. Hollow, soulless statues controlled by a single being, driven by a single will. Only they were statues of flesh and blood. They were living people, deprived of spirits.

"Greetings, King," Alaji proclaimed. As she spoke, the music dipped the slightest bit, and the King cringed. The crowd of dancing figures ceased and froze in place. Then, with a slight wave of the King's hand, the dancers shifted to either side, clearing a path towards his throne. He gazed down the empty corridor and looked directly at Alaji.

"A moment, if you please," he said to her. "There was a viola out of time. He clapped his hands together twice, and a shimmering mist swept over the court. A raised alcove made of pale energy appeared surrounding them. It was filled with the forms of frightened spirits: spectral servants with human forms. Some held instruments, and these looked uneasily towards a solitary figure gripping a curved object in one hand and a bow in the other. The King motioned for him to approach. The figure floated slowly down to the King on the lower level. The other spirits turned away as he passed.

"I'm sorry, my King. I was distracted by your guest's outburst."

"I know," the King said, still seated on his throne. "And I have sympathy. I take pain in the position I am placed in. Know I find no joy in punishing those who serve me faithfully. You understand this, I hope."

"I do, my Lord," the musician's spirit said.

The King nodded. "And yet, there can be no improvement without correction. Do you not agree?"

"I… I agree," the spirit said, shaking.

"Good. I hope you may reflect on this as your punishment is carried out." He raised his voice and added, "I hope you all reflect on it." Then he held his palms open and whispered a word. The spirit was flung backwards towards the stage; not the spectral one overhead but the real one, where he snapped into a real body sharing his features and form.

The musician collapsed to his knees and dropped his instrument. He ran his fingers over his arms, feeling them, and he began sweating. He looked up with an expression of horror.

Then the King clapped his hands again. A quarter of the assembled bodies turned simultaneously towards the musician, who began shaking and scrambling backwards on the stage, only to be caught by several other musicians, who pushed him forward to the edge. Other than him, Alaji, and the King, the eyes of the living were empty. They weren't even looking at him, only facing him. Waiting for him to topple over.

Then they fell on him. They made no sound as they grabbed at him, leaned down, and bit into him. None of them feasted—they each took a single bite: a finger, an ear, or a chunk of flesh. His body screamed until he was dead, then he kept screaming as a spirit again. Eventually, he grew silent, though he remained there, visible, watching as his body was devoured, one bite at a time. They ate everything—clothes, hair, and nails. Alaji turned away from the gruesome execution. When she finally looked back, there was nothing left. Whether they'd removed the bones or somehow ate those as well, she didn't know, but all that remained was the spirit.

Then, with a nod from the King, the pale spirit returned to the alcove and took his place beside the other musicians. Again, the King moved his hands, and the shimmering servants faded from view along with their platform. The King lifted his hand beside his head, raised a single finger, and the music started again, softer than before. He raised both palms and swayed them to the music. The men and women of his court, mouths still red with blood, began dancing in rhythm, all while leaving a passageway for Alaji.

"You are here before me," the King said solemnly, as though the execution had never taken place. "That demonstrates strength of character. Or perhaps you are merely mad. I have yet to decide."

"I'm here, because I need your help," Alaji said.

The King snickered. "It's madness then. You sided with my enemy against me. I should kill you for that alone."

"I gave the Bleak Queen strength, and you became stronger in turn. Do you really think you could have stood against Graillinde if your magic hadn't been tempered by war?"

"You expect me to believe you gave the Queen visions of the future just so I'd one day be able to rival Graillinde's power?"

"Of course not," Alaji said. "I don't care much about any of you. I am looking at a larger picture. A war against our common enemy."

The King with the Red Arm squinted. "You are speaking of the Citadel. I am growing skeptical this 'enemy' even exists."

"Without me, it will be only thing that exists. Everything else is a figment, an idea without structure, to be forgotten and lost. None of us are enemies in the scheme of things. Not you or the Queen or even Graillinde."

"And I've your word on this," he said dismissively. "That in the scheme of history we will all become allies?"

"I'm not looking for allies," Alaji said. "I am weaving a weapon."

"What are your weapons to me?" the King asked.

"You misunderstand. You are part of that weapon. All of you are. The Bleak Queen, the Collective she'll become, the Storm, Graillinde, the Acolyte, and all the others. Even the Anomaly."

"She will kill you in the past and rid us all of your meddling," the King said. "That is the only reason I haven't killed you already."

"She already killed me," Alaji said. "I am still here. But that's part of why I've come. I have reconciled with her."

"You have aligned with the Anomaly?" the King asked. His voice boomed, but he sat back in his throne as he spoke.

"She should be there at the end. She deserves to be. But I need your help to make that possible. You alone know how to reverse her condition."

"This is a trick, a gambit to get me to remove the threat she poses."

"I want to take you to a time before I existed," Alaji said. "Her opportunity to find me will have elapsed anyway."

"Why should I trust you?" the King asked.

"The same reason she came to trust me," Alaji said. "I told her the truth. I told her my story…"

44: THE CITADEL'S DEFENSES

"A weapon," Yemerik said, as soon as Alaji stopped speaking.

"Are you angry?" the crone asked.

"Angry?" Yemerik shook his head. "No. I'm only… I'm disappointed. That you'd think of something like that, let alone believe it could work. You realize others have attempted things like this, right? You're not the first to weaponize time travel and spectromancy against the Citadel. Others have attempted to build magical constructs to attack us before."

"That really isn't important," Reilla said.

"No," Yemerik muttered, "I suppose it isn't."

"Oadeth told me," Alaji said. "He told me stories of attacks and enemies from your past."

"Past isn't the right word," Yemerik said. "Nor is 'enemies.' They were confused, and—"

"Yemerik," Reilla interrupted.

"—and they were delusional," he added defiantly. "They learned enough about time travel to become terrified by the implications but not to grasp the correct philosophical conclusions. They decided they needed to destroy us to protect themselves or at least avenge their timelines."

"Yemerik!" Reilla said louder than before. She was no longer even concealing the fact he was out of line.

"But they couldn't!" Yemerik added, practically yelling. "Because, no matter how advanced, no matter how much they were willing to rely on the same tools or time travel they despised, their magic was rudimentary compared to our defenses. The Citadel is protected from everything. We have existed outside time for a relative duration that's unfathomable to them or to you. So whatever weapon you've made we've dealt with. Spectromancy is a blight upon time. It is a horror to its victims and practitioners both. But it is no threat to the Citadel or our work."

He took a deep breath as he finished and felt a wave of relief sweep over him. Then he waited for Reilla's obvious response.

"Yemerik," she said calmly. "Leave this room immediately."

Yemerik, however, stayed seated. He turned to Alaji and asked simply, "Is that what you'd like?" Then he turned to face Reilla, so he could watch the expression on her face when Alaji responded.

"Yes."

He turned back to Alaji in shock. "What?"

"I want you to leave now, as Reilla asked. Everything else I have to say is for her alone."

"Fine," Yemerik said, standing. "I'll go." He paused to give her one last chance to stop him, but she simply continued staring at him. So, feeling a mix of emotions, Yemerik stepped to the wall, which opened for him to pass, and walked away.

45: THE LIGHTS OVERHEAD

"I'd like to apologize for that," Reilla said, as soon as they were alone. "Yemerik has been having a difficult time with this, and I'm afraid he let his emotions get the better of him." The old crone simply listened and watched quietly. Reilla nodded, adding, "I would certainly understand if you need some time to rest. I just want you to know I'm happy to listen whenever you're ready."

Alaji smiled. "I'm not upset. Not at all."

"I'm glad," Reilla said, returning the smile and concealing her puzzlement. "If you'd like to continue—"

"Of course," Alaji said. "I'd like to finish my story." She cleared her throat and added, "I didn't ask him to go because I was upset with him."

"I understand," Reilla replied. "I'm sorry I implied otherwise."

Alaji laughed and shook her head. "No, no. I'm not chastising you. I'm telling you, so you'll understand. This is part of it. Part of my story."

Reilla nodded politely, as though Alaji was making sense. There was no point in pushing her further, after all.

"I wonder about him in this moment. What's going through his head. What he's thinking. What he's piecing together and what he simply can't. I've thought about you—all of you—for a great deal of my life, you know. I didn't know your names or faces, aside from the handful of you I've met, but I've pondered you ever since… I'm sorry. I'm getting ahead of myself."

"Not at all," Reilla said. "Please, take your time."

"Time," Alaji repeated the word with a sigh. "That's just it. You must think about the people outside of your Citadel; you must consider them children. They don't understand the world as you do. They simply can't."

"I wouldn't use those terms," Reilla said, "but I understand your point."

"Of course you do," Alaji said. "People who are born in time, who never experience it from another perspective, most of them never dream of things like this. Even the ones who do, like Xayra—she was a historian who traveled with me for a while—it's only a simple, vague idea. Xayra saw time as events and possibilities. She'd dreamed of the sort of power you have here, but the reality of it was too much for her. Because everyone, including me, has concepts and notions they can't escape."

"You're describing paradigms," Reilla said. "It's a rather advanced philosophical concept in itself."

Alaji shrugged. "Call it what you like. What's important is that it's insufficient. It's enough for people in history to live their lives by, but there comes a limit. It's not just time, but magic, too. I've been to era after era where people believed there were laws of nature that magic couldn't overcome."

"There actually are limits to magic, but they're far beyond what most civilizations imagine. It's a common misconception," Reilla agreed.

"Even when confronted with evidence to the contrary, they can't see it," Alaji said. "When Phaesha and I went to Iasyia, people couldn't believe what we could do. Even when they saw it, they doubted it. Or they tried to explain it in their own terms. Helgwin, even—he took me for a god! And all because I produced a man he thought was dead. There's no mystery to it when you understand, but for him it was… impossible." She said the word slowly.

"I wonder if you're not implying that we're no better," Reilla said with a wry smile. "We can't understand how you altered and broke the talisman, for example."

Alaji shifted her staff in her hand so she was holding the broken shard embedded in the top. "You want to know how I altered it," she said. "How I transmuted an object made to reject all alteration." Then she leaned a little closer. "I will tell you. I didn't."

Reilla tilted her head to one side. "You're saying it's some sort of forgery?"

Alaji laughed. "No, you already know better than that. But that only proves my point. You're as limited as everyone else."

"I'm willing to admit as much," Reilla said.

"I think you would admit a great number of things, if it meant getting the answers you want," Alaji said. "It's not about admitting them. It's about accepting them. Realizing them. It wasn't all that hard for me, because I came from a simple time. The more complex the civilization, the harder it is to see. That's been my experience, anyway."

"Then help me understand," Reilla said, using her tone to convey a hint of a challenge.

Alaji nodded. "Yemerik," she said calmly.

"You want me to go get him? To bring him back?" Reilla asked.

Alaji laughed. "There's no need. This next part is about him, in the hallway, as I said before. He'll mostly likely have wandered off by now. I imagine he's thinking about what happened here, trying to understand where he went wrong. I'm not sure how he'll feel, whether he'll be scared or excited, when it happens."

"When what happens?" Reilla asked.

"When the lights change," Alaji said.

"Lights," Reilla said, repeating the word. "What lights?"

"The lights," Alaji said, pointing up at the glowing energy overhead. "When they shift from orange to red."

"I don't think that's likely," Reilla replied. "Even under normal conditions, the Gathering's security manages to prevent breaches or accidents that would necessitate a Citadel-wide alarm. It hasn't happened in my lifetime."

"I remember," Alaji said.

"And these conditions aren't normal. There's a great deal of uncertainty around the state of the—" She cut off abruptly as the lights overhead turned red, giving the entire room an eerie glow. Reilla could feel herself growing tense, and she knew she wasn't managing to hide it, at least not completely. She drew in a long breath through her nose, forced a smile, and began to rise from her seat. "I'm sorry, but I should really check on what—"

"If you leave, you'll never know the truth about the talisman," Alaji said.

Reilla froze and settled back into her seat. She swallowed and said, "Please. Go on."

"I don't know for certain how much he figured out on his own," Alaji said quietly. "I like to think, deep down, it was enough. I referred to this timeline as a weapon, after all, and I all but laughed when you two boasted about your defenses."

It was absurd, but Reilla felt a surge of fear through her body. The Citadel's protections were perfect. She knew this to be true, just as she knew Alaji's allusion to the alert had to be coincidental. But sitting there, in the red glow of an alarm whose cause she couldn't imagine, Reilla couldn't help but be afraid.

"The Jar," Alaji said after a brief pause. "Whatever the reason, that's where he runs. To the Jar."

46: THE JAR

Yemerik ran past countless panicking archivists arguing about readings and artifacts. A team of thaumaturgical operation specialists were standing on floating disks to examine the magical ray. "Calm down!" one of them shouted as he hurried past them. "It's almost certainly a malfunction."

"Or a drill!" another added.

But Yemerik didn't stop. He felt nauseous in the pit of his stomach, and he was sweating heavily. He didn't care that he wasn't supposed to be anywhere near the central core, nor did anyone move to stop him. Even as he ran into the depths of the Citadel where only a handful of experts were cleared to work without an escort, no one prevented him from continuing.

Normally, there'd have been someone stationed here. But then, with everything going on, the guards were stretched thin. Most of them would have been reassigned to other work as the Gathering's resources were focused on recovering their lost agents.

He was nearly there before he saw the first body. A young archivist lay bleeding on one side of the hall. Yemerik ran to him, checking for a pulse. "Help!" he shouted as loud as he could manage. But no one was in sight, and he didn't hear an answer. Besides, this man was already dead.

Yemerik climbed back to his feet, cringing as he felt his joints strain. Then he ran on, passing two more bodies, both stabbed and left in the hallway. He darted into the final room. The large domed enclosure where the Jar was kept. And he paused, momentarily speechless.

"Hello, Yemerik," the young woman said, as she turned to face him.

"This is impossible," Yemerik gasped.

Alaji shook her head in disapproval. Then she looked behind her at the round, glass structure. "This is it. The Jar you kept referring to. Where every soul is collected, so you can measure the effect you're having on the timeline. The one place in the Citadel that's not safeguarded from what you do." She was holding something small in one hand. The other was empty, and she reached out to touch the clear surface. "It's beautiful," she said.

On the other side of the glass, millions of miniature swirling lights with blue and purple hues danced and wove together. When she drew her hand away, she'd left a smear of blood behind.

"It's one of the great ironies," Yemerik said, still dazed. "That the worse the world gets, the better the lights look. It's one of the ways we measure them. The glass alters the light to make it visible and colors it."

Alaji nodded. "Spirit. You bring it in and trap it here."

"So, if someone wanted to construct a weapon against us, what could be better?" Yemerik asked. "There's just one problem. We're not stupid." Alaji turned back and looked at him. He cleared his throat and said, "We filter for the spirits we allow to be reborn. And we've ensured there's no way others are released. I've told you—or at least I told some version of you—we've dealt with spectromancy." He paused and asked, "How are you here?"

"It's impossible," Alaji said.

"It should be," Yemerik agreed. "There's an older version of you. The Citadel… it functions just like the talismans. It overwrites duplicate individuals."

Alaji shifted to reveal a bag at her side. The egg-shape of one of their talismans was visible through the fabric. "Breaking the talisman was also impossible, remember?"

"How did you do it?" he asked in a frustrated tone. "And why?" He gestured to another body, this one slumped over a desk. "Those people… they did nothing to deserve this. I don't know what you hope to accomplish here. All this nonsense about the Jar and

Graillinde… it won't work. If you just want to hurt me, go ahead. I'm unarmed, like they were. Kill me, if that's what you want."

"This isn't about you," Alaji said quietly. "I'm sorry for your friends, and I'm sorry for what comes next. But it's necessary."

Yemerik laughed. "I don't understand much of what's happening here, but the one thing I know is that none of this is necessary."

"Maybe not. But if it's a choice, it's the right one."

"She told you that, I'm assuming," Yemerik said. "Your older self."

Alaji shook her head. "I figured it out on my own. I realized I could change everything. And then I realized I already had. I always had."

Yemerik shook his head. "None of what you're saying makes sense. I'm sorry. I'm sorry, because I know this was all my fault. I turned you into this."

"No—I created myself. You didn't bring me into this quest. I'm going to summon you."

"So your older self said," Yemerik replied sarcastically.

Alaji nodded. "But you didn't believe her?"

"No. Time travel doesn't work that way. Not here, anyway."

Alaji grinned. "And your talismans can't be broken. And the same person can't be in two places in the Citadel at the same time." She rapped against the glass behind her and added, "And this can't be broken."

"It can't," Yemerik said, but his voice wavered.

"I'm not going to lie," Alaji said. "On the disk. I won't need to. I'll trick you, but I won't lie."

"Just tell me!" Yemerik said, raising his voice. "Or don't. I'm sick of these games. What are you talking about?"

"I broke your talisman by striking it against a piece of itself. That's all it took. The energy patterns matched and conflicted at once, and whatever magic protected it faltered."

"It's impossible," he said, before realizing how absurd he sounded. "You can't… the same talisman can't occupy the same time, let alone the same space. The older will overwrite itself."

"The Citadel overwrites it," Alaji corrected him.

"Yes, fine," Yemerik said, irritated. "The Citadel uses the talismans as anchor points and overwrites duplicates. How could you disable that?"

"You were looking for the answer the whole time," Alaji said. "Another Citadel. Another Gathering. You believed that was what the disk meant, and you were right. But you couldn't see it. None of you could, in all the time you've existed. With everything you've done. It's so obvious. This is it. This is the other Citadel you were looking for."

Yemerik shook his head, unsure if she was trying to confuse him or if she was mad. "What is that supposed to mean?" Behind him, echoing down the halls, someone screamed, and footsteps began striking stone. If Alaji heard, she didn't seem concerned.

"It took countless iterations to create this place," she said. "Entire timelines developing magic, time travel, and spending their last days attempting to make the Citadel."

"What of it?"

"What happened before that?"

Yemerik shook his head. "The concept of before is meaningless in this context. The Citadel and Gathering are the final evolutionary step in meta-time."

"No," Alaji said. "There was a Citadel before this one. And another before that. They created talismans, they sent agents back to fragment the timeline."

"Even if that were true, the temporal scale would be immeasurable. All trace of that would be lost. It wouldn't matter."

"The shard of talisman used by my older self," Alaji said. "It's the same but different. It's still connected to the last Citadel, the last iteration of the entire Citadel. It could occupy the same space and time as the talisman connected to this place. The older me wouldn't part with her staff, right? And I won't part with these." She patted her pack again. "The stolen talismans. Not the ones I took—the ones she took. We traded, so we'd each have different talismans connected to the Citadel before this one. That's how two of me can be here— it's maintaining us by keeping this Citadel's functions from overwriting me, and this Citadel's presence is keeping the last one's from doing the same. They're functioning and canceling each other simultaneously. That's how I'm going to break your talisman when my time comes."

Yemerik's mouth hung open. He took a deep breath and managed a single word. "Why?"

"Which part? I'm going to break the talisman for the same reason I'm going to leave the skin of Verow's Brew and whisper about places I've seen. I'm planning all this out. Even now, I have so much more to piece together. Especially about them," she added, glancing quickly towards the Jar. "It was mostly war and madness. I need them together. I need them to understand. Do you see? I need to work on this for decades to ensure it keeps working. There's too many pieces, stretched over different timelines."

"I still don't understand," Yemerik said. In response, Alaji held up the object in her left hand. "What is that? It looks like a stick." Something caught the light at the tip, but he couldn't make it out.

"It is a stick," Alaji said. "With a piece of glass stuck on the end." The voices and footsteps were coming closer now. In a moment, they would burst through into the room. Alaji turned and paused, as if reconsidering. Then, with a single deep breath, she thrust the stick down against the glass dome and fell back as a loud noise echoed through the chamber.

For a moment, everything was still. Then, a crack appeared.

47: THE MIDDLE OF HER STORY

As soon as she regained her footing, Alaji hurried towards Yemerik. His arms dropped to his side, and he held his head up in case she wanted easy access to his neck. He watched her reach into her coat and took a deep breath.

"Stay behind me," she said, pulling out her amulet. "This won't stop them, but they'll be able to recognize me."

"You're not going to kill me?" he asked, confused.

"Of course not," Alaji said. "I have more to say."

"Stop!" someone shouted, running into the room. It was a guard of some sort, and he was holding his hand up. A metallic orb floated in front of his palm, moving with him. "Lay down all magical devices you're holding and surrender!"

Alaji looked at him sadly. Then she glanced back at the cracked glass. The guard followed her gaze, and he froze when he saw the fracture in the dome. Glowing wisps of light congregated behind the crack, which was growing, forking in different directions, and spreading quickly.

The crack itself seemed to glow as radiant spirits pressed against it. "Run!" Yemerik cried out to the guard. "Get help! Get everyone!"

But of course there wasn't time. The first spirit seeped through within seconds. Instantly, it transformed into a trail of light leading to the petrified guard. The metallic orb dropped uselessly to the ground, hitting with a loud thud. The guard shook once, and his eyes rolled back.

"You don't want to see this," Alaji whispered to Yemerik.

But Yemerik watched as the guard rose into the air and began convulsing. Dark veins appeared in his arm, and he screamed in pain and terror. A spectral form sharing his appearance began emerging from his body, which reached out to grab the spirit and hold onto it. The guard's former body stared into his spirit's eyes for several long seconds before releasing its hold.

The body descended to the floor, touching lightly and looking around. Its eyes glowed purple, and its breathing sounded laborious. "You are Alaji?" it asked, setting its eyes on her and Yemerik.

"There are more guards coming," Alaji said to the figure. She gestured down the hallway behind him. Dozens of voices were shouting.

"Will they know more than this form?" he asked.

"I don't know," Alaji said. "Someone here will."

"Know what?" Yemerik asked.

"How to destroy the Citadel," Alaji answered.

"I don't know if the Citadel can be destroyed," Yemerik replied.

"It can, and it will," Alaji replied. "No one of you knows how, but there are tens of thousands here. Your knowledge together will be enough, and they have the power to gather it."

"From our souls, you mean," Yemerik said sadly. "As they rip us apart and steal our bodies and memories."

"It was the only way," Alaji said.

"The only way to damn history to anarchy," Yemerik said.

Alaji laughed and shook her head. "I thought you'd understand by now. You still think I'm doing this to destroy the Citadel?"

"You just boasted about destroying it!" Yemerik said angrily.

"I'm also creating it. You once told me there was a limit to how many versions of history the Citadel could maintain, that creating new ones was selfish. Do you remember?"

"No," Yemerik said, "But it's true."

"Oadeth told me the same thing, more or less. You'd need an infinite number of Citadels to hold on to everything. I spent a lot of time thinking about that, and I realized something. I realized I was already working towards that. The other me—the one who'd destroyed the talisman—she wouldn't have done that without a reason."

"It's a recurrence," Yemerik said dizzily. "You're talking about a loop in… it's beyond time. Our time."

"Good," Alaji said. "You understand. An endless line of Citadels generating countless timelines. All of them woven together by these." Alaji patted her pack. "Talismans from one maintaining the stability of the next iteration. And the sheer force of repetition maintaining the worlds within. All the iterations, interwoven and maintained together."

Yemerik's lips quivered. He looked behind Alaji as several more guards charged in then froze as additional lights broke free and flew towards them. Their fates were no different than the one before. Then, with a deafening crash, the dome shattered. Thousands of lights sped away in every direction.

Spectral forms emerged, some taking human forms even without hosts. Alaji turned to watch one as it drifted towards a wall and placed a shimmering hand on the surface.

"Is that… is it him?" Yemerik whispered.

Cracks began appearing on the wall beneath the spectral figure's fingers, though these healed almost immediately. The figure's mouth opened, and a haunting voice filled the room. "It is I. Different than either of you remember me. Dead and reborn a million times, then reborn again when death overtook all. I still fought them for a time. When the world was nothing but spirits, I fought to be their emperor, but for all my power, I could not win."

"Of course not," Alaji said. "There were more of them."

"So I joined them, as you asked," Graillinde said. "And in time, they shared their minds with me and I with them. We are still connected, and we are learning quickly." He paused, tilted his head, and added, "You lied to us."

"I doubt it," Alaji said. "I expect I'll leave things out. And perhaps I'll trick you, but the core of what I'll tell you will be the truth."

"Perhaps," Graillinde admitted. "But it is still a betrayal. It is not our world alone we're fighting for. And what we do this day will be undone."

"Destroying the Citadel creates the Citadel," Yemerik whispered, looking to Alaji for validation. She responded with a simple nod.

"We could kill you," the spirit said. "We could take this place for our own."

"You won't," Alaji said, shrugging. "Even if you're tempted, the others will understand. If you tried, you'd only take up the quest of its last occupants. The timeline you want to save would be gone."

"You are right, of course. I will not be denied my fate. Even if it unfolded long ago, it will be mine."

"The Citadel will fall," Alaji said. "And all of this—all the time-lines that result, including the one you know, will come to pass again in turn."

"These walls will shatter," Graillinde replied. "But it will not be easy. We will need their knowledge. All of it." He glared at Yemerik as he said this.

"I'm sorry," Alaji said quietly to Yemerik.

"Wait," he said, glancing down at the floor. He bent over and lifted a small shard of glass that had landed near them when the Jar had broken. "For the next iteration," he said sadly.

Alaji accepted it and nodded her head. Then she opened her mouth to say something, but he shook his head. "You don't have to," he said.

She nodded and took a deep breath. "Goodbye," she said anyway.

"Until the next cycle," he replied as she vanished.

—

"You don't believe me?" the crone asked Reilla, who was sitting silently across from her. Every few seconds, the light above them flickered as the crackling red energy dissipated then reappeared.

"I'm not sure what to believe," Reilla replied. "What you're say-ing seems…" She paused, smiled uneasily, then said, "Impossible. But I have no better explanation." She tapped the magical device beside her for no obvious reason. It had ceased glowing a moment earlier and was no longer recording. "I have another question, if you'll answer it," Reilla said. "Why come at all? Your younger self, I understand, but why you? Why tell your story, if you knew we were going to die?"

"Distraction," Alaji said. "I'm sorry. I wish I had a better answer. Something profound or meaningful. But if my younger self came alone, the Citadel would have detected her. You'd have captured her."

"But if the two of you came together, she'd be hidden. The enchantments preventing an unauthorized individual from appearing outside of the entryway wouldn't activate if that person was already in the Citadel."

Alaji nodded. "You trusted too much in your rules. That one person couldn't exist here twice. I really am sorry for what this will mean for you."

"You mean my death?" Reilla asked as calmly and with as little emotion as she could manage.

"Please, don't mince words. I am killing you. No, that's not quite right—I killed you. Long ago, I sacrificed you and everyone in this place."

"But not you?" she asked.

"It would be right for me to stay, wouldn't it? There'd be some justice in dying here, at least. But I am not a just woman."

"If the Citadel is really broken, the talismans won't work," Reilla said. "I'm not sure how you'll be able to leave."

"My count," Alaji said simply. "It's an anchor set in time. I once leapt a thousand years by accident and almost froze to death in the ocean. Since then, I've learned to slow it to a crawl, to draw days into numbers. I began counting before I came here. While the Citadel's defenses were intact, it didn't matter—I was held here by your people's magic. But those defenses are falling now. In a moment, the flow of time will return, and I'll be able to step into it, as will my younger self. She's been counting, too."

"She's been hiding here all along. Since the moment you appeared."

"I do not have time to tell that tale in detail, and if I did, I do not think you would enjoy hearing it. I hid in the archives and explored the corridors as I searched for the Jar. I killed a dozen men and women, one at a time, without my magic, and kept my count through it all. It was one of the hardest things I ever did."

"You aren't from this place, and you weren't raised with our philosophies, so I can't challenge your ethics. But I question the wisdom of this. If this act has the effect you claim, it means there will be an immeasurable number of timelines. That every possibility the Citadel created exists."

"I am certain," Alaji said. "I've learned to move between them." She shrugged and added, "How else could I have found my way here? There was an eternity of eternities between the moment this place fell when I was young and now. Countless iterations before the Citadel was even remade, then countless more before it reached this point. But I had the shards and the talismans I'd given myself. Held together, the ripples intersected, and I found other ways to move. I found a way through the time beyond itself."

"Scotheck's readings," Reilla whispered. "We were looking at them, and we couldn't understand them."

"Of course not," Alaji said. "It is as I said, people in complex times find it hard to accept truths beyond their understanding."

"You were right," Reilla said.

"I wish I'd been able to visit more. I wish I'd had time to find versions of the people I loved living different lives," Alaji said, sighing. "Or explore more of those other eras. But so much of my life was spent on this. It was worth the cost, but still… I'd have liked to see more of it."

Reilla cleared her throat and said, "I still do not like your decision. The world, I think, would have been better with one Citadel and one timeline progressing towards perfection."

But Alaji shook her head. "No. I don't think that's right. You said yourself life and culture are worth pain, and I've found that to be true. If I can say that after the things I've seen..." Her expression was one of sorrow, nostalgia, and joy, all at once. "If I can still say that, I think it must be true. That life has value. And if it's true overall, it is true for each possible world, the greatest and least of them. It's true for you, as well. And, for what it's worth, I really am sorry."

With that, and with a step back to the start of a count she'd begun hundreds of millions of years before, the old crone vanished.

48: A FAREWELL

The crone appeared at her cabin beneath the towering oak. She was tired and cold, and she felt tears welling in her eyes. They were tears of sorrow and guilt, but also relief. Once again, she'd done something terrible, but it was something terrible that had to be done.

She'd saved everyone. Not their lives or even their souls, but something deeper.

"Witch!" she heard a familiar voice call out from the branch of a tree. "You are different now than a moment ago! And there is only one of you once more!"

"Thrush," Alaji said, brushing her eyes with the back of her wrist. "I'll bring you some seed." She shook her head and hurried into her cabin, grabbed a handful of seeds out of a porcelain pot, and tossed these out the door. The thrush, however, left them on the ground and flew in.

"Where is the other you? The younger?"

"She is gone," Alaji said. "She has no business here, not for a long time."

"You are sad of it," the bird said.

"Not about her, but I am sad. I am surprised you can tell."

"Your face is like Wolf's," the thrush replied, and Alaji laughed through her tears.

"I have one more piece of business to attend to," Alaji said softly. Her clothes were dirty, so she changed into a black dress she'd received as a gift long ago, in the distant future. She took some jewelry as well, hoping it would make her a bit less recognizable.

Then she went to her cabinet, an ornate wooden piece she'd stolen from yet another age, and opened the drawer. She removed a simple wineskin and added this to her pack. She sighed and lifted an object from the top, the last of her talismans. She'd traded two with her younger self and returned those to the Citadel; the last, the one she'd taken from Oadeth, she'd left here for this purpose.

She lifted it and held it in one hand, then recovered her staff with the other. Then she hurried. She whispered softly, giving a command that she'd spent months fine-tuning to ensure she reached the right time and place.

And, like that, she was home. She was standing alone in a wooded section bordering Boars Lake, looking out over the still water. Everything felt familiar, even after all these years: the air, the water, the muddy ground, and even the feel of time.

She sat and waited for nightfall. She could have skipped the day, of course, using her talisman or her count, but she was anxious enough as it was. Besides, the lake and the land were beautiful.

Finally, when it was dark, she called out to her feather, which carried her into the air. She floated upwards until the trees became spots, and she looked down at the hills, at the village she'd grown up in, the five dark lakes, and the field to the north where distant fires burned. And it all seemed so small.

She drifted north, passing over the field. She spotted lovers who'd snuck away from the northern camp, spies from both sides, and horses grazing. There was no danger of her being seen—it was a dark night with only a sliver of moon visible, and then only when the clouds were thin. And besides, they wouldn't be looking for a woman in the sky. Such magic was far beyond their understanding.

At last, she saw who she was looking for. She floated over him, looking down as he made his way awkwardly through tall grass. He wasn't much of a spy, she decided, but then he was young and inexperienced.

She used her count to appear behind him, so he wouldn't see her descend. She paused, unsure how to start, while the same conflicting feelings surged through her. It would be so easy to save him.

To take him to another time or even help him here. She had so many ways she could have changed the outcome of the coming night and subsequent battle.

But there were larger things than the life of this young man. She was here to give him the wine, not to change his fate. So, she took a deep breath and prepared herself to speak with her brother for the first time in almost fifty years, and to finally bid him farewell.

* 9 7 9 8 6 4 9 8 3 9 7 8 5 *